Some Will Not Sleep

Other books by Adam L. G. Nevill

Novels

Banquet for the Damned

Apartment 16

The Ritual

Last Days

House of Small Shadows

No One Gets Out Alive

Lost Girl

Under a Watchful Eye

Some Will Not Sleep

Selected Horrors
by
Adam L. G. Nevill

Ritual Limited
Devon, England
MMXVI

Some Will Not Sleep

by Adam L. G. Nevill

Published by

Ritual Limited

Devon, England

MMXVI

www.adamlgnevill.com

rituallimitedshop@gmail.com

Cover design by ClarkevanMeurs Design Ltd

Cover artwork by Mister Trece

Paperback cover layout and text design by The Dead Good Design Company Limited

Ritual Limited logo by Moonring Art Design

Printed and bound by IngramSpark

ISBN 978-0-9954630-3-5

For my wife, Anne, who must endure my horrors, daily,
but who has always managed them and soothed them too.

'I heard one cry in the night, and I heard one laugh afterwards.
If I cannot forget that, I shall not be able to sleep again.'
M. R. James, 'Count Magnus'

Contents

Author's Preface

I began writing my first horror novel in September 1997 and I was writing short horror stories from the beginning of the same decade. I'm now eight novels deep into producing a body of work as a horror novelist, and although I have written enough short stories to squeeze out three collections, this Johnny-come-lately is my first collection. I have selected the stories from a period in my writing that ranged from 1995 to 2011 (though they were first published in the middle of that period, and after it). I've chosen these stories because I still like them enough in 2016 to give them a second life in a volume of selected stories. They were all key works in terms of who asked me to write them, who published them, and what I tried to achieve with voice or style or effect. More details on these matters can be found in the 'About These Horrors' section at the back of the book.

In the current publishing environment, that continues to change in significant ways, many new opportunities exist for writers. And new technology and the new era of independent publishing finally unlatched the gate, let loose my hounds, and made me want to publish this first collection myself, through my own company, Ritual Limited. Not least to put to use eleven years of experience as an editor in traditional publishing. All of the excitement and anguish, the satisfaction and disappointment, and all of those long days in my working life in editorial roles, left me sufficiently equipped to try and produce a book in my own way. In effect, to complete a personal vision of how I wanted my stories jacketed, text-designed, and presented to a reader.

In such a broad field, literally teeming with writers old and new, I specifically wanted this collection to represent *what I'm all about* as a horror writer. I felt that I could only do that by going it alone. If I made mistakes, I could rectify them quickly too. I could also keep the book in print for ever. And, as the publisher and the author, I would never let it sleep *out there.*

With a novel published each year since 2010, and with life taking over in the way that it does, only 2016 provided me with an opportunity to finally develop my company (into something more than its original function in business administration), and to produce the debut title. It was always going to be hard work. It was always going to require lots of time to produce multiple formats. And it was probably going to be an education in a rapidly changing publishing arena too. Producing *Some Will Not Sleep* has been all of these things.

Finally, the title of the collection was inspired by the First Epistle of *Corinthians* (15:5), written by Paul the Apostle: "We shall not all sleep, but we shall all be changed". As with much of the Bible, there are multiple interpretations of the meaning in this statement. But there are several interpretations of the title of this book too. Some within it do not sleep, some who read it may not sleep, and he who wrote it often doesn't sleep.

Manes exite paterni
Adam L. G. Nevill
Devon. June, 2016.

Where Angels Come In

One side of my body is full of toothache. Right in the middle of the bones. The skin and muscles of one arm and one leg have a chilly pins-and-needles tingle. They'll never be warm again. That's why Nana Alice is here; sitting on the chair at the foot of my bed, her crumpled face in shadow. But the milky light that comes through the net curtains still finds a sparkle in her quick eyes, and gleams on the yellowish grin that hasn't changed since my mother let her into the house, made her a cup of tea and showed her into my room. Nana Alice smells like the inside of overflow pipes at the back of the council houses.

'Least you still got one half,' she says. She has a metal brace on her thin leg. The foot at the end of the caliper is inside a baby's shoe. Even though it's rude, I can't stop staring. Her normal leg is fat. 'They took me leg and one arm too.' Using her normal fingers, she picks the dead hand from a pocket in her cardigan and plops it onto her lap. Small and grey, the hand reminds me of a doll's hand. I don't look for long.

She leans forward in her chair, and I can smell the tea on her breath as she says, 'Show me where you was touched, luv.'

I unbutton my pyjama top and roll onto my good side. At the sight of the scar, Nana Alice wastes no time and her podgy fingertips press around the shrivelled skin at the top of my arm, but she doesn't touch the see-through parts where the hand once held me. Nana Alice's eyes go big and her lips pull back to show gums more black than purple. Against her thigh, her doll hand shakes. Cradling the tiny hand and rubbing it with living fingers, she coughs and sits back in the chair. When I've covered my shoulder, Nana Alice still watches that part of me without blinking and seems disappointed to see it covered so soon. She wets her lips. 'Tell us what happened, luv.'

Propping myself up in the pillows, I peer out the window and swallow the big lump in my throat. Feeling a bit sickish, I don't want to remember what happened. Not ever.

Across the street, inside the spiky metal fence built around the park, I can see the usual circle of mothers. Huddled into their coats and sitting on benches beside pushchairs, or holding the leads of tugging dogs, they watch the children play. Upon the climbing frames and on the wet grass, the kids race about and shriek and laugh and fall and cry. Wrapped up in scarves and padded coats, they swarm among hungry pigeons and seagulls; thousands of small white and grey shapes, pecking around their stamping feet. Eventually, the birds all panic and rise in a curving squadron, raising their plump bodies into the air with flap-cracky wings. And the children are blind with their own fear and excitement in brief tornadoes of dusty feathers, red feet, cruel beaks and startled eyes. But they are safe here – the children and the birds – and closely watched by their tense mothers, and are kept inside the stockade of iron railings: the only place outdoors the children are allowed to play since I came back, alone. A lot of things go missing in our town: cats, dogs, children. And they never come back. Except for me and Nana Alice. We came home, or at least half of us did.

Lying in my sickbed every day now, so pale in the face and weak in the heart, I drink medicines, read books and watch the children play from my bedroom window. Sometimes I sleep, but only when I have to. At least, when I'm awake,

I can read, watch television and listen to my mom and sisters downstairs. But in dreams, I go back to the big white house on the hill, where old things with skipping feet circle me, then rush in close to show their faces.

For Nana Alice, she thinks that the time she went inside the big white place, as a little girl, was a special occasion. She's still grateful for being allowed inside. Our dad calls her a silly old fool and doesn't want her in our house. He doesn't know she's here today. But when a child vanishes, or someone dies, lots of the mothers ask Nana to visit them. 'She can see things and feel things that the rest of us can't,' my mom says. Like the two police ladies, and the mothers of the two girls who went missing last winter, and Pickering's parents, my mom just wants to know what happened to me.

'Tell us, luv. Tell us about the house,' Nana Alice says, smiling. No adult likes to talk about the beautiful, tall house on the hill. Even our dads who come home from the industry, smelling of plastic and beer, look uncomfortable if their kids say they can hear the ladies crying again, above their heads, but deep inside their ears at the same time, calling from the distance, from the hill, and from inside us. Our parents can't hear it any more, but they remember the sound from when they were small. It's like people are trapped up on that hill and are calling out for help. And when no one comes, they get real angry. 'Foxes,' the parents tell us, but they don't look you in the eye when they say it.

For a long time after 'my accident' I was unconscious in the hospital. When I woke up, I was so weak I stayed there for another three months. Gradually, one half of my body got stronger and I was allowed home. That's when the questions began about my mate, Pickering, whom they never found. And now Nana Alice wants to know every single thing that I can remember, and about all of the dreams too. Only I never know what is real and what came out of the coma with me.

For years, we talked about going up there. All the kids do, and Pickering, Ritchie and me wanted to be the bravest boys in our school. We wanted to break in there and come out with treasure for proof that we'd been inside, and not just looked in through the gate like all the others we knew. Some people say the white house on the hill was once a place where old, rich people lived after they retired from owning the industry, the land, the laws, our houses, our town, us. Others say the building was built on an old well and that the ground is contaminated. A teacher told us the mansion used to be a hospital and is still full of germs. Our dad said the house was an asylum for lunatics that closed down over a hundred years ago, and has stayed empty ever since, because it's falling to pieces and is too expensive to repair. That's why kids should never go there: you could be crushed by bricks or fall through a floor. Nana Alice says it's a place 'where angels come in'. But we all know that it's the place where the missing things are. Every street in our town has lost pets and knows a family who's lost a child. And every time the police search the big house they find nothing. No one remembers the big gate being open.

So on a Friday morning when all the kids in our area were walking to school, me, Ritchie and Pickering sneaked off the other way. Through the allotments, where me and Pickering were once caught smashing deckchairs and beanpoles; through the woods full of broken glass and dogshit; over the canal bridge; across the potato fields with our heads down so the farmer wouldn't see us; and over the railway tracks until we couldn't even see the roofs of the last houses in our town. Talking about hidden treasure, we stopped by the old ice-cream van with four flat tyres, to throw rocks and stare at the faded menu on the little counter, our mouths watering as we made selections that would never be served. On the other side of the woods that surround the estate, we could see the chimneys of the big white mansion above the trees.

Although Pickering had been walking out front the whole time telling us he wasn't scared of security guards or watchdogs or even ghosts – *Cus you can just put your hand froo them* – when we reached the bottom of the wooded hill no one said anything, and we never looked at each other. Part of me always believed that we would turn back at the black gate, because the fun part was telling stories about the house and planning the expedition and imagining terrible things. Going inside was different because lots of the missing kids had talked about the house before they disappeared. And some of the young men who broke in there, for a laugh, always came away a bit funny in the head. Our dad said that was because of drugs.

Even the trees near the estate were different, like they were too still and silent and the air between them was real cold. But we went up through the trees and found the high brick wall that surrounds the grounds. There was barbed wire and broken glass set into concrete on top of the wall. We followed the wall until we reached the black iron gate. The gate is higher than a house, and it has a curved top made from iron spikes, fixed between two pillars with big stone balls on top. Seeing the PRIVATE PROPERTY: TRESPASSERS WILL BE PROSECUTED sign made shivers go up my neck and under my hair.

'I heard them balls roll off and kill trespassers,' Ritchie said. I'd heard the same thing, but when Ritchie said that, I knew that he wasn't going inside with us.

We wrapped our hands around the cold black bars of the gate and peered through at the long flagstone path that goes up the hill, between avenues of trees and old statues hidden by branches and weeds. All the uncut grass of the lawns was waist-deep and the flower beds were wild with colour. At the summit was the tall white house with the big windows. Sunlight glinted off the glass. Above all the chimneys, the sky was blue. 'Princesses lived there,' Pickering whispered.

'Can you see anyone?' Ritchie asked. He was shivering with excitement and had to take a pee. He tried to rush it over some nettles – we were fighting a war against nettles and wasps that summer – but got half of the piss down his legs.

'It's empty,' Pickering whispered. 'Except for hidden treasure. Darren's brother got this owl inside a big glass. I seen it. Looks like it's still alive. At night, it moves its head.'

Ritchie and I looked at each other; everyone knows the stories about the animals or birds inside the glass cases that people find up there. There's one about a lamb with no fur, inside a tank of green water that someone's uncle found when he was a boy. It still blinks its little black eyes. And someone said they found skeletons of children all dressed up in old clothes, holding hands.

All rubbish; because I know what's really inside there. Pickering had seen nothing, but if we challenged him he'd start yelling, 'Have so! Have so!' and me and Ritchie weren't happy with anything but whispering near the gate.

'Let's just watch and see what happens. We can go in another day,' Ritchie said.

'You're chickening out!' Pickering kicked at Ritchie's legs. 'I'll tell everyone Ritchie pissed his pants.'

Ritchie's face went white and his bottom lip quivered. Like me, he was imagining crowds of swooping kids shouting, 'Piss pot! Piss pot!' Once the crowds find a coward, they'll hunt him every day until he's pushed out to the edges of the playground where the failures stand and watch. Every kid in town knows this place takes away brothers, sisters, cats and dogs, but when we hear the cries from the hill, it's our duty to force one another out here. It's a part of our town and always has been. Pickering is one of the toughest kids in school and he had to go.

Standing back and sizing up the gate, Pickering said, 'I'm going in first. Watch where I put me hands and feet.' And it didn't take him long to get over. There was a little wobble at the top when he swung a leg between two spikes, but not long after that he was standing on the other side, grinning at us. To me, it now looked like there was a little ladder built into the gate; where the metal vines and thorns curved between the long poles, you could see the pattern of steps for small hands and feet. I'd heard that little girls always found a secret wooden door in the brick wall that no one else can find when they look for it. But that might just be another story.

If I didn't go over and the raid was a success, I didn't want to spend the rest of my life being a piss pot and wishing I'd gone in with Pickering. We could be heroes together, and I was full of the same crazy feeling that makes me climb oak trees to the very top branches, stare up at the sky and let go with my hands for a few seconds knowing that if I fall I will die.

When I climbed away from whispering Ritchie on the ground, the squeaks and groans of the gate were so loud that I was sure I could be heard all the way up the hill and inside the house too. When I got to the top and was getting ready to swing a leg over, Pickering said, 'Don't cut your balls off.' But I couldn't smile, or even breathe. It was much higher up there than it looked from the ground. My arms and legs started to shake. With one leg over, between the spikes, panic came up my throat. If one hand slipped off the worn metal I imagined my whole weight forcing the spike through my thigh, and how I would hang there, dripping. I looked at the house and I felt that there was a face behind every window, watching me.

Many of the stories about the white place on the hill came into my head at the same time too: how you only see the red eyes of the thing that drains your blood; how it's kiddie-fiddlers that hide in there and torture captives for days before burying them alive, which is why no one ever finds the missing children; and some say that the thing that makes the crying noise might look like a beautiful lady when you first see it, but soon changes once it's holding you.

'Hurry up. It's easy,' Pickering said, from way down below.

Ever so slowly, I lifted my second leg over, then lowered myself down the other side. He was right; it wasn't a hard climb at all; kids could do it.

I stood in hot sunshine on the other side of the gate, smiling. The light was brighter over there; glinting off all the white stone and glass on the hill. And the air seemed weird, real thick and warm. When I looked back through the gate, the world around Ritchie seemed grey and dull like it was November or something. He stood on his own, biting his bottom lip. Around us, the overgrown grass was so glossy it hurt my eyes to look at it. Reds, yellows, purples, oranges and lemons of the flowers flowed inside my head and I could taste hot summer inside my mouth. Around the trees, the statues and the flagstone path, the air was wavy and my skin felt so warm that I shivered. Closing my eyes, I said, 'Beautiful.' A word that I wouldn't usually use around Pickering.

'This is where I want to live,' he said, his eyes and face one big smile.

We both started to laugh and hugged each other, which we'd never done before. Anything I ever worried about seemed silly now. I felt taller, and could go anywhere, and do anything that I liked. I know Pickering felt the same. Anything Ritchie said sounded stupid to us, and I don't even remember it now.

Protected by the overhanging tree branches and long grasses, we kept to the side of the path and began walking up the hill. But after a while, I started to feel a bit nervous. The house looked even bigger than I'd thought it was, down by the gate. Even though we could see no one and hear nothing, I felt like we'd walked into a crowded but silent place where lots of eyes were watching us. Following us.

We stopped walking by the first statue that wasn't totally covered in green moss and dead leaves. Through the low branches of a tree, we could still see the two stone children, naked and standing together on the marble block. One boy and one girl. They were both smiling, but not in a nice way, because we could see too much of their teeth.

'They's all open on the chest,' Pickering said. And he was right. Their stone skin was peeled back on the breastbone, and cupped in their outstretched hands were small lumps with veins carved into the marble – their own little hearts. The good feeling I had down by the gate went.

Sunlight shone through the trees and striped us with shadows and bright slashes. Eyes big and mouths dry, we walked on and checked some of the other statues that we passed. We couldn't stop ourselves; it was like the sculptures made you stare at them so that you could work out what was sticking through the leaves, branches and ivy. There was one horrible cloth-thing that seemed too real to be made from stone. Its face was so nasty that I couldn't look at it for long. Standing under that thing gave me the queer feeling that it was swaying from side to side, and ready to jump off the block and come at us.

Pickering was walking ahead of me, but he stopped to look at another statue. I remember he seemed to shrink into the shadow that the figure made on the ground, and he peered at his shoes like he didn't want to see the statue. I caught up with him, but didn't look too long either. Beside the statue of the ugly man in a cloak and big hat was a smaller shape covered in a robe and hood with something coming out of a sleeve that reminded me of snakes.

I didn't want to go any further and knew that I'd be seeing these statues in my sleep for a long time. Looking down the hill at the gate, I was surprised to see how far away it was now. 'Think I'm going back,' I said to Pickering.

Pickering never called me a chicken. He didn't want to start a fight and be on his own. 'Let's just go into the house quick,' he said. 'And get something. Otherwise no one will believe us.'

The thought of getting any closer to the white house, and the staring windows, made me feel sick with nerves. It was four storeys high and must have had hundreds of rooms. All the windows upstairs were dark, so we couldn't see beyond the glass. Downstairs, they were all boarded up against trespassers.

'It's empty, I bet,' Pickering said, to try and make us feel better. But it didn't do much for me. He didn't seem so smart or hard any more. He was just a stupid kid who hadn't got a clue.

'Nah,' I said.

He walked away from me. 'Well, I am. I'll say you waited outside.' His voice was too soft to carry the usual threat. But all the same, I imagined his triumphant face while Ritchie and I were the piss pots. I'd even climbed the gate and come this far, but my part would mean nothing if Pickering went further than me.

We never looked at any more of the statues. If we had, I don't think we'd have reached the steps that went up to the big iron doors of the house. Didn't seem to take us long to reach the house either. Even taking slow, reluctant steps got us there real quick. And on legs full of warm water I followed Pickering up to the doors.

'Why is they made of metal?' he asked me.

I never had an answer.

He pressed both hands against the doors. One of them creaked but never opened. 'They's locked,' he said.

But as Pickering shoved at the creaky door again, and with his shoulder and his body at an angle, I'm sure that I saw movement in a window on the second floor. Something whitish, behind the glass. It was like a shape had appeared out of the darkness and then sunk back into it, quick but graceful. It made me think of a carp surfacing in a cloudy pond before vanishing as soon as you saw its pale back. 'Pick!' I hissed.

There was a clunk inside the door that Pickering was straining his body against. 'It's open,' he cried out, and he stared into the narrow gap between the two iron doors.

I couldn't help thinking that the door had been opened from inside. 'I wouldn't,' I said. He smiled and waved for me to come over and to help him make a bigger gap. I stayed where I was and watched the windows upstairs as the widening door made a grinding sound against the floor. Without another word, Pickering walked inside the big white house.

Silence hummed in my ears. Sweat trickled down my face. I wanted to run to the gate.

Pickering's face reappeared in the doorway. 'Quick. Come and look at the birds.' He was breathless with excitement, and then he disappeared again.

I peered through the gap at a big, empty hallway. I saw a staircase going up to the next floor. Pickering was standing in the middle of the hall, looking at the ground, and at all of the dried up birds on the wooden floorboards. Hundreds of dead pigeons. I went inside.

No carpets, or curtains, or light bulbs, just bare floorboards, white walls and two closed doors on either side of the hall. On the floor, most of the birds still had feathers but looked real thin. Some were just bones. Others were dust.

'They get in and they got nothin' to eat,' Pickering said. 'We should collect the skulls.' He crunched across the floor and tried the doors at either side of the hall, yanking the handles up and down. 'Locked,' he said. 'Both locked. Let's go up them stairs. See if there's somefing in the rooms.'

I flinched at every creak our feet made on the stairs, and I told Pickering to walk at the sides like me. But he wasn't listening and was just going up fast on his plump legs. When I caught up with him, at the first turn in the stairs, I started to feel real strange again. The air was weird, hot and thin like we were in a tiny space. We were both sweaty under our school uniforms too, from just walking up one flight of stairs. I had to lean against a wall.

Pickering shone his torch at the next floor. All we could see up there were plain walls in a dusty corridor. A bit of sunlight was getting in from somewhere upstairs, but not much. 'Come on,' he said, without turning his head to look at me.

'I'm going outside,' I said. 'I can't breathe.' But as I moved to go back down the first flight of stairs, I heard a door creak open and then close, below us. I stopped still and heard my heart bang against my eardrums from the inside. The sweat turned to frost on my face and neck and under my hair. And real quick, and sideways, something moved across the shaft of light falling through the open front door.

My eyeballs went cold and I felt dizzy. From the corner of my eye, I could see Pickering's face too, watching me from above, on the next flight of stairs. He turned the torch off with a loud click.

The thing in the hall moved again, back the way it had come, but it paused at the edge of the rectangle of light on the floorboards. And started to sniff at the dirty ground. It was mostly the way that she moved down there that made me feel as light as a feather and ready to faint. Least I think it was a *she*, but when people get that old you can't always tell. There wasn't much hair on the head and the skin was yellow. She looked more like a puppet made of bones and dressed in a grubby nightie than an old lady. And could old ladies move that fast? Sideways like a crab she went, looking backwards at the open door, so I couldn't see the face properly, which I was glad of.

If I moved too quick, I'm sure that she would have looked up and seen me, so I took two slow steps to get behind the wall of the next staircase, where Pickering was already hiding. He looked like he was trying not to cry. I thought about them stone kids outside, and what they held in their little hands, and I tried not to cry too.

Then we heard the sound of another door opening downstairs. We huddled on a step together, trembling, and we peered round the corner of the staircase to make sure that the old thing wasn't coming up the stairs, sideways. But another one was down there. I saw it skittering around by the door like a chicken, and all the air leaked out of me before I could scream.

That one moved quicker than the first one, with the help of two black sticks. Bent over with a hump for a back, it was covered in a dusty black dress that swished over the floor. What I could see of the face, through the veil, was all pinched and was sickly-white as the grubs you find under wet bark. And when she made the whistling sound, it hurt my ears deep inside and made my bones feel cold.

Pickering's face was wild with fear and it was like there was no blood left inside his head and I was seeing too much of his eyes. 'Is they old ladies?' he said in a voice all broken.

I grabbed his arm. 'We got to get out. Maybe there's a window, or another door round the back.' Which meant that we had to go up the stairs, run through the building and find another way down to the ground floor, before breaking our way out.

I took another peek down the stairs to see what *they* were doing, but wished I hadn't. There were two more of them. A tall man with legs like sticks was looking up at us with a face that never changed, because it had no lips or eyelids or nose. He wore a creased suit with a gold watch chain on the waistcoat, and was standing behind a wicker chair. In the chair was a bundle wrapped in tartan blankets. Peeking above the coverings was a small head inside a cloth cap. The face was yellow as corn in a tin. The first two were standing by the open door so that we couldn't get out through the front.

Running up the stairs into a hotter darkness, my whole body felt baggy and clumsy and my knees chipped together. Pickering went first with the torch and used his elbows so that I couldn't overtake him. I bumped into his back, and kicked his heels, and inside his fast breathing I could hear him sniffing at tears. 'Is they comin'?' he kept asking. I didn't have the breath to answer and kept running through the long corridor, between dozens of closed doors, to get to the end. I just looked straight ahead and knew that I would freeze if one of the doors opened. And with our feet making such a bumping on the floorboards, I can't say that I was surprised when I heard the click of a lock behind us. We both made the mistake of looking back.

At first, we thought it was waving at us. But then we realised that the skinny lady in the dirty nightdress was moving her long arms through the air to attract the attention of the others that had followed us up the stairwell. We could hear the scuffle and swish as they came through the dark behind us. But how could this one see us, I thought, with all those rusty bandages around her head? Then we heard another of those horrible whistles, followed by more doors opening real quick, like them things were in a hurry to get out of the rooms.At the end of the corridor, there was another stairwell with more light in it, which fell from a high window three floors up. But the glass must have been dirty and greenish, because everything around us on the stairs looked like it was under water. When he turned to bolt down the stairs, I saw that Pickering's face was all shiny with tears and the front of his trousers had a dark patch spreading down one leg.

It was real hard to get down to the ground. It was like we had no strength left in our bodies, as if our fear was draining us through the slappy, tripping soles of our feet. But it was more than terror slowing us down; the air was so thin and dry, and it was hard to get our breath in and out of our lungs fast enough. My shirt was stuck to my back and I was dripping under the arms. Pickering's hair was wet and he'd almost stopped moving, so I overtook him.

At the bottom of the stairs, I ran into another long, empty corridor of closed doors and greyish light that ran along the back of the building. Just looking all the way down it made me bend over with my hands on my knees to rest.

But Pickering just ploughed right into me from behind and knocked me over. He ran across my body and stamped on my hand. 'They's comin',' he whined in a tearful voice, and stumbled off, down that passage.

When I got back to my feet I followed him, which never felt like a good idea to me, because if some of them things were waiting in the hall by the front doors, while others were coming up fast behind us, we'd get ourselves trapped. I even thought about opening the door of a ground-floor room and trying to kick out the boards over a window. Plenty of them old things seemed to come out of rooms when we ran past them, like we were waking them up, but they never came out of every room. So maybe we would have to take a chance on one of the doors.

I called out to Pick to stop. I was wheezing like Billy Skid at school who's got asthma, so maybe Pickering never heard me, because he kept on running. As I was wondering which door to pick, a little voice said, 'Do you want to hide in here?'

I jumped into the air and cried out like I'd trod on a snake, and stared at where the voice had come from. There was a crack between a door and the door-frame, and part of a little girl's face was peeking out. She smiled and opened the door wider. 'They won't see you. We can play with my dolls.' She had a really white face inside a black bonnet all covered in ribbons. The rims of her eyes were red like she'd been crying for a long time.

My chest was hurting and my eyes were stinging with sweat. Pickering was too far ahead for me to catch him up. I could hear his feet banging away on loose floorboards, way off in the darkness, and I didn't think I could run any further. So I nodded at the girl. She stood aside and opened the door wider. The bottom of her black dress swept through the dust. 'Quickly,' she said with an excited smile, and then looked down the corridor, to see if anything was coming. 'Most of them are blind, but they can hear things.'

I moved through the doorway. Brushed past her and smelled something gone bad. It put a picture in my head of the dead cat, squashed flat in the woods, that I found one time on a hot day. But over that smell was something like the bottom of my granny's old wardrobe, with the one broken door and little iron keys in the locks that don't work.

Softly, the little girl closed the door behind us, and walked off across the wooden floor with her head held high, like a 'little Madam', my dad would have said. Light was getting into this room from some red and green windows up near the high ceiling. Two big chains were hanging down and holding lights with no bulbs, and there was a stage at one end, with a heavy green curtain pulled across the front. Footlights stuck up at the front of the stage. It must have been a ballroom once.

Looking for a way out, behind me, to the side, up ahead, everywhere, I followed the little girl in the black bonnet to the stage, and went up the stairs at the side. She disappeared through the curtains without making a sound, and I followed because I could think of nowhere else to go and I wanted a friend. But the long curtains smelled so bad around my face that I put a hand over my mouth.

She asked me for my name and where I lived, and I told her like I was talking to a teacher who'd just caught me doing something wrong. I even gave her my house number. 'We didn't mean to trespass,' I also said. 'We never stole nothing.'

She cocked her head to one side and frowned like she was trying to remember something. Then she smiled and said, 'All of these are mine. I found them.' She drew my attention to the dolls on the floor; little shapes of people that I couldn't see properly in the dark. She sat down among them and started to pick them up one at a time, to show me. But I was too nervous to pay much attention and I didn't like the look of the cloth animal with its fur worn to the grubby material. It had stitched up eyes and no ears; the arms and legs were too long for its body too, and I didn't like the way the dirty head was stiff and upright like it was watching me.

Behind us, the rest of the stage was in darkness, with only the faint glow of a white wall in the distance. Peering from the stage at the boarded-up windows along the right side of the dancefloor, I could see some bright daylight around the edge of two big hardboard sheets, nailed over patio doors. There was a draught coming through the gaps too. Must have been a place where someone got in before.

'I got to go,' I said to the girl behind me, who was whispering to her toys. And I was about to step through the curtains and head for the daylight when I heard the rushing of a crowd in the corridor that me and Pickering had just run through; feet shuffling, canes tapping, wheels squeaking and two hooting sounds. It all seemed to go on for ages; a long parade I didn't want to see.

As the crowd rushed past the ballroom, the main door clicked open and something glided inside. I pulled back from the curtains and held my breath while the little girl kept mumbling to the nasty toys. I wanted to cover my ears. A crazy part of me wanted it all to end; wanted me to step out from behind the curtains and offer myself to the tall figure down there on the dancefloor. Holding the tatty parasol over its head, it spun around quickly like it was moving on tiny, silent wheels under its long musty skirts, while sniffing at the air for me. Under the white net attached to the brim of the rotten hat and tucked into the high collars of the dress, I saw a bit of face that looked like the skin on a rice pudding. I would have screamed but there was no air inside me.

I looked over to where the little girl had been sitting. She had gone, but something was moving on the floor. Squirming. I blinked my eyes fast, and for a moment, it looked like all of her toys were trembling. But when I squinted at the Golly, with the bits of curly white hair on its head, the doll lay perfectly still where she had dropped it. The little girl may have hidden me, but I was glad that she had gone.

Way off in the stifling distance of the big house, I then heard a scream; a cry full of all the panic and terror and woe in the whole world. The figure with the umbrella spun around on the dancefloor and then rushed out of the ballroom towards the sound.

I slipped out from behind the curtains. A busy chattering sound came from the distance. It got louder until it echoed through the corridor, and the ballroom, and almost covered the sounds of the wailing boy. His cries were swirling round and round, bouncing off walls and closed doors, like he was running far off inside the house, and in a circle that he couldn't get out of.

I crept down the stairs at the side of the stage and ran to the long strip of burning sunlight that I could see shining through one side of the patio doors. I pulled at the big rectangle of wood until it splintered and revealed broken glass in a door-frame and lots of thick grass outside.

For the first time since I'd seen the old woman, scratching about the front entrance, I truly believed that I could escape. I imagined myself climbing through the gap that I was making, and running down the hill to the gate, while *they* were all busy inside with the crying boy. But just as my breathing went all quick and shaky with the glee of escape, I heard a *whump* sound on the floor behind me, like something had just dropped to the floor from the stage. Teeny vibrations tickled the soles of my feet. Then I heard something coming across the floor toward me, with a shuffle, like a body was dragging itself real quick.

I couldn't bear to look behind and see another one close up, so I snatched at the board and I pulled with all my strength at the bit not nailed down. The whole thing bent and made a gap. Sideways, I squeezed a leg, hip, arm and a shoulder out. My head was suddenly bathed in warm sunlight and fresh air.

One of *them* must have reached out right then, and grabbed my left arm under the shoulder at the moment I had made it outside. The fingers and thumb were so cold that they burned my skin. And even though my face was in daylight, everything went dark in my eyes except for the little white flashes that you get when you stand up too fast.

I wanted to be sick. I tried to pull away, but one side of my body was all slow and heavy and full of pins and needles. I let go of the hardboard sheet and it slapped shut like a mouse trap. Behind my head, I heard a sound like celery snapping and something shrieked into my ear, which made me go deafish for a week.

Sitting down in the grass outside, I was sick down my jumper. Mucus and bits of spaghetti hoops that looked all white and smelled real bad. I looked back at the place that I had climbed through and my bleary eyes saw an arm that was mostly bone, stuck between the wood and door-frame. I made myself roll away and then get to my knees on the grass that was flattened down.

Moving around the outside of the house, back toward the front of the building and the path that would take me down to the gate, I wondered if I'd bashed my left side. The shoulder and hip had stopped tingling but were achy and cold and stiff. I found it hard to move and wondered if that was what broken bones felt like. My skin was wet with sweat too, and I was shivery and cold. I just wanted to lie down in the long grass. Twice I stopped to be sick. Only spit came out with burping sounds.

Near the front of the house, I got down on my good side and I started to crawl, real slow, through the long grass, down the hill, making sure that the path was on my left, so that I didn't get lost in the meadow. I only took one look back at the house and will wish for ever that I never did.

One side of the front door was still open from where we went in. And I could see a crowd in the doorway, all bustling in the sunlight that fell on their raggedy clothes. They were making a hooting sound and fighting over something; a small shape that looked dark and wet. It was all limp too and between the thin, snatching hands it came apart, piece by piece.

In my room, at the end of my bed, Nana Alice has closed her eyes. But she's not sleeping. She's just sitting quietly and rubbing her doll hand like she's polishing treasure.

The Original Occupant

Reasons for the male mid-life crisis are well documented, so I need not trouble the reader with too detailed an interpretation of the affliction. But the consequences arising from the death throes of youth, and an individual's grapple with a more precise awareness of its own mortality, were extraordinary in the case of William Atterton. Word of his dilemma came to me through Henry Berringer.

William Atterton, Henry Berringer and I were all fellows of St Leonard's College and shared the same alumni affiliations, including a club in St James's where Henry and I enjoyed a regular dinner on the first Friday of each month, complemented by a stroll along The Mall with cigars to close. There were many predictable aspects to our dining ritual, chief among them a discussion of Atterton and the precarious life he led.

It was towards the end of June that Henry updated me on the latest 'Atterton news'. Only a few weeks earlier Henry had bumped into our mutual acquaintance in Covent Garden carrying 'a hundredweight' of travel books and self sufficiency manuals. Over an impromptu luncheon, Atterton told Henry of his intention to resign from his position in the City in order to pursue a 'far simpler existence in the sub-arctic forests of Northern Sweden. Four seasons, if nothing else. I'll see it through for one entire year. And for the first time in ages I'm going to be aware of my surroundings, Henry. The changes in nature, the sky, the birdsong, the very air –'

'The ice and snow,' Henry was compelled to interject.

'Yes, damn it! The ice and snow. And I shall lovingly observe every crystal and flake at my leisure.'

'Which will be considerable,' said Henry. 'Would not a couple of weeks or even a month out there be more prudent?'

'No! I'll not be one of those look-at-little-me chaps, alone in a cabin for a fortnight. You won't understand, Henry, but I'm realising more and more that my whole life has been a matter of compromise and half-measures. To tell you the truth, I'm not sure I ever pursued a real dream of my own. I can't even recall how I came to be this person, or what I ever wanted to do in life. But I do know one thing: that after thirty years in the City I've not done it.'

On hearing this news, I immediately drew the same conclusions as Henry. We were both unsure precisely what Atterton was escaping from this time, because this plan certainly had the makings of an escape and there were plenty of reasons for one. Though I risk sounding like a gossip, Atterton had always been something of a meddler. Particularly in the pockets of others. Some years ago, he made property speculations in which several dear friends lost considerable sums of money. His involvement in a restaurant is alleged to have caused its swift closure, and his mismanagement of several accounts led to the impoverishment of at least one pension fund. To exacerbate his fiscal troubles, at the start of what we shall call his *crisis*, there was evidence of meddling both in a friend's marriage and then with a colleague's daughter, working as an intern at his firm, with barely a weekend to spare between the two affairs. As to his resignation from the company, there has been some talk in the City that it was not entirely a matter of choice.

But during discussion of this Scandinavian venture, Henry had never seen the man's face so animate. He described

Atterton's eyes as being fixed with a peculiar quality akin to euphoria. Atterton was a committed man.

'And what, dare I say, will you do for one entire year in the woods?' Henry had asked him, shortly before paying the bill for their lunch. This was the only question that Atterton wished to be asked on the matter. Beside his fondness for Thoreau's *Walden*, and his long eulogised backpacking holiday in Scandinavia as a student, Atterton had this to say: 'Walk. Swim in the Alvar. Sleep outdoors. Explore. Get back to my sketching. I haven't touched a pencil in twenty years. There won't be enough hours in the day. And you should see the place I have purchased for my exile, Henry. What they call a *Fritidshus*, or *Stuga*, meaning summer house. It's thirty kilometres from the nearest town, and situated in a prehistoric forest festooned with runestones. There's even a wooden church that has been around since the fourteenth century. I shall be suffering from brass rubber's elbow by the end of summer.'

Henry was beginning to share Atterton's excitement and feel the first twitches of envy, until he inquired how they might stay in touch.

'Now there's the rub, Henry. No phone masts where I'm going. And I'm not even connected to the mains. I shall be drawing my bath from a well, running a generator on oil and cooking my freshly caught fish on a wood-fired stove. It's all very basic. I plan to spend my evenings by the fire, Henry, reading. I'm taking the complete works of Dickens and Tolstoy for starters. So I anticipate we will be corresponding by letter.'

Henry is not the sort of man to dampen a friend's spirits, but as Atterton held forth about his plans for isolating himself in the backwoods of another country, he was filled with a schoolmarmish suspicion that things had not been properly thought through.

'I want to be tested again, Henry. Really tested.' As indeed he was, but not in the manner that he anticipated.

So, in early August, into the wild ventured Atterton accompanied by a large collection of books and several cases of warm clothing, leaving Henry with the sole task of checking on his flat in Chelsea to flush the toilet from time to time, and attend to other matters in a bachelor's absence. And so too, towards the end of August, began their correspondence. Which swiftly failed to take the course that either man envisaged.

I spent the remainder of the summer and most of autumn abroad, but on my return Henry and I fell into our first Friday of the month routine. But my dear friend was much changed. At his request, we took possession of a table close to the kitchens of the club's dining room, rather than our usual seats overlooking Green Park. During dinner Henry also displayed all the signs of a high agitation, which were only partially relieved when the staff closed the curtains. 'I tell you, I've had enough of damn trees in a high wind,' he said, and waved away my invitation to take our stroll along The Mall. Instead, we retired to the library with a decanter of brandy, where he promised to explain his mood and the events of the summer, which served as the cause of his discomfort. It became immediately apparent that Atterton, or 'poor Atterton' as Henry now referred to him, was to be the sole topic of conversation as tradition dictated. Only this time the tale Henry told was different from any other that I had ever heard, and must have influenced my decision to take a cab home to Knightsbridge, forgoing my usual walk home around the leafy perimeter of Hyde Park.

'I can well understand a sophisticated man's desire for solitude in a more natural environment, and even his yearning for a more historical way of life, but I did fear that a lack or, in Atterton's case, a total absence of society could lead to an excess of inner dialogue, which can only result in one's consciousness turning upon itself. And during our brief correspondence, it appeared that just such a thing had befallen the poor fellow.

'There were three letters, and only the first one contained any trace of his initial enthusiasm for this Swedish venture. I can be prone to an underestimation of my fellow man, but it was never the selection of supplies, gathering of fuel, the workings of the generator or the outdoor orientating skills that gave him trouble. On the contrary, during his second week out there, he'd removed a ghastly decoration of horseshoes from the property, was repainting the house in the traditional deep red of the area and replacing roof slates with an enthusiasm befitting a scout on a camping trip. He was hiking well into the bright nights, had begun fishing in local waters and had completed the Everyman editions of both *Bleak House* and *Little Dorrit*.

'But after reading the second letter, I couldn't help but suspect that Atterton had become uneasy in his surroundings. The valley – no more than twenty kilometres across, in northeastern Jämtland – was entirely cut off. I mean, that was the whole point, to get away. But the area's sparse, and mostly elderly, population seemed to have exercised a wilful obstinacy in remaining divorced from modern Sweden.

'Despite the incredible beauty of the land, and its abundance of wildlife, Atterton believed that the local population were committed to turning tourism away at the door. Atterton's Swedish was almost non-existent, and their English was uncharacteristically poor for Scandinavia, so what little contact he had with his nearest neighbours, during his walks, was only ever conducted at the border of the valley, and he found it to be entirely unsatisfactory in nature. The people there had either taken to some sect of Protestantism with a fanatical bent, or were observing the dictates of some kind of folklore to an irrational degree. They spent far too much time in church, and any building or fence or gate he came across on his wanderings was festooned with iron horseshoes.

'And what's more, they seemed wary of him. Not afraid of him, but *for him*, he felt. Once or twice, at the general store and post office, that he cycled ten kilometres to reach, he'd been told about "bad land", or some kind of "bad luck" in the area. An elderly man who had learned some English in the merchant navy advised him to leave well before the end of September, when what little summer congress that frequented those parts would migrate to other places before the long night fell. What was equally alarming was the manner in which other Swedes appeared only too happy to avoid the place. Odd, considering the plethora of standing runestones and several wooden churches of immense antiquity dotted about the woods. Even trails for hikers seemed to circumnavigate the region on every map.

'Atterton did admit, however, that his curiosity about the region far outweighed his reservations; a remark which sounded a chime of alarm inside me, knowing how our mutual friend could be impervious to reason and logic in his passing enthusiasms.

'Anyway, another four weeks passed before I received the next letter. And moments after reading his hastily scribbled handwriting, I made a cursory inspection of airline timetables and looked into car hire in Northern Sweden.

'Here, see for yourself.' Henry handed me the third letter from Atterton.

Dear Henry

I plan to be gone from here by the week's end. I anticipate arriving in London a few days after you receive this letter. I cannot alarm you any more than I have alarmed myself, Henry, but there is something not right about this place. With the late sun gone, the valley has begun to show me a different face. I no longer spend much time outdoors if I can help it.

Do not think me foolish, but I am not at all comfortable with the trees after midday. As for this wind, I had no idea that gusts of cold air could create such a sound of violence amongst deciduous woodland; it's unseasonably strong and cold too for autumn, and savage. The forest is restless, but not quite in the same way that a wood is animated by air currents alone; I believe the core disturbance comes from the standing stones.

They were benign in midsummer; though even then I was not particularly fond of that hill on which the circle stands. But I have made the very grave error of visiting that place when the sun is behind the clouds or going down. And I believe I may have interfered with some kind of indigenous custom.

I can only imagine that it was some of the locals who had tethered the pig inside the stones. You see, while I was out walking yesterday evening, I heard the most desperate and baleful cries, carried on the north wind from the direction of the circle. I went up and found a wretched boar tied to the central plinth. Surrounded by enough dead fowl, strung up between the circle of dolmens, to satisfy a large appetite. Some kind of barbaric ritual in progress. The plinth had been literally bathed in the blood of the birds. I found it appalling. So, I cut the boar free, and wished him well as he made haste into the forest. But, in hindsight, I believe he had been installed there for my protection. As some kind of trade.

You see, the entire time I was among the stones, I felt that I was being watched. You get an extra sense out here in the wild, Henry. You come to trust it. And I believe the scent of blood, and the shrieking of a pig, had attracted something else to that place. I felt a presence in the wind that seemed to come at me from all points of the compass. Air that cut to the bone and left me damp inside my clothes and hair and the very marrow of my bones.

I didn't hang around. I set off for home feeling more peculiar than I can adequately describe. To be honest, I became more frightened than I had ever been as a child at night. But my fear was combined with a sort of disorientation, and a conviction of my utter insignificance out here amongst these black trees. The noise of them, Henry. It felt like I was being shipwrecked by an angry sea.

I'd not gone far before I heard a dreadful commotion from the direction in which I had just come: the freed boar in some considerable distress. Though it sounded frightfully like a child at the time. Then its cries ceased with an abruptness worse than the preceding shrieks.

I fled. Fast as I could. Ran till I thought my heart would give out. Cut my head badly on a tree branch and smashed up a knee on a tree root when I fell. And through the trees the cold air chased after me. Among its whining gusts came a howl of a nature that I am convinced will echo within me for some, if not all, time. There are wolves and bears and arctic foxes this far north. Perhaps I had even heard a wolverine, or so I told myself. I've heard the baying of jackals and the roar of great baboons on safari too, but yesterday I was ready to wager that nothing in the animal kingdom could utter such a cry in the mêlée of the hunt. There was an awful note of triumph in it. And I'm convinced that whatever issued the howl followed me back here, Henry. Last night I heard something outside, in the paddock at the rear of the house. And this morning, I found prints. Not even bears make such tracks.

Suffice to say I have seen and heard enough. This Friday I shall make my way to the airport in Östersund. By then, the rest of my things will be packed and the house shuttered for the winter. The sun is still bright and strong in the morning and I can sense things are more reasonable here at that time of day. I shall wobble and wince up to the postbox this morning on my bike to post this letter. And while I am there, I shall arrange from the callbox for the transport company to come for me and my gear in two days' time.

Your fond friend
William Atterton

In silence I passed the letter back to Henry, and he continued with his story.

'I waited anxiously for the week to end and even made a hasty call to the Swedish consulate, only to discover the nearest local authority to Radalen was some eighty kilometres away from Atterton's *Fritidshus*. As I had no crime or accident to report, and was frankly too embarrassed to paraphrase the content of his third letter over the phone, I decided it best I set off for Sweden myself the following Monday. Even if we passed each other in transit, so be it; I'd like to think that one of my own friends would act as I did, should they ever receive a letter of a similar nature from me, while I'm abroad. The least I could do was accompany poor Atterton home and assist him in procuring professional treatment for his nerves.

'On the first plane to Stockholm early on Monday morning, an elderly Swedish gentleman sitting beside me asked if I required any assistance with the map that I'd spread across my lap. He had seen me struggling with four reputable travel guides too, in which I sought some information about Radalen. There was mention of the counties inside Norrland, but little on Jämtland, and nothing at all on Radalen. So I took advantage of the passenger's kind offer and made some inquiries about getting to Radalen. To which the gentleman immediately asked me a question as direct as his gaze. "And why would you wish to see Radalen?" Just like most of his fellow countrymen, the man spoke excellent, direct and concise English.

'I was temporarily at a loss for an explanation, but the gentleman informed me that he was originally from the south of Jämtland, though hadn't lived there since his teens and rarely visited any more. But though most of Sweden was ignorant of the reputation of Radalen, those of his generation who originated from the area were unlikely to forget the stories that they were told as children. Many other parts of Sweden were more *amenable* to visitors, he said, than Radalen. As a youth, he was forbidden to ever roam that far north.

'Of course, I humoured the man, and tried my best to keep an expression of scepticism at bay. I asked him for more detail about this *reputation* and mentioned my friend's recent residence there.

'He proceeded to tell me of things that had survived in the oral tradition, as opposed to those recorded by historians, which detailed the survival of... I guess you would call it folklore, or a belief system that had been observed long before the aggressive colonisation of Sweden by the Christian Church. Apparently, even during the early twentieth century, animal sacrifice was still common at the end of each summer to placate the original occupants of the forests, prior to the privations of winter.

'It was claimed that these original occupants of the woods – or *Ra* – were ghastly things, and the basis for monsters in local legends and so forth. And it had always been believed that the forests were unsafe if certain precautionary measures were not taken. Foresters and huntsmen could no longer roam, women could no longer collect firewood, and children would be unable to play freely. Then, in the seventeenth century, the custom of offering gifts was violently suppressed during a period of puritanical fervour, intended to sweep away the last vestiges of pantheism in Northern Sweden. But immediately after the censorship, this fellow claimed, a spate of disappearances ensued in northern Jämtland. First livestock, then the more vulnerable human elements of the local communities went missing. And it was from this period that a particular warning originated – *Det som en gang givits ar forsvunnet, det kommer att atertas* – which the gentleman translated into English for me: *What was once given, is missing. One will come to fetch it back.*

'This script was erected on gateposts and signs as a warning to visitors, and was usually accompanied by the horseshoe, a symbol that made the *Ra* particularly uncomfortable due to its aversion to men on horseback.

'Though temporarily suppressed, the late-summer gifts were soon offered again from the places designated for such transactions. And this originally began in an age when colonising Norsemen, and the original occupants, had made these uneasy treaties. This time, the church turned a blind eye, silently acknowledging a local problem beyond its brief and power to correct.

'But things were different. The tastes of the original occupants were said to have changed. Changed back to an older *baseness*. During the interference of the church, the *Ra* had rediscovered a taste for a different kind of flesh. And unscrupulous members of the local populace were soon said to be giving succour to the revival of such an enthusiastic appetite. Hence the long-standing tradition of missing travellers in Radalen.

'Gradually, the local communities withdrew from the affected area to put themselves beyond reach of the very territorial *Ra*, abandoning homes and churches as they migrated south and east. And in time, such observances of old lore struggled to survive in the age of reason and science. The local lore was seen as folly by all but a few who lived closest to the valley. This area is now a long-neglected portion of the national park, though the gentleman did hear something about a property developer rebuilding or renovating old villas to sell off as summer houses. But the idea had never taken off. With such a slender population, there is little infrastructure and almost no local services in the area. "It must be one of these your friend has purchased," he said in closing, just as the smoked salmon and caviar were served to us by a stewardess.

'I had listened with interest and some disquiet, but my unease soon turned to irritation. I was willing to venture that such talk and spurious conjecture amounted to nothing more than the fairy tales composed to prevent children from getting lost in the forest. Somehow, it must have all taken root in Atterton's isolated imagination, and then the foolishness must have flourished; no doubt cultivated by the dying of the light as winter approached. So, the sooner I reached him and returned him to the observable world, the better. I say "observable" because I've always championed a motto among those with a bent for psychics, ghosts and visitors from other galaxies, and that is that *I trust my own eyes. If it exists, then let it show itself.*'

At this point in the narration, I was surprised at the manner in which Henry gulped at his brandy.

Descriptions of travel by untutored pens can be as dull as slide-shows of holiday photographs, so I will not blunt the reader's concentration with details of Henry's journey through Sweden to the Jämtland region, and then onto the periphery of Radalen. Suffice to say, he acquired his rental vehicle and a better map. But the closer he drew to Atterton's location, the more difficult the journey became.

'The moment I left the main arteries, to move inland on secondary roads, I found myself overwhelmed by the impenetrable nature of the forest. I'd never seen such a place in Europe before. A true, virgin wilderness, as much of northern Scandinavia still remains; Boreal forest surviving from prehistory, unmanaged, and probably still boasting miles of woodland where no human has ever set foot.

'About sixty kilometres from Radalen, there was some evidence of summer housing scattered about through the trees; small wooden houses built in the vintage rural style and painted a dark red. These must have been the remnants of the settlements that drew away from Radalen in the eighteenth century, and the buildings were now used for summer holidays, but were empty that late in the season.

'The buildings thinned and then practically disappeared when I couldn't have been more than twenty kilometres from the valley. The road surface turned from tarmac to gravel and, in places, was barely wide enough for a single vehicle. And even in the late sun of the afternoon, I couldn't prevent myself thinking that the last of the buildings that I spied through the trees, on higher ground, suggested a greater air of abandonment than the others. The very structures seemed to suggest that they had not drawn back far enough from the darkest, ageless fathoms of the valley. I even fancied that some of the little *Stugas* were in the process of peering over their gabled shoulders in fearful anticipation of what might be approaching through the trees.

'Chiding myself for a betrayal of reason, I shut down that train of thought. But even the unimaginative, in whose number I would include myself, retain enough of their primal instinct to fear the shadowy expanses of uncultivated forests.

Particularly as dusk settles through the clouds to tint the very air before your eyes, promising a nightfall so dense as to cancel visibility in every direction. It was no longer any surprise to me that legends of the *Ra* and human sacrifice lingered in these valleys. It was the perfect setting for such fables. But stories they were, and I had a troubled friend to find.

'When I could not have been more than ten kilometres from Atterton's *Fritidshus*, I found myself making repeated stops to study the map. The light was fading and the road curved about to such an extent that I no longer knew which direction was north and which was south. I'd become lost. I was tired and hungry by this time too, the best of my concentration was long gone, my temper was beginning to spark, and my sense of awe at the forest was fast turning to dread. I wondered if I'd have to spend the night on the backseat of the car.

'But, to my relief, after another five minutes behind the wheel, I spied a church steeple through the passenger window, during a brief break in the woodland bordering the road. Hoping to find someone who could direct me to Atterton's house, I drove toward the steeple on what amounted to no more than a track.

'The church was a long, single-storey, timber affair, with a steeple that also served as a bell tower, surrounded by a well-tended meadow cemetery. But my brief optimism began to drain when I noticed that all of the windows were shuttered. And around the arch that topped the little gatehouse, providing access to the grounds through the dry-stone wall, an inscription had been carved into the wood between two black horseshoes: *Det som en gang givits ar forsvunnet, det kommer att atertas – What was once given is missing. One will come to fetch it back.*

'Alone, lost in a national park, hours' drive from the nearest town, and before a churchyard with a chilly dusk assembling about me, this warning was just about the last thing that I wanted to come across. And no sooner had

I advanced through the gate and approached the church doors than I noticed another configuration of horseshoes nailed about the porch canopy, to protect the entrance of God's house. If indeed these primitive iron symbols were used to ward off evil spirits, then why would a crucifix not suffice? *Perhaps*, an irritating voice cried out inside me, *because a cross is not recognised by eyes older than the origin of that symbol.* I turned an involuntary shudder into a vigorous shake of my cramped limbs, my tired muscles and frazzled senses, and I investigated the building.

'My knocks went unanswered, as did my calls, and there was not so much as a single notice in the glass-fronted display case beside the door.

'At the rear of the property I discovered a collection of large granite runestones, suggesting to me this was the sight of a far older cemetery. And while I looked at them, all about me the shadows thickened between the boughs and trunks of the trees, the leaves darkened as the light thinned, and I pulled up my collar against the buffets of a cold wind. I was forced to remember Atterton's last letter. I didn't linger long and made my way back to the car.

'Eyes burning and head thumping, I made another frustrating scrutiny of the map under the overhead light. Pretty soon the headlights would have to go on as well. I was just about to utter another string of curses, when I noticed the tiny symbol of a cross on the map, which seemed to be an indication of the church that I was currently parked beside. If this was the case, then all I needed to do was turnabout, drive to the crossroads that I had passed no more than two kilometres back and take a left. A road or single track would then take me to Atterton's *Stuga*.

'With my sense of direction recovered, I managed to find the house, without further mishap, at 6.45 p.m. A small, pretty red building with white awnings and porch, set in a grass paddock about which the white picket fence was not so much surrounded as engulfed by the encroaching forest.

I could see no more than a few feet along the leafy tracks that ran between the great trees and then vanished into a darker immensity.

'There was no answer to my rapping on the door, or to my calls as I circled the house with a growing sense of alarm. I recalled Atterton mentioning his removal of a plethora of horseshoes from the walls of the house, but it now appeared that they had been nailed back, and with haste and little regard for symmetry. The windows had also been boarded over with any material at hand: bits of broken furniture, firewood, planks torn from the outhouse. Surely this was not what he referred to as shutting up for the winter? So, had he come to believe himself besieged by a creature from a fairy tale?

'Upon a closer inspection of the windows, even in the failing light, I happened to notice a disturbance in the flower beds beneath the windows at the rear of the property. The soil had been thoroughly trampled and the plants had been raked out. So had some inquisitive moose come nosing up to the windows to eat flowers or peer in through the glass? Or perhaps a bear had been enticed out of the woods by the scent of Atterton's fish supper? And had the noises from such a commotion transformed themselves, inside Atterton's unstable thoughts, into what he perceived to be a threat from some monstrous intruder?

'Running my fingers along the woodwork of the sills, I discovered a series of deep scratches in the timber, which may have resulted from his hasty and inept attempts to seal the windows. And yet, despite my stubborn recourse to reason, I was struck by a notion that these marks suggested the attempt of a powerful animal to gain access to the interior.

'But one thing did seem irrefutable: isolated and overstimulated by the oppressive forest once that summer had gone, Atterton must have succumbed to panic and fled. For I was sure that he was no longer a resident of Radalen.

'By this time, night was falling fast and an icy wind

was causing a noisy commotion in the treeline. After over fourteen hours of continuous travel – including two plane journeys and a long drive – I needed shelter, food and rest. Going back the way I had come in the darkness would have been idiotic, so I made a quick decision: I would break in and get a fire going, first forcing the door with a tyre iron or a tool from the shed.

'But I'll admit, by that hour, it was not only exhaustion that spurred me on: I found the heavy, tense valley air peculiarly unpleasant. From out of the gloom came the odours of leaf rot and wet soil, and, if I'm not mistaken, the night air was also tainted by the smell of animal spoor. Not as searing as the pig, but less earthy than the cow. Something sharp and doglike. Perhaps Atterton had been using a local manure to cultivate the gardens? At any rate, I wanted to be spared the stench.

'Using a spade from the shed, I levered the lock out of the door-frame, and into the dark house I made my way. Guided by the twilight, I found an oil lamp in the kitchen and got it lit before checking the rest of the ground floor. The ceilings were much lower than I expected and the whole place reeked of timber, wood smoke and paraffin. Wherever I found them, I lit the lamps.

'As Atterton had promised, it was basic. Plainly and simply furnished and painted white throughout. The interior of the place reminded me of both a skiing chalet and a child's play house; everything seemed small, and cramped, especially the beds in the two upstairs bedrooms: little wooden boxes built beneath the slope of the roof.

'And while I searched about, I realised that Atterton had never finished packing. It appeared to me that he had started stuffing his clothes into cases, in the master bedroom, and to box his books in the parlour, only to have stopped, or been interrupted.

'In the kitchen, the surfaces were also littered with the rubbish produced by the last few days of his occupancy, and the metal bin beside the back door was full. That door was now sealed by uprooted floorboards. He'd been eating out of tins and rationing water out of a collection of enamel jugs. There was a pile of firewood beside the range, brought up from the dry goods cellar, in which I found the remainder of his supplies.

'So, I reasoned, Atterton had nailed himself inside the house, remained there for a few days and then fled. What else could I make of the evidence?

'I helped myself to some cracker breads, pickled herring and some interesting local beer, while pondering his disaster. I decided that I would wait until dawn and then make a cursory inspection of the surrounding terrain, in case he had injured himself, or completely lost his wits and was out there now like King Lear, raving on the blasted heath. I'd then drive to the nearest settlement to notify the authorities of the condition of the house, and Atterton's mind, in case a more thorough search of the locale needed to be arranged, or his whereabouts traced through airline records and so forth. Until then, I'd make camp in the parlour where I would get a fire going. I'd sleep in the chair, wrapped up in blankets.

'With the majority of the oil lamps arranged about the room, and a fire roaring in the grate, I tried my best to relieve the oppressive gloom of the place. I'll admit it, the place and its atmosphere unsettled me greatly; every window nailed shut and reinforced with oddments of wood, horseshoes hammered on the outside of every interior door, the wind crashing about in the trees outside, or buffeting the walls and whining under the room beams. And as night fell, the entire structure of the house was beset with all manner of groans, creaks, bangs and sly draughts. How Atterton could have even contemplated a year alone, out here, was beyond me. In itself, such a decision suggested the onset of mental illness, and it seemed his sanctuary had quickly become a prison – a theory confirmed by what I found amongst his papers.

'Besides his jottings detailing his chores and repairs and intentions to begin a vegetable patch, I discovered some heavily scored maps; they indicated the paths he'd trekked, waters he'd fished, the circle of stones on the high ground to the east of the property, and a loose folio of charcoal sketches. Amongst his drawings, there were depictions of the house from various angles, trout he'd caught and the church I had seen; all of which I took to be his earlier work, before his obsession with the stones took precedence. You see, there were scores of rubbings from the runestones on the hill, and dozens of sketches of the circle from within and without its rough boundary. And as I flicked through the papers, I noticed how he'd begun to incorporate text with the pictures. One page in particular caught my eye. It was titled 'From The Long Stone' and featured a rubbing from a weathered granite dolmen. Below, he'd added definition and detail to the etching's crude suggestiveness with a set of cutaways and expansion sketches. It was these convincing embellishments to which I took an instant aversion. *So what am I to make of this?* he'd written at the foot of the page.

'What indeed? If Atterton's sketch was to be believed, upon the stone was carved a silhouette of something both too tall and too thin to have been a man. A creature with long simian arms and clawed feet and hands, that appeared to stride across the face of the stone, while pulling behind itself a smaller figure, by the hair. The second character in the piece must have been a child, and it was being taken to what seemed to be a depository of bones chiselled on the far side of the stone; that is, if the pile of sticks were skulls, ribs and femurs and so forth.

'My eyes didn't dally upon the sketch, I can assure you, and I began to take a keener interest in the violence of the wind about the little house. The timbers were being harangued by these swooping blasts, from every direction, and I was at once reminded of how the noise of a strong wind in old timbers can produce the sounds of occupancy in empty rooms, particularly those above one's head. I had another suspicion that the elements were building to something, or heralding an arrival. I could have sworn there was some kind of anticipation in that wind.

'After perusing Atterton's final sketch, I confess to getting out of my chair in order to move it away from the window behind my head.

'You see, the last picture contained a rough impression, made by an unsteady hand, of the tracks Atterton claimed to have discovered *outside the gate*, *at the rear of the garden* and *under the parlour windows*. They were certainly the prints of a biped, not dissimilar to the human foot in shape, apart from the size and the length of the clawed toes, including a sixth on the heel; this was akin to that of the cat, used for disembowelling its prey. As a footnote, Atterton had added the date of composition too: four days prior to my arrival. He'd embellished that drawing with a comment: *No longer deterred by horseshoes or fire, it meant to get in.*

'I tried to persuade myself that this was more concocted evidence produced by a deeply disturbed mind; one driven to extremes of fancy and conjecture, delusion and suspicion, by the windy rigours of this climate and the haunting aspects of the landscape.

'I put down the sketches and took a firmer grip of the fire poker, longing for a more fitting distraction from the dark and the relentless wind than Atterton's illustrations. I had a go at *Great Expectations*, but my concentration was repeatedly fractured by sudden squalls against the walls of the parlour that made the foundations shudder and the lamps flicker. But some time after midnight, I mercifully succumbed to a fatigue peculiar to travel, fresh air and new surroundings, and I nodded off in my chair. Neither the angry roar of the gale nor the thumpings about the roof could stay my eyelids any longer.

'But a heavy crash, filled with the splintering of wood, brought me around soon enough and straight to my feet.

'About me in the parlour, the fire was no more than red embers and two of the lamps had gone out.

'The terrific noise had originated from the front of the house, and the most vulnerable spot, or so my senses cried out. Even with two metal latches in place, I had broken the main lock earlier, and it was the only access point not secured by six-inch nails and timber. I surmised that Atterton must have left that exit clear to make his final escape. Unable to spend another night trapped like a rabbit in a burrow, he must have made a dash for it, during his last morning.

'With the lamp and the small axe, used for breaking up the kindling, I stumbled through the parlour, into the dark kitchen and towards the little reception room that housed the front door. And the thought came to me then: *it could be Atterton trying to get inside.* Who knows what hours he kept out there? He could have been half-lunatic by then. But when I saw the state of the door, I soon shook off the last swaddling of sleep. At once, I abandoned my theory about Atterton breaking in. And besides that, I never had the breath to call out his name.

'Both hinges and latches had been ripped from the wall and now hung from a flattened door. It had been smashed inwards from the outside by considerable force. Did a man have such strength? Even a madman?

'The freezing night air hit me with a *whump* that failed to dispel what I would call an intensification of the stench that I had smelled seeping from the trees around the garden earlier: the damp of an unlit forest floor tinged with a bestial pungency; the raw miasma that strikes one near the stained concrete of the zoo cage. And it filled the house.

'I found it impossible to even step onto the porch and investigate. I dithered in the hall and suddenly comprehended Atterton's belief in the necessity of barricades: someone, or *something*, was terrorising the property under the cover of moonless nights. An assailant of significant size and power.

'I held the lamp up and tried to shed some light on the doorway and whatever lay beyond. Screwing up my eyes, all I could make out was the end of the porch and a murky impression of the grass below the steps.

'The lamp flickered and was nearly doused by another gust of wind that whipped across the paddock from the treeline. "Who's there?" I called out, and in a voice that broke like an adolescent's.

'I put the lamp on the floor beside my feet and went to raise the door when I heard the sound of a footfall. Behind me. In the kitchen. The dark kitchen that I had just come through, wide-eyed but drowsy.

'Then another floorboard creaked. Followed by the sound of a snort; the kind a bullock might make.

'Whatever had smashed down the door was inside the house with me. I stopped breathing and felt disoriented by an acute terror that I cannot begin to articulate. I whimpered like a child and I cringed as if anticipating a blow from behind. One more sound from the darkness and I was sure that my heart would stop beating. I could not bear to turn my head and see what now stood behind me.

'Then I heard it again. The squeak of a floorboard beneath another step taken, closer. And there was something at the end of the sound, a scratching, that inserted the picture from Atterton's sketches into my mind: a long foot, tipped with claws, but now moving across a wooden floor toward me.

'I sprang about-face and knocked the lamp onto its side with a clatter that made me suck in my breath, and cry out, "Oh, God!" At that moment, I saw the intruder, bent over and tensing long limbs inside the kitchen.

'I say I saw *something*. I mostly saw a silhouette for a moment before the lamp spluttered out. But in that crouching figure I am sure I detected a wet snout, yellow canines and blood-spoiled eyes in a black face. The head was close to the ceiling, against which it was stooped over, unable to stand upright, even with its spindly legs bent at the knee.

'I ran out of the building and into the darkness, and in the direction of the car. Which I hit with my knees at the very same moment as the door to Atterton's house was slammed hard against the floorboards by a heavy weight landing upon it. That noise, I assumed, was of the door being trampled, or run over, and it signalled that the trespasser was now outside *with me.*

'From force of habit I'd locked the car and activated the alarm, which I set off after striking the vehicle at full pelt. It was the shrieking of the alarm, I believe in hindsight, that saved my life. It must have momentarily stunned my pursuer, and given me enough time to get the keys from my jacket pocket and get the car unlocked and my body eventually into the driver's seat. Had those valuable few seconds not been purchased, I am sure that I would never have left Radalen. And leaving the place, I am convinced, is something that Atterton never managed to achieve.

'I stalled the car three times. Once because I had left it in gear. The second time because the engine was cold. And the third time because, when I turned the lights on, I caught sight of something in the rear-view mirror, all lit up in red, that made me take both feet off the pedals in shock.

'When I managed to get the car moving, across the paddock and onto the narrow entry road, driving faster than caution advised, *it* kept pace with me. Sometimes behind, loping along the track, a few feet back from the bumper, and sometimes alongside me in the trees at the side of the road. At least I think it was my pursuer that rubbed and scratched up against the car like that. And as I slowed down to take the bends in the road, something outside the vehicle tried to hold the car still. It meant to have me that night, and I believe it tracked me for over ten kilometres.

'I drove through the night and into the welcome dawn, straight onto Kiruna, where I raised the alarm about Atterton. That was before paying over two thousand pounds for the damage sustained to the car's paintwork and, in some places, to the actual steel of the door panels.'

It was a much paler and strained figure who finished the story for me in the library of our club. The epilogue Henry only managed to deliver after another glass of brandy:

'They never found him. A removal company sent a van the Friday before my arrival, but found the property much the same as I found it: deserted and crudely boarded up. Atterton never set foot on the plane. He never left the valley.

'Just as the first snow began to fall, the forestry commission and army searched the area and found no definite trace of him either, and could shed no light on his disappearance. They even used a helicopter to search the valley, but found nothing unusual except an abandoned bicycle, about three kilometres from the *Fritidshus*. Though the ownership of the bike was never established, I think it must have been his.

'In Sweden, poor Atterton is still listed as a missing person.'

Mother's Milk

Exiled like a degenerate king on a cardboard throne, Saul sleeps down here in the gloom, same time every day. All seven feet of his bulk rest. Thick limbs splay amongst the boxes and acres of bubble-wrap. His big head is thrown back and making strangled sounds. There is a moon of a face above a neck tiered with fat, luminous from afar in the dusk of the warehouse.

Left among empty factories on the edge of the city, just the two of us work here in this metal labyrinth, where aisles of skeletal shelves the colour of battleships go on for ever. Above us the buzzing fluorescent suns on the corrugated ceiling bleach our skin. Together, we are neglected by the managers in a distant office block and avoided by the drivers who come for our packages: square mountains of boxes that we pack, seal, stack and then stuff into the lorry that is parked inside the giant roller doors at the end of the day.

As I watch Saul sleep until the afternoon period, when our shuffling under the weight of boxes begins again, I fancy I could run away. But he makes sounds like gas escaping whenever I stray far. Through those sticky lids, I think he can see me.

Saul, I whisper. Saul, Saul, it's time. My voice is quiet and I keep my distance from the alabaster mass as I try to rouse it. Rising without a sound from sleep or out of the shadowy aisles, he still frightens me.

Before me, an eye opens: a blank, grey shark eye. Soon joined by the other eye to move inside the doughy curves of his eye sockets. There is a sound from dewy lips as if a billiard ball is passed from one cheek to another. Then Saul speaks. Oversized tongue speech that I have learned to understand. Milk. He wants milk. And then we work some more before the pickup.

After lifting the metal flask from the little white table, I cradle the sloshing torpedo in my arms and deliver it to his moist paws. Big hands gently take it with a touch like cold cheese. Turning my face away I hear guzzling sounds but do not watch the feeding. It reminds me of her, the *mother*. Saul's mother. My mother, she likes to think.

Signalled by a grunt, I collect the flask when he's finished. Watching my own hands tremble on the lid, screwed tightly down, my stomach flops over as I carry the flask back to the little white table. Hunger starts in me with a growl and I can feel Saul smiling behind me. In the past I would only take the milk in tea, but now there's no resisting such delicious cream. At night I dream of milk.

With the work done we go again to the place Saul calls home: a house on the top of a hill, protected by a fence and hidden by the trees and the dark. We are the last people to leave the bus and dismount by the big oaks at the bottom of the hill. Then the bus turns around, almost by itself because the driver never stops staring at us.

Old iron bars, with spikes on top, run around the base of the hill, but Saul has a key for the heavy gate I can't move. He opens the gate and we pass through. It slams shut behind us.

Walking in silence, we go through the black gaps between tree trunks. Pine needle and weedy smells rise thickly from the ground. Above, the leafy canopy shuts out the light. Darkness presses against us and I feel peculiar as the odours of the forest pad my brain with a thick creamy drowsiness, flowing through me and over me and getting behind my eyes too. But with nowhere else to go, I follow Saul's shambling up the path and into the restless woods where I imagine children running away from the dewy-faced thing in front of me; flitting like little ghosts like they did when I escaped and ran blind into the shopping centre full of Christmas lights. What a commotion I caused. Seeing my reflection in a shop window made me weep like a baby; a big, fat, white baby. That was a long time ago and I haven't run away since.

Carrying the can of milk, which is now empty and must be brought home every day, I whip my head from side to side. Birds the size of dogs are flapping out there. They crash about in the undergrowth and their wings make wet leather sounds. I can't see them but Saul told me they're what's left of unfarmed game. Can't picture pheasants. My mind tries to see greeny-blue birds pecking the ground nearby but my heart still gallops inside my mouth when I hear them. Same every night and there have been many journeys up through the trees.

As we climb Saul makes a smell amongst the huge oaks and conifers. Something bubbles from his flabby body and smells of sulphur. I make the same smell now. It comes from the milk; gallons of frothing sweetness that we slurp down.

After passing through acres of woody darkness we come to the houses that have been owned by Saul's family for longer than they can remember. Looking up from the bottom of the hill, you can't see the houses because they are smothered by the trees where the forest suddenly thickens around the two white buildings. Upper boughs and branches then curl over the pointy, red-tiled roofs to blot out the stars. And only when you're in the centre of the garden can you see the sky through a small hole, up in the top of the trees, like you're at the bottom of a huge bowl with curved sides and a rim.

After returning from my first escape, I spent ages trying

to find the garden gate on my hands and knees, so frightened by the loud flapping in the woods around me. And in the end only my stomach was able to lead me back to the gate and the houses where the milk is kept.

When we pass through the hidden gate and go through the corral of trees the first thing we see is a pale lawn. Milky green grass grows here. It's short and soft, on dirt that is black if you dig down with a finger. The lawn is perfectly flat and smells sweet too. It's amazing, in all these trees is this circle of grass like the top of the hill has been chopped off for the houses, and the dances that I dream of.

This evening, soon as I'm in the garden the grass catches my eyes and holds my stare. It grows in my dreams. Sometimes in the middle of the night I imagine I've woken up face-down, and that I'm pushing my nose and mouth into the lawn's soft pelt, sucking the sugary blades. Shining under the strongest moons, the lawn often looks like a big pond too. I like to watch it from my window to bring the dreams back. The good dreams; not the bad ones when things move across the bright surface.

Silence and darkness inside the houses now. No lights on behind the windows in the square white walls that remind me of the sheds that farm animals live inside. There are no flowers or shrubs around the great solid building. It is divided into two houses by a thin inner wall. Each back door faces the milky pasture and leads into a kitchen. Like lonely sentinels the houses watch the sky and are lost to the world below.

In the kitchen of our house, we light the lamps full of pink oil and wait. But never for very long. Over they come, rushing through the back door: the mother and the brother, Ethan. In the days before I drank the milk, I used to wonder what they were doing next door with the lights out. Soon as I started to drink, I stopped thinking about it.

Be humble, stay quiet, lower the eyes; in the mother's presence it is best not to stare. Her shape is vaster than the first son Saul, but the pallor of the flesh is the same.

With my eyes on the floor I can see the bottom of the floral dress that sticks to her bulk in places. In the pinky light and rushing shadows I see sparrow legs under the hem, as if her pudding body has been smashed down on two bone pins to stop it rolling around on the floor. But she's fast on those legs. Usually, I barely have time to run upstairs and hide in my room when I hear her feet skittering around from next door.

She speaks to me in a deep voice. With booming words she says I have done wrong. Moving my eyes I look at the tiny 'Dainty Maid' sign on the enamel cooker that is next to the rickety kitchen table. Reading the letters to take my mind off her voice, I see they are made from chrome, like the names on the metal grilles of old cars.

Look at me, little bastard, she says.

I shake my head. I don't want to look. She makes me sick; even more than my own bulbous shape looking out of a mirror. Perhaps this is why there are no mirrors in our house, but in the bus window I can always see what the milk has done to my face.

Shadows flick around her stick-legs, made by the quick movements of her short arms. Her gruff voice rises. Slowly, I turn my hot face from the 'Dainty Maid' and look at her naked arms. There is no elbow. Dimpled stumps end in baby hands. Puppet fingers move like anemones in a rock pool.

Look at me, little bastard.

This time I obey.

White eyes with a purple iris are pressed like studs into the cushion of her face. On top of her head is a messy thatch of fine white hair. Around the wet mouth there is more hair.

I have done wrong, she says. Never bring milk and bread home from the outside. How many times have you been told? She thought I was ready. Ready for what? Doesn't she realise that I will always hold onto the last bit of myself, what is left of me; those fuzzy images I have in my memory before the milk cravings start fires inside my body?

This scolding means that she has been in my little room and gone through my things. All alone in the unlit house, cleaning and sweeping while I'm at work, she searches about. I imagine her face when she found the loaf and the carton of normal milk that I brought home yesterday. I bet she screamed.

The telling off is soon over. She has a good mind not to give me milk tonight. On my face there must be a look of horror. I feel it tighten my podgy cheeks and crease my forehead. But then she smiles. I will be allowed my share after all. Now where is the dirty washing? she asks. I want all of it.

Ethan appears from around the hem of her yellow and brown circus-tent dress. Glad to see me and pleased the telling off is over, he frolics like a puppy. He jabbers at me in his strange buzzing voice that I can hardly make sense of, even after all this time. To please the watching mother, for it is my job to amuse Ethan, I hold a stupid grin on my face until it aches. His small body speeds around the kitchen like a fleshy barrel on tiny legs, covered in old man's hair. Jabber, jabber, jabber. Will he ever shut up? Sometimes I want to smack his little pig face. But he'll only run next door and tell the mother.

After the mother collects the washing in white pillow cases, she leaves the kitchen and returns to her house next door. Saul, Ethan and I sit around the wooden table in the flickering pink kitchen and wait. Our elbows make the table rock where the oil lanterns sit. Light ripples against the brown cupboards, shining on all the glass windows and off the china dishes we are forbidden to touch.

Groaning and yawning sounds start inside us all when we hear her coming back. Outside, she waddles across the lawn to make us wait, like a big plucked goose with no beak and chin feathers.

Milk! Here is the milk, frothing and slopping in big, ivory-coloured jugs. It's brought around on a broad tin tray, painted with green, blue and red stripes. Her foetal paws hold the tray under her chin and it always looks so heavy for her. There's one flagon each. Little squalls and squirts of excitement start in Saul, Ethan and me. Warm cream smells fill my nose and I can almost see the little bubbles in the soupy fluid. It's like starving and dying of thirst when you're near the fresh stuff. You have to have it quickly. Slug it down with big gulps and let it thicken inside you, all the way down until your belly is full. There is bread too. Oily bread soaked in cream. Steady, boys, she says, but all we can hear is the rushing sound when we close our eyes and feed.

After the meal I run upstairs to make sure that the mother hasn't been stealing again. I know she has been in my room to take my normal bread and milk, which is so bland and thin and makes me sick now. Straight out it comes like a fountain after it touches my stomach. But maybe, I tell myself, outside milk will help water down the strength of her produce.

In the bedroom I go rummaging through the bottom of the cupboard with the mothball smell, to check my little stash. There should be a comb, a wallet and a broken watch in a shoebox. Everything else has gone. There used to be letters held together by a rubber band but the mother took them. This house doesn't have a number and no one writes to the family anyway, but people used to mail letters to the store where I work with Saul. A girl used to send letters and cards for a while too, and I liked the one with 'happy birthday' written on it. Big pink letters on the front and a blue number thirty inside.

Although nothing more has been taken from the shoebox, I see the contents are disturbed. The mother's little hands have been in here then. Fortunately I keep the photo of the girl safe under my mattress. I want to remember the girl. Like I do in the store before the hunger grows and I circle the little white table with the metal flask on top. But when I look for the photo of the girl with the charcoal eyes, thin body and long brown hair, the rage comes out. The mother has taken the photo along with the bread and milk.

Anger boils inside me and sweats across my skin. I decide to escape again. These are the same feelings as before, when I ran down through the trees and managed to get over the gate. Back then I wasn't so fat or sleepy and the cold snow kept me awake. I hate myself for taking the milk. If I had left it alone back in the beginning of the tenancy, I would be with the girl I can't remember properly, and not with the mother. My hate adds to the rage.

I run downstairs and smash the milk jug on the kitchen floor. Upstairs, Saul closes his heavy book with a thump that I hear through the ceiling. Ethan appears from under the table to buzz and jabber and run around the kitchen as if the house is on fire. Shouting and slamming, I run from the house, through the back door and into the garden. Heading for the gate and the woods beyond, I cross the lawn. Anger drives my podgy legs and I don't even care about the pain between my rubbing thighs. My heart gurgles and my little lungs feel raw but I keep running.

Shouldn't have turned around by the gate. I only look to see if Saul or Ethan are following me. They aren't, but I see movement in the mother's house. At the kitchen window is a face, pressed against the glass. What looks like a huge white hare with buck teeth stares at me with pink eyes. It is the father.

My slippery hand goes still on the ring-shaped gate handle. I don't like those eyes one bit. He's the one the mother keeps locked away next door; the one with the hiccupping voice that used to come through the wall at night when I first moved here. He was angry back then and he's angry now, watching me trying to escape. Out come his hiccupping shrieks making the glass tremble, and up go his goaty legs with the hard bone at the end to rattle, scratch, rattle on the glass like he wants to get to me. Now the mother's face appears in the gloom behind the father, all red and howling because she's heard the jug smash. From the mother's kitchen, there is a sound of a door being unlocked and I watch the father's grimace turn into a grin. She's letting him out to catch me.

I run from the gate, back across the milky green grass to our house, and don't turn my head. But he's so fast. When I reach the kitchen, I can already hear his bone feet on the tiles behind me, getting louder as he gets closer. Soon, I can smell his goaty breath as he snorts over my shoulder and all I can think of are his yellow teeth and how they must bite with a wooden clacking sound. I want my heart to stop; then it will be over quickly.

Jabbering, Ethan runs into his legs and stops him from catching me. There is a crash behind my back. One of the pinky lamps smashes on the floor and the table skids across the tiles and hits the 'Dainty Maid' enamel cooker. Ethan is hurt and I hear him squeal as the father stamps on his hairy back with those clip-cloppity feet.

Up the stairs I run and hear the mother start to bellow at the father for crushing Ethan. There is more smashing and howling in the kitchen as I slip into my room. The truckle bed goes against the door.

Now I am ill, laid up with a fever, and the dreams are worse. For two days I've been off the milk and it has made me sick. Ethan is outside my bedroom door, buzzing. His words are madness. He is saying the milk will make me better and the mother is angry. When she is angry we all suffer. He tells me the mother has said that I am never to go to work again. I have done wrong, she says. I'm a little bastard who can't be trusted.

And I'm hurting inside now; dry and gritty and sawn in my throat and lungs. It's like there's broken glass inside my stomach too, cutting my softness, and a little voice tells me to drink milk because it will fill in the slashes and take away the pain. And all I can think of is the creaminess inside the ivory jugs. Cravings make me weep salty tears and I hate myself even more. All I want to do is go back to the time of the debts and say no to the warehouse job where I first met Saul. Then I could also say no to the little room and the sweet, sweet milk.

Back in the days of my early tenancy, I wanted to be sick whenever I saw the milk. Laden with tins and packages of normal food I would struggle up the hill through the black forest, resisting her. There was no way I wanted to drink that brew with the offal taint and soupy thickness. But every night, it would be brought across in huge jugs, slightly steaming, and left upon the kitchen table for the sons to feed from. The sounds they made when feasting made me think of new accommodation. I would have moved out too if I hadn't touched the milk.

As if it were poison, whenever I left a carton or bottle in the otherwise empty 'Dainty Maid' fridge, she would pour my normal supermarket milk away. With no other choice, I got into the habit of storing a little emergency container under my truckle bed. But once, when it ran dry with a last rattle and I had a desire for hot tea to stave off the night cold, I was trapped into tasting her produce. To whiten my tea, I used a teaspoon of her milk from the jug that had been left on the kitchen table. And it was delicious; the best tea I ever tasted. Thick and sweet and warming me up like a shot of whisky, while filling my belly like a big roast dinner. Then, a few days later, I tried it on some cereal. Just a few warm dollops with my nose turned away from the smell. As I ate, loving spoonfuls wrapped my body in warm feather pillows and filled my head with sleepiness and the promise of good dreams. In secret, I went to that jug again and again, like a drowsy bear who found a honeycomb in a log. Eventually, Ethan saw me and sped next door. When he returned with the mother, she was smiling and her cheeks were ruddy. That was the start of my troubles.

If only I'd trusted my instincts. Maybe the last tenant did and escaped. There was another, you see, before me in the little room upstairs with the cupboard, greasy wallpaper and child's truckle bed that my feet hang over. I have seen his markings and know he had the dreams. Maybe he hid under the bed after dreaming of the dances down on the milky green grass and scratched the last of himself away on the wooden slats beneath the tiny springs. Milk, milk, milk, he scratched over and over again with a nail or belt buckle. He knew the craving, when a thousand fish-hooks snag in your belly, and a shrill inside voice screams until it's smashed all of the windows in your head. But where is the last tenant now? If he escaped then so can I. Soon.

Locked in my room without the milk, I'm struggling to fight off the rolling waves of yellowy fever. Sometimes my head gets a little clearer, but not in the cool way it used to at work before I supped with relish. When I'm not so sick and can move a bit, I write tiny notes under the bed for the next person who takes this room, drinks the milk and has their clothes washed by the mother.

The father is outside the door now. Up he comes every day and chitter-chatters like an ape, but I won't let him in. Before I smashed the milk jug the mother used to threaten me with the father. My husband will bite you, she'd say, if you don't go in with Ethan at night. Ethan gets lonely in his little box, but the straw smells like the meaty chairs downstairs and I always hated going in with him. I'll have to wait until

Ethan and the father have gone from outside the door of my room before the next escape is attempted.

There are noises too at night. The worst sounds come out of Saul's room.

Since I've been here, Saul follows the same routine. After work and the feeding he always goes to his room, which is next door to mine, to read his heavy books and he never comes out until the following morning. In the early evening when the mother's curfew is announced by her banging on the walls, the rest of us go to bed and dream. But now I'm awake for most of the night, rolling and turning, I hear her moving up the stairs. I know it's her because their feet make different sounds like their voices: Ethan scrabbles, Saul shambles, the father clip-clops and the mother skitters like a chicken in straw. Most nights, she scratches up the stairs on her bird legs and goes into Saul's room. It is then I cover my ears, unable to listen to the bumping sounds.

But dreaming is the most frightening part of being a prisoner. I'm never sure whether I'm awake or asleep now and all the good dreams have gone. Stuck in my tiny room, passing in and out of sleep, sometimes disturbed by the shifting sounds the father makes outside – I think he sleeps by the door now – I dream of the dances. The whole garden is lit up by a yellow moon, the colour of the fever inside me, with thin clouds drifting across its brightness. It's as if the stars are closer to the earth too when the family forms the circle. Croaking and bellowing, Ethan and the father hop and skip round and round the mother, who moves slowly on her hands and knees with her face in the grass, while Saul chants things from the side in his singing bark. He has a book open and sits beneath my window like a white whale glowing on a strange beach. They are calling out to something in the sky with words I have never heard and don't understand. But these names and words pull me from sleep, sometimes with a scream.

When I wake up, I am always standing by the window looking down at the milky green grass, with my body all moist. The garden is empty, but there is a faint ring still left on the lawn as if it has been trampled by skipping feet. Then the soft blades of grass straighten themselves, and in the centre of the slowly vanishing circle the lawn is silvery with midnight dew.

I could break the window to lick that moisture down. To stop the yellow fever and parched throat that has stolen my voice. Nothing has passed my lips for three days and nights and much of my strength has gone. Maybe a final slurp of the milk will allow me to escape, but you can never trust yourself after swallowing that creamy sweetness.

Fourth day, maybe the fifth, and my room is starting to smell. If I don't drink soon I'll dry out and die. Feeling my face with slow-moving fingers, I touch the loose flesh. All over my body the skin has gone yellow. Even the little white hairs are dying on my tummy. Cramps have taken over from the fever and sickness, but they're half-hidden by weakness.

No matter how stained and sharp the father's teeth are, or how fast he can run, or how big the forest birds are, I must escape tonight. You see, they've all been up today and talked through the door. It's no good, staying in there. Come and drink the milk, Saul said. Tonight is very important, he said. Everything is ready and you don't want to miss out. We've all worked very hard to welcome you into the family. Ethan just buzzed and squealed, but the mother made threats. This is your last chance, she said. If you come out right now I won't let my husband bite and we'll forget about how bad you've been. But if you don't come out, I'll put you to sleep for good. I'll put your big head in a bowl of water and drown you, like the last one. You'd grown so well, she said. Almost ready. All you had to do was grow some more for the joining.

Rage keeps me awake and I hold the bed against the door with my body on top. Joining will be the end of me.

There was glee in her voice when she mentioned it. Let them dance beneath the vapours and the yellow moon. When they gather on the grass, I won't be here.

Now it's quiet outside, thoughts of escape give me a shiver and start a dripping in my gut. I make my move and ease the truckle bed away from the door, bit by bit, while listening out for the father. Silence fills the house. Maybe they're next door. All I have to do, I tell myself, is go out of the house, leave the garden, run through the woods and then climb over the gate by the bus stop. And this time I won't come back when the children start screaming.

Peering through a tiny gap between the door and the frame, I can see no one outside between the grubby walls on the landing. So out I go, breathing softly with little shudders in my lungs, into the dark house.

Creamy smells surround me on the unlit stairs, like soft hands reaching out from the stains on the walls. Even the bricks beneath the dirty wallpaper must have milk inside them and I hold my sagging face to stop the spinning inside my skull.

I'm getting nearer the kitchen, with the pinky glow and the flicker of shadow against the table and the cabinets, which I can see from the bottom of the staircase. I continue past the old parlour with the horsehair chairs that smell of bad meat. I think of sitting in there for a while to catch my breath and to stop the dizzies, but then the idea of sitting on those fleshy things, surrounded by the silk wallpaper gone brown with damp and smelling of sulphur, makes me go all seasicky.

In the kitchen, the lamps are lit but the jugs are empty. I look inside them and dry belches rise to my mouth. My eyes screw up from the hot-fire cramps that pinch my inner softness between tweezer fingers. Nothing in the enamel 'Dainty Maid' fridge either. Vanilla light glows thickly around the frosted-glass shelves and sends me reeling back to the table. I can't stop my snorting sounds or the licking tongue, dry as toast, that comes through my puffy lips to touch the cool ivory jugs.

Then I hear the song. Saul's chant is coming through the kitchen wall that attaches us to the mother's house. Strange barking music with the family's chorus beneath his dog sounds. Slipping to the cold, tiled floor, neatly swept by the mother, I feel their rhythms and howls pulling at my clammy body. Making sucking sounds with my belly, I squirm across the floor and out the back door to the milky green grass.

Now there is a fight inside me between two voices. Something whispers about the gate and escape, pulling my squinty eyes across to the arch in the trees, where the metal ring hangs against the dark planks. But the other voice is screaming.

I go looking for milk.

Crying, I move like a thing, yellow and soft, that has fallen from a fisherman's rough hand into the grass. Slowly, I make my way to the back door of the mother's house. I can't stop myself and the screaming voice inside me softens. That's it, just a sip to feel better, it sings.

The expectation of milk eases the gritty feeling inside the pipes and tubes beneath my skin, and my naked flesh shines under the biggest moon, set low in the night sky over the milky green grass whose caressing blades sweep and brush beneath me, feeding me towards her kitchen. Crawling over the little step before the door, I wince at the roughness of stone against my pale underside.

Pink oil has been lit in four lamps inside her kitchen and it's as if I am still on the floor of our house. Things are much the same in here, save for the wooden service hatch set between the wall cabinets and work surface. Little curved dents on the swept tiles, made by the father's feet, make me stand up. The family's song has eased to a halt. A smacking of lips begins on the other side of the hatch.

Snuffling takes over from my dry-mouth panting and I see my hands reach for the hatch. Thick fingers work by themselves to nudge and press about for the plastic hole, big enough for a thumb. The wooden doors of the hatch slide through the runners soundlessly and make a hole for the kitchen light to fall through. Staring into the moving darkness, my eyes follow a funnel of pink light, dropping like a ray through a church window.

Before my eyes, pallid shapes move about the floor. Wet and tangled, the family squirms before the mother who sways back on her haunches. A moist face pauses in its feeding and whimpers a message up to the provider. Another's lips part to show rows of small square teeth before turning away from me. They all mewl, then twist aside, and the pinky light strikes her.

Tiny fingers pinch the hem of the floral dress and hold it under her chins. Her eyes are full of excitement. Unveiled is the swollen belly with its pasture of teats among the white hairs. Opaque tears of sweet milk, so thick and dangly, fall to the family and melt something inside me.

With a broad smile, mother invites me to join them.

Yellow Teeth

I made a terrible mistake.

It's hard to remember how he came to be here. The precise transaction of words that allowed Ewan inside escape me now. Did I ever actually invite him across the threshold of my home? I cannot remember doing that. All that remains is a sense of an awkward, fretting reluctance on my part to permit any intrusion into my orderly existence. A resistance that he brushed aside with the waft of one dirty hand. And in no time, the silence, the white walls, the absence of dust, the right angles, the open spaces were lost, for ever.

His need for shelter and support became a wheedling insistence. I remember that much. A cry for help from an old *friend*, though he was never more than an acquaintance at best. He had nowhere else to go. He just kept calling and calling and calling.

The frequency of his visits to my one-bedroom flat in Bayswater, and the first home that I'd ever owned, increased over the summer until he began to cry in my presence. Dishevelled and drunk before noon, with his big, shiny face held in a cage of long fingers, the nails black with dirt, he would sob. Paralysed by discomfort, I would just watch and fidget.

But at times, I also wanted to laugh out loud at the long, oily hair hanging like old rope from beneath a baseball cap that was jammed onto the crown of his unusual skull: flat at the back, but flush with the flabby neck and showing no definition to the shoulders. The squashed-up face was immediately monstrous to an onlooker too, with that low brow above the dark eyes, the nose a porcine snout, and those damn teeth creating an orifice both bestial and curiously feminine. Yes, there was something peculiarly sexual about his mouth that compelled me to stare and to experience a disgust akin to the revulsion I once experienced when suddenly confronted by the genitals of a female baboon in a zoo. Perhaps it was the fringe of black beard that made his lips appear so red, so engorged, and perhaps it was the contrast of the bright, wet lips that made his square teeth appear so yellow. A prehistoric mouth, I remember thinking; there was simply nothing contemporary about it.

I'd not seen Ewan once in the ten years since he dropped out of university in his first year. He'd just arrived in London that spring, fresh from a decade of disappointment and mishap, of which the details remain unclear to me. But he claimed to have been betrayed, mistreated and set upon many times. And he always spoke in grand platitudes about his plight, as if he'd endured a form of biblical suffering alone, for so long.

Blinking bloodshot eyes at the vaulted ceiling of King's Cross station, one huge hand holding a single bin-bag full of paper, he seems to have begun searching for me as soon as he arrived in the city. Where else could he go? He was tired of being alone.

When I think back now, I realise how soon, in my own home, I became his hostage. Even before he spent a night under my roof, the roles had been assigned, with Ewan slouched in my favourite chair, where I used to sit and read beside the sash window that overlooked a chestnut tree. The place I felt most comfortable. A spot that protected me. And there I was, always diminished in shadow on the sofa, merely listening.

I'd arranged the room around my favourite chair. It was an apex of a triangle that offered the best reception from the stereo speakers, and the most ideal view of the television, the prints and photographs on the walls, my book collection, my towers of CDs and my collection of absinthe bottles. All gone now. But pushing me aside in the hallway the moment I had the front door open, Ewan would make straight for that chair, like some impostor with pretensions to a throne. He'd never pause to remove the ripped anorak, or to kick off the worn-out schoolish shoes, split across the bridge of the toes, the soles ground down to a rubber membrane by his endless, directionless walks around the city.

Twice I had seen him in West London before he came to call the first time; a tall but hunched figure in an old raincoat, muttering anxiously to himself, never looking another in the eye. Pacing, agitated, jobless, alone, whispering and getting closer to the one thing that he considered companionable and safe, and twice I'd avoided him. Ducking into a second-hand clothes shop the first time, and back-pedalling into the mouth of Queensway tube station during the second sighting.

So how did he find me? Who gave him my address? Few of my crowd at university that I remained in contact with even remembered him. And none of them had heard from him since he'd dropped out. He must have followed me home from the street. Come across me as I shopped for organic produce, or antiques on the Portobello Road. But then how did he know where to look in the first place? How did he find the specific area in West London? Am I to believe that it was coincidence? I don't know. He would never tell me and only smile whenever I asked him how he found me. He liked to know things that I did not.

But then he was there, with me, all of the time. He and I and that awful smell that he brought with him.

Whenever I opened the front door, the smell would rush out to embrace me from the long hall. One week after his status changed from visitor to resident, the odour still startled me: the sweat of cattle, sharp and choking; a foot odour close to the waft of regurgitation; the kidney and shellfish of a male groin too long unclean; and something else, like burned bone, binding all of the other flavours together.

Coughing to clear my airways was no use; the entire flat had filled with his scent. Seeping from the living room he occupied, clouding down the hallway, filling the kitchen and bathroom, lingering fresh in my room to the ceiling, the smell was everywhere and on all of my things. Absorbed by upholstery and fabric, thick in the confined spaces of wardrobe and drawer, drifting from every book cover and ornament, his spore was ever present.

And I remember our first confrontation clearly. It was a Monday evening after I'd returned home from the studio, one week since his 'stay' began, and as I unlaced my shoes in the hallway I broke out into a sudden and uncomfortable sweat. Even though it had been a hot day, all of the windows in the flat were closed and the curtains were drawn in each room. From the kitchen I heard the whoosh of the central heating boiler. Electric lights burned in every room save the lounge, where only the television screen offered any illumination, and a white-blue light flickered under the closed door. He never switched the set off and sat far too close to the screen, like a child that had never been told otherwise. He'd already staked out that room as his own territory, and turned it into an unnerving facsimile of his room in halls at university. A disorderly nest, I thought, with the smell of a landfill.

I hung up my coat and dropped my briefcase in the kitchen. My nails cut half-moons into the palm of each hand. Clenching my teeth until my jaw ached, I surveyed the mess he'd made. Pools of milk, scattered granules of sugar and dregs of tea were spilled across the steel surfaces around the cooker. Something red had dried hard over a gas ring and trickled down the glass of the oven door: tomato sauce from a can of Scooby-Doo pasta shapes I found abandoned and sticky on a stool before the breakfast bar. A brown clump of exhausted teabags stained the draining board. A clutter of soiled crockery and long black hairs filled the dry sink. Two saucepans encrusted with dried soup sat on the breadboard beside a tub of my butter, congealing with the lid off. Beside the kettle, with his black fingerprints on the plastic handle, four of my compact discs lay face-down in a galaxy of scattered sea salt.

A gravity of exhaustion dropped through me and I leaned against a wall. The place had been spotless that morning. Before work, I'd already cleaned his mess from the weekend. Since I'd granted him a few days to sort himself out, a similar soiling had awaited me each evening. I was too tired for this. Too fatigued for my run in the park. Couldn't face cleaning up in order to cook. Already he was eroding my routines, sapping my will and ruining the place that I considered a sanctuary. *Enough of this*, I said to myself, *again*.

But the stench outside the living room was worst of all, almost pulsing from under the door. I went to knock, then paused and loathed myself for this enduring but pathetic display of courtesy. Why maintain the charade of playing the perfect host? He had no respect for me, my privacy or my possessions.

Strangled by an anger that I recognised as unhealthy, I turned away from the living-room door. Too enraged to articulate my grievances, to speak to Ewan in a coherent manner, and to appear reasonable, I walked away. Or was it something else? If I am honest, I now acknowledge that I was also afraid to enter the lounge and to confront him. It was fear, but not a fear for my own safety. More an emotion similar to wandering through a smell of corruption in a wood and declining to investigate in case some tortured image in the undergrowth was impressed upon the memory.

Even then, at the beginning, I was afraid of what I might see in the rooms that Ewan had occupied.

I'd snapped at him before. I'd lost my temper and raised my voice, but only succeeded in driving him deeper into self-pity and an absorbing despair, in itself fatiguing to watch.

I went to my room to change. A territory that I had been increasingly withdrawing inside, as if driven into the very keep of my castle by the intrusion of noise, and the filth of a plague that had blithely breached the walls. I decided to take a shower too, and to try and calm down before the impending confrontation; I'd need a clear head and steady voice to penetrate his peculiar childlike reason, and his convenient inability to comprehend most of what I said that was not in his favour.

But my attempt to calm down was derailed the moment that I set foot inside my bedroom. That day, he had been in there. *Again*. Either he lacked the intelligence to cover his tracks or he exhibited a wilful disregard for my wishes. After the last time, I asked him not to go into my room. But I could clearly see open drawers in my filing cabinet and the indent of his backside on my duvet as he'd sat and examined things. Private things.

Into the lounge I burst.

And was immediately disoriented. Canned laughter crackled from the speakers. The floor vibrated. I coughed. Covered my nose and mouth. In my mind I saw an image of long, yellow toenails and underwear soiled brown like a corpse's shroud. In my mouth I could taste his body. I coughed again, though it sounded more like retching.

In the gloom I spied his dark shape slumped into my favourite chair. One shoe had been removed and the pale foot was placed in his lap. In the cartoon on the television something exploded white and, for a second, I saw the full horror of that foot. Yellow teeth gritted and nose ruffled, eyes slit, brow furrowed, he concentrated as two of his dirty claws scratched against the crispy red psoriasis on his instep.

'Jesus,' I said, as my foot kicked an empty beer can and sent it skidding into the teacups beneath the littered coffee table. I snatched the remote control off the table and turned the television volume down. Ewan pulled the remnant of the sock over the foot and ankle.

'It itches,' he said, smiling.

'I'm not surprised.' My chest was tight. My mind blocked. What was I going to say? I was choked with rage. Did this make me forget what I was going to say? Perhaps the intense way he stared at me was disarming. He seemed uninterested in the glance; his eyes were always still. He looked at me like a cat that my family used to have when I was a child. A cat that would sit and stare. Its black eyes made me feel vulnerable and guilty somehow, as if its suspicions of my unacceptable thoughts were something more than a hunch. But he, like the cat, was really expecting some kind of challenge or attack. These were the eyes of someone incapable of trust.

I looked away. I suffered an aversion – one that writhed in my gut – to meeting his eyes and I loathed myself. If I could not hold and return his stare then it was no surprise that he was ruining my home.

Around the living room I saw all of the books that he'd taken off the shelves, flicked through and then discarded open and face-down. He could concentrate on nothing but cartoons and pictures in magazines. I saw my hardback first edition of Walter de la Mare beside his chair. There was a mug of tea placed upon the dust jacket.

I rushed across the room and retrieved the book. The jacket was marked by a cup ring. 'Jesus Christ.'

He sniggered.

'Do you know how valuable this is?'

Ewan shrugged. 'It's just a book.'

'My book!'

'Sorry,' he replied in an automatic, placid tone of voice.

'How many times have I told you about this?' I stared about the room and waved a hand at the debris.

He sniggered again. 'Would you listen to him.'

Briefly, I closed my eyes, took a breath, and I sat on the sofa. 'We need to talk.'

'What about?'

'What do you think? Like I've told you nearly every night this week, you can't stay here any longer.'

He stared at me, his expression blank.

'Look at this place. Look at what you've done to it.'

Nonchalantly, he surveyed the room. 'Sorry, what am I looking at?'

I slapped my hands against the leather sofa. 'Can you not see?'

'Sorry, what do you mean?'

I stared up and through the ceiling as if appealing to some other for support. No, I would not be drawn into another of these endless, circular exchanges that were baffling, devoid of reason and conducted in an atmosphere of his unwashed body and clothes. 'You can't stay here. I want you out. Tonight.' Something squealed in my tone of voice, which made me sound foolish and impotent.

'Sorry, why?'

A blockage was finally removed from the well. 'The mess! The fucking mess. The garbage. The old newspapers. The dirty cups and plates. The food spilled everywhere. The heating is on full. It's twenty-four degrees outside. The windows and curtains are closed. It stinks in here! You are ruining my books. My things. Everything.'

His expression never changed from a weary puzzlement. 'But I get cold.'

I tried to control my voice. 'I know you have problems. But you are your own worst enemy. You make no effort.'

'In what way, sorry?'

Holding my head in my hands, I said, 'Jesus, Jesus, Jesus.'

He sniggered.

'It's not funny. This is not a joke.' I heard my voice begin to break again.

He reached over the side of his chair, picked up a beer can and took a throaty swig. I watched, transfixed by frustration. Observing this simple, unapologetic, seemingly carefree act made me realise that I despised him. 'Did you hear what I said? You have to go.'

'Sorry, where?'

I raised both hands into the air. 'I don't know. Anywhere that's not here. Home. You have parents.'

'No,' he said conclusively, with a shake of his head. 'Can't go there. I never want to see them again.'

I cut him off, not wanting to kick-start another self pitying ramble in which he moaned about those who had wronged him, without ever possessing the gumption to acknowledge his own role in the dispute. In his mind, he was blameless, always, like now. 'Well, you have to go somewhere. Find a place. I can't live like this any more.'

'Like what, sorry?'

'If you can't see it, then I'm not explaining it to you.'

'But you're not making sense. You want me to go somewhere else' – he embellished his point by waving a long hand above his head – 'but you can't tell me where. So how do I know where to go?' He finished with a smile. Pleased with himself, he showed me his yellow teeth.

With a tremendous concentration of will, I kept my voice steady. '*Loot.* The newspaper. Buy Loot. Find a room in there and move into it.'

Considering my advice, he took another leisurely swig of beer. 'Not really my scene. And you're still not making sense. It all sounds a bit cuckoo to me.' He started to laugh. He was also drunk. 'You need a deposit to get a room in there. I don't have enough money. And the rooms are terrible places. I lived in one and I'm never going back. I like it here.'

'Does any of what you're saying strike you as absurd?'

'I don't follow, sorry?'

'You just show up here. At my flat. It's been ten years. We were never even close. And you… you get inside here and just…'

'What, sorry?'

'Make this terrible mess and refuse to leave when I ask you to.'

He looked around the room again. 'It's not so bad. I've seen worse.'

'That doesn't surprise me. But to me, it's terrible. Horrible. We clearly have different standards. And as it's my flat I decide who lives here and what happens here. Do you understand that?'

'I think you're missing the point –'

'No! You are missing the point. This is a private residence. Not a drinkers' hostel. You have no rights here.'

He looked at the can in his hand and a glum, doleful expression returned to his face.

'Look,' I said, 'I'm a very private person. I don't ever want to live like a student again. I need my own space.'

'So do I,' he said.

'Then move out. This place is too small for two people. It's a one-bedroom flat for one person. Me.'

'I don't agree. It's big enough.'

'What you think is irrelevant. You're just not listening to what I'm saying, are you?'

'I am.'

'Then you're going to leave.'

'No.'

'What?'

'You're confused. You've just missed the point.'

'What point is this?' I began to think about who I should call first: the police or Social Services.

'Somewhere along the line, you got it all wrong,' he said, utterly sure of what he was saying.

My face was in my hands again. I clawed at my scalp with my fingers. I couldn't bear to look at him. 'I'll find you somewhere to live. I'll pay the deposit.'

There was a long silence. 'It's a nice offer. But I'm not so sure it's the right thing to do. You see, I don't want to live on my own again. It's too hard to keep everything going.

It's better if I stay here.'

I stood up, wrenched open the curtains and threw the sash windows up through their frames.

Ewan blinked in the tangerine light.

I clutched at the piles of old newspapers and flyers and leaflets and sandwich wrappers strewn around the floor, all collected by Ewan during his forays outside the flat. Each day's refuse was arranged in a little rubbish pyramid.

He leaped out of the chair. 'Leave them!'

Startled, I stepped away from him and stared at his wild eyes, red cheeks and trembling lips.

'Don't touch them.'

'It's rubbish.'

'But I need them.'

'Why?'

'They're not finished with.'

'But it's rubbish. The papers are days, weeks old.'

'Just leave them.' It was the first time that I had seen Ewan angry and my scalp prickled. He began to weave and pointed a dirty fingernail at my face. I recalled what I had read of shut-ins living with their stacks of old newspapers and heaps of garbage; every item of vital importance to some incomprehensible inner life; landfills secluded inside flats or single rooms that they eventually expired within. Ewan was mad, and this was his goal; to surround himself with refuse and filth in my home. To seal himself off from a world that he could not function in, with me for company, so that he didn't get lonely. I was to be a provider of victuals and companionship, a guardian. I wanted to laugh.

I dropped the papers on the floor. 'It's all garbage. I want all of it out of here and all of these dishes washed. Then I want you gone.' But my voice held no strength. It sounded like a rehearsed platitude, half-heard at best, ignored almost certainly. Something that just dispersed around Ewan's head.

I stalked out of the living room and went into the kitchen. I switched the heating off at the boiler and opened the two windows overlooking the Greek restaurant.

'What are you doing?' he said from behind me, calm again, now that his precious newspapers had been returned to disorder and chaos. He was standing in the door-frame, holding a two-litre bottle of Dr Pepper.

'What does it look like?'

'But I get cold.' The gangly figure, with the anorak zipped up to its throat and the baseball cap jammed onto its head, pretended to shudder.

'Tough. You're not going to be here for much longer and I'm going to make a start on getting rid of that smell.' Now I was one of them – I could read it in his face – one of his tormentors. 'And get ready for some hard physical labour. You're cleaning the bloody mess you've made before you go.'

'I don't know how, sorry.'

'Clearly.'

'What do you mean, sorry?'

'Those clothes need to be thrown away. I'll give you something to wear, otherwise you'll never get a room.'

'Some things are the way they are for a reason.'

'Not in my flat, they're not. You can't just invade someone's life and fill every room with that awful smell, and leave garbage all over the floor. I mean, what were you thinking? This is my home. My flat. A private space.'

'But how is it private? Julie comes over.'

He was referring to my girlfriend at the time, who used to stay over at least three times each week. But since Ewan had arrived I'd been sleeping over at her place, which I realised had been a mistake. She'd met Ewan once and subsequently refused to visit again until he was gone. The very fact that he had mentioned her as some kind of obstacle to his occupation made me angrier than I had ever been. 'What the fuck has that got to do with you?'

'Well, think about it,' he said, the grin back.

'Think about what?'

'I have no place to go when she's here.' He looked triumphant. 'It's not a very nice thing to do to a person.'

I suddenly realised that the surreal, childlike debate

could run for ever. Was he trying to wear me down? Was he a congenital idiot, or was this some carefully rehearsed obfuscation? I didn't know, but I was exhausted by the drunken imbecile. I looked about myself at the kitchen that I would now have to clean again. In one week, I'd fallen into a role of obscene servitude to his beguiling will. It seemed so long ago that I would prepare a meal after work and eat it with wine, read a book, fall asleep in my chair by the window. Or lie on the sofa with Julie and watch a film. *How did this happen? How did this come about?* These situations are unexpected. There are no defences against them. 'I'll have whoever I want here. Especially Julie. You have no say in anything.'

'I'm right about this. You know I am.'

'No, I don't!'

He smiled, as if patronising a misguided child. 'Oh, yes, I think that you do.'

'I'll tell you what, you can leave now. Right now. Leave the keys. Go.'

He sniggered and shook his oily head. 'Where? I asked you before and you couldn't give me an answer. Where do I go? Do I just vanish? What you're saying doesn't make sense.'

'So, you're going to stay here for ever, turn my flat into a compost pit, destroy all of my possessions, and I'm not allowed to have guests over. Is that it? Is that the plan? Can you not see why I might object? Why I am seriously alarmed by your behaviour?'

He laughed and shook his gigantic head, as if pitying my delusions. 'Now you're being dramatic. Getting ahead of yourself. We're not there yet. All I am saying is it's not fair, not considerate when you bring people here. Because they're not my friends and not my girlfriends. And I have no place to go when they're here. It's quite simple.' He turned and left the kitchen and I stood alone in silence, stupefied.

From the living room, I heard the rattle and thud of closing windows. Followed by the shriek of the curtains, tugged across plastic rails to seal out the beauty and light of a summer's evening. With a blare, the television erupted back into life.

I walked, as if possessed, into the living room. My lips moved rapidly. I was close to violence and tears; which would come first, I did not know. Livid with anger, I stood in the doorway. Ewan looked at me, his face inscrutable, or perhaps vaguely puzzled by my insistence. 'You are fucking mad,' I said.

And a change occurred in his expression, his posture, in the very energy that seemed to project from the slumped, dark form in the chair. By the light of the television I could see how his face purpled with rage, how the watery eyes darkened. Leaping from the chair, he rushed at me.

My breath caught in my throat.

He raised one long clumsy arm, the nylon of the anorak whipping through the air like a sail on a boom.

But paused, when a moment of sense in his eyes became restraint in his ungainly body, and he stopped short of striking me, and brought that arm down against the wooden drying rack beside the radiator. Wooden struts snapped and splintered before being silently engulfed in the bathroom towels that were hanging there. The clothes horse collapsed upon itself.

'You know nothing!' Long thin arms swept around his head. Spittle frothed on his vulval lips. 'You got it all wrong! You missed the boat!' And with that final exclamation, he seized the handle of the living-room door and slammed it with all his might, sending me reeling backwards into the hall.

From Ewan's first night in the flat I had slept badly. A fretting anxiety made it difficult to fall asleep, and would continually bring me back to either full consciousness or a troubled half-sleep in which I found it impossible to become physically comfortable. In retrospect, I realised that I had completely lost the ability to relax after his odoriferous intrusion into my life. But the quality of my sleep the night following our row and his destruction of the drying rack was not only fitful but harassed by awful dreams that I only partially recalled in the morning.

Thinking as rationally as I was able, I put the nightmare down to the intensification of my feelings of victimisation and powerlessness, through the loss of control that I was suffering within my own environment. But the experience of these disturbing dreams made me resent Ewan even more; his physical pollution of my home and maddening, autistic will were but the first level of my torment. At the time, it seemed to me that he had reached far deeper into my life, and that it wasn't enough that he was now my only topic of conversation with Julie, or the only thought that continuously distracted me from my work at the studio. No, his intrusion went much further; I felt that Ewan was now unwilling to be without me at any time. Even as I slept.

The setting of the nightmare was my apartment, though the landscape was much enlarged – big enough to hold me for ever – and much changed. Physically diminished, I was a skeletal and hairless thing with no genitals. Some crude operation had been performed between my legs and the wound had been stitched shut with the brown twine that I kept under the kitchen sink. And I stumbled and fell about, exhausted by a long march down the even longer hallway. My flesh was cut by the floor of broken toenails. His yellow toenails. My discomfort from the quickly infecting incisions on my knees, the soles of my feet and the palms of my hands was constant, and I repeatedly collapsed on the strange beach that had been formed from his discarded foot claws.

A naked thing, luminous as a pale worm in dark clay, I also found it difficult to see in the stinging blizzard of dandruff and scurf that constantly blew at us from the direction in which we headed: the living room. In my ears, mouth and nose, the oily matter built up and had to be scraped away. Dirty light seeped from above us to partially illumine him in this storm of decay. Thin-limbed, large-footed, pot-bellied, he forged ahead and swept one arm about in the air as he read aloud from a cluster of dog-eared sheets of A4 paper torn from a refill pad. Incanting words that I could not catch, he forced a quick march onward while I scurried behind on a lead, choking on the stench.

The flat was also insufferably hot, which served to intensify the ever-present miasma. But Ewan was indifferent to my choking and sobbing. There was to be no delay in our reaching the far-off flicker of whitish light that crackled through the storm. And there was something else in the flat with us that I never saw. Never laid eyes upon, because I was too afraid to look at it. Crouched behind the naked, ranting giant whose crown of black hair stuck to his skull and neck as if his head had been revolved round a basin of grease, I felt safer. I had to stay close to Ewan and remain concealed from the thing that was waiting up ahead in the streak-lighting static of the living room. I instinctively knew that it was old and full of glee and looking forward to seeing me.

In the dream, Ewan, the naked, bearded prophet with that paunch, was soon swinging one of his old shoes like a bishop's censer. The shoe was full of excrement, and, as he paraded through my flat, he finger-painted figures onto the walls. Childish figures, but all the worse for it, those hunched-up things in matchstick trees that he daubed on the walls. And I had crawled behind him, holding aloft my best Habitat salad bowl, a vessel choked with filth, so that he might refill the tatty shoe. And down that hallway we went with Ewan spreading graffiti all the way down to the place that I soon feared with a ferocity. A flashing room inhabited by a third presence, something that existed in the whitish blue crackles. Something on the ceiling that Ewan worshipped.

He had to tighten the belt around my throat to drag me inside the white flickers where sound travelled backwards. A place inside which I began to suffocate, while being unable to flee because my whole body was beset by a paralysing sensation of pins and needles. And as I crawled upon a floor that reeked of an ape's enclosure, I would slip back to the place directly beneath whatever it was that I feared upon the ceiling.

When I awoke, my face was taut with dried tears.

It was still dark outside my bedroom. I sat up in damp sheets that still contained vestiges of his smell, from where he'd sat on the bed while inspecting my room the day before. And I immediately became aware of the light burning under my door from the hallway, and also of the loud music, partially muffled by the walls, that boomed from the living room.

Music? I looked at my alarm clock. It was not yet three in the morning, but a rumble of drums and cacophony of buzzing guitars assaulted my senses the moment I opened the bedroom door. I thought of my neighbours upstairs, Holly and Michael, and became convinced that a knock at the front door was imminent.

Wrapped in my bathrobe, I scurried down the hall to the lounge. Wincing, I covered my mouth and nose from a fresh assault of his peculiar smell. It seemed fresher than ever, but mere hours ago I had thoroughly disinfected the hallway, bathroom and kitchen floors. How was this possible? Not even bleach could withstand him.

I thrust open the door of the living room. And saw Ewan dancing. Leaping drunkenly from foot to foot and throwing his arms out wide, and shaking his big head about so that coils of wet hair lashed and stuck to his shiny face. His dirty shoes, with their flap, flap, flapping soles, skittered through the newspapers and empty beer cans on the floor. His cracked lips pulled apart at the sight of me, and he stuck out a tongue better suited to the maw of an ox. And even with me there, he never stopped the clumsy prancing, but instead unleashed a deep moan, utterly discordant and bestial. Opening his mouth even wider, he wiggled his tongue across those yellow teeth obscenely, before issuing another hoarse roar into the punishing din that erupted from the speakers.

Ewan was playing his Necrophile Autopsy album. The only CD he owned, recorded by some Scandinavian black metal outfit that I'd never heard of before he came to stay. The case was long lost and I was surprised the disc even played; there were scratches and oily fingerprints all over the playing surface.

I moved into the room and shut the music off. I was afraid. I had no idea who this person was, or what the misfit I had vaguely known at university had been doing for the last decade. But there was no point in reprimanding him. Little point even talking to this inebriated oaf who lived exclusively on a diet of children's party food and beer. He was in control; I was just there to listen.

Ewan flopped his entire weight down into the chair and the frame cracked. The legs dug grooves into the floor boards. Two cans of extra strong beer were balanced on the arm of my chair. He must have gone out at some point to buy the chips, the king-size Mars Bar and the half-dozen bags of crisps that were also piled upon the coffee table.

Drunk and excited, Ewan tried to keep his slurred words together to make sentences. 'I've been walking, walking. I've walked miles. I went to William Blake's old house. And then Peckham Common. The place where the angels are in the trees. They're still there.'

As if my body temperature had suddenly dropped, I began to shiver and closed the robe around my neck. 'It must have been dark.' My voice sounded tiny.

'There's plenty of things you can see without light.' He stretched his legs out and slurped from a beer can, then gasped with satisfaction.

'I bet.'

His expression became challenging, then hateful. Ewan had always been ugly, but at that moment I thought he looked particularly primitive and dangerously delinquent. Despite his delusions about being a poet at university, I suddenly understood that I'd underestimated him; when drunk, he could become a thug and a bully. 'You'd better not be thinking of laughing at me,' he said, and the subtext was obvious. He grinned, and showed me those yellow teeth, satisfied with my reaction. Yes, Ewan wanted to be feared and respected. 'I've done a lot of thinking about you,' he slurred. 'About what you said. And you were wrong. I was right.'

I turned to go. 'I have work in the morning. There are neighbours upstairs. No more music.'

'No, no, no, no, no.' Ewan swayed out of the chair and tumbled across the room at me. I flinched to the side and he slammed the door shut, trapping me inside the sordid lounge. And he began to weave in front of my face. 'I have something very, very, very, very, very –'

I made to move past him, but he stumbled in front of me and pushed me backwards with his index finger. Repulsed at the thought more than the reality of his touch, I stepped out of his reach.

'You're going nowhere. You see, this is very, very, very, very important. I've something to tell you. No… show you. Yes, tell you and show you. So just stay where you are. I think you'll be rather surprised.'

I now thought him boring and rude. Woken in the middle of the night to be cornered and intimidated by a drunken stranger in my own home: had I ever suffered such abuse? 'I doubt it,' I said in defiance. 'So make it quick. Some of us have to work in the morning.'

'Tut, tut, tut. That's not the spirit.'

My tolerance of drunks and their self-important babble has never been good. 'Just get it over with. I want to go to bed. I have to go to work.'

'That's not important. As you shall see, it hardly matters in the order of things.'

'Order of things?' I hadn't the energy to pursue another of his ridiculous assumptions. My salary paid the mortgage on the flat that he was now staying in against my will: could he not fathom that much out? The mere thought of explaining it brought on another wave of fatigue.

'Oh, yes. As you shall see.'

'What will I see?' Impatience now replaced the fear that had accompanied me from my sleep. 'What could you possibly tell me, or show me, that could have any bearing on anything of importance?'

He held a broad hand up to command silence. Then unzipped his anorak and slipped a hand inside. There was a brief struggle with an inside pocket until he pulled out a dirty roll of paper. 'I want you to read this.'

The ends of the paper were brown and the dog-ears compressed. I thought of the dream and felt uneasy. This whole situation, the coincidence, seemed unreal. It was as if I was no longer part of the ordinary world. I even began to feel slightly ill-defined. 'It's three in the morning.'

'It's all nicely written out.' He walked across to the coffee table. Swiped the bags of crisps onto the floor. One of them was open and the contents scattered noisily across the floorboards. Ewan smiled and said, 'Oh, dear.' In an exaggerated, mocking posture, he then bowed and laid the manuscript on the table. He wiped the top sheet open and straight, but as soon as he removed his hands, the page curled back upon itself.

'So here it is. If sir would be so kind.' He pointed at the sofa, motioning for me to sit.

I sat down. I'd read it quickly and placate the lunatic.

Ewan drummed his black fingernails on the manuscript, cleared his throat and said, 'I give his lordship *The Gospels According to the Goddess*.' He then stood back, his eyes wide with excitement, expecting that I would share his awe at the presence of the soiled paper. I didn't want to touch it. The man was insane. He needed a psychiatrist. Pressed against an unwashed body and sealed inside a hot plastic coat in all weathers, while he wandered endlessly to find angels in trees, the paper was moist. I could smell it from three feet away and shivered with disgust. 'It's not even typed.'

'You keep asking what I was doing for ten years. Well, there's your answer.'

It could not have been more than forty pages long. 'You spent ten years writing that?'

'Not just writing it. A lot of preparation was involved. And other things. Poetry just doesn't happen, you know. You may think it, it, it…'

The great poet couldn't express the thought. My face fell into my hands.

Ewan paced the room. 'You have to read it.' Teeth clenched and on display, he paused to strum an imaginary instrument. Took the baseball cap off and scratched the tight scalp beneath. It was the first time I had seen the hat removed, and his hair still retained the shape of the cap. He was ridiculous. Drunk, unwashed and ridiculous. 'Everything will make sense and you will see why I'm right.' The cap was slapped back onto his head and contentedly he strummed the invisible instrument again. He was happy. This is what he wanted: someone to pay attention to him and his crazy ideas.

I wanted to physically destroy him. Smash his head against a steel radiator with my fists entangled in his wet hair. I stood up. 'Forget it.'

Ewan ran to the lounge door and blocked it. 'You have to read it. It's important.'

'Not to me it isn't. Step aside.'

'No, no, no, no, no, no,' he said in a sing-song voice.

My vision was starting to tremble. 'You solipsistic moron. I'm tired. Can you not see that? You never get up before two in the afternoon. You sit around watching cartoons and eating kids' junk food. What do you know about responsibility? Look at yourself. You can't even dress yourself. When was the last time you washed your clothes or took a shower?'

He pursed his generous lips. 'Mmmm. Let me see. Two years? About that.'

I actually felt my face pale.

And then he was angry again. Almost panting at me. 'Two years since water touched my flesh. The flesh must be prepared. Same as the mind. These things take time. It's what she says. Read my book and you'll see. You'll see things a little more clearly. You've missed the point. Same as everybody else. You've all missed the boat.' He tapped his head. 'But I haven't.' And he refused to move away from the door.

The next day, at the studio, one of my colleagues remarked that I was 'on another planet'. But her remark was justified. I made mistakes. Misheard things. Couldn't concentrate. I was preoccupied, listless, and exhausted. The other designers and the familiar surroundings of the company buildings struck me as being incongruously clean and absurdly ordinary.

I'd awoken late that morning, after no more than two hours' sleep. Anger had kept me awake. Disgust too, at what I had read on those sticky pages of *The Gospels According to the Goddess*. When I'd finally roused myself and climbed out of bed, there was no time for a shower or breakfast. There were no cups left in the cupboard for coffee either. They were all soiled and sealed within the living room, where Ewan slept and would sleep until the afternoon to ready himself for the night's fresh festivities.

His manuscript had been written in a beatific style that seemed to me a clumsy attempt at an antiquated idiom. Each line was numbered like the Bible too, and the text was separated into cantos. There was no metre or rhyme, just a relentless, self-important barrage of statements allegedly transmitted by the Goddess and recorded by Ewan, her earthly conduit and representative.

If anything, the passages reminded me of a quasi prose-poetry written by someone hopelessly arrested in their development. Morbidly adolescent, self-aggrandising, deluded: a manifesto for a paranoid man's persecution fantasies and odd spiritual beliefs. The *Gospels* made me think of Charles Manson and *Helter Skelter*; the testament of a shabby misfit with a messiah complex. Only this author was an uncharismatic prophet without a single disciple.

As I read, Ewan had sat perched on the armrest of the sofa, his eyes intense with a kind of euphoria, because someone was finally paying his manuscript the attention he thought it deserved, even if it was a hostage taken after midnight and dressed in a bathrobe.

Given Ewan's inebriation, how could I have been honest with him? I had found the *Gospels* to be creepy, the work of a man paralysed by an undiagnosed personality disorder. Thinking only of rest and sleep, I had lied to Ewan and said that it was 'interesting'. I had promised more of a critique the next day. I'd then edged out of the living room and into the bathroom, intent on washing my hands, while he'd tripped over my feet, pleading for more applause. Ewan waited outside the bathroom too, and then crowded me down the hall. He even tried to enter my bedroom, wheedling and desperate to squeeze more acclaim from his reluctant reader. Eventually, I had to push him out of my room, with two scrubbed hands pressed into his sticky breastbone, before shutting the door in his face.

He entered my room another three times shortly afterwards and switched the light on, before I fell into a coma of fatigue. When I woke at 8 a.m., the light was on in my room and the door was wide open.

> 1. All doors shall be open unto him. 2. And lo, none shall mock him. 3. For he is a king among men. 4. A god-man who has been given the sight of her and things too holy for other men to withstand. 5. Lo! And woman neither

> shall lead him astray. 6. This is my will and I am his true love at the centre of all things.

I was angry at myself for remembering the rubbish, and for allowing the impact of Ewan's unexamined conceit to intrude so far into my mind, where it then recited itself at the studio. And even there, in my office cubicle, another unpleasant consequence of Ewan's occupation awaited me. Sat before the Head of Human Resources before lunch, I was asked several questions in a benign interrogation, the kind adopted by management to delve into a member of staff's personal problems. Alice Fairchild was smiling when she asked me if things were 'all right at home'. She was still smiling when she explained 'how difficult it always was to discuss the issue of personal hygiene' with someone whom she considered 'a friend and not just a valued colleague'. Several people in my studio had complained about me, and she had noticed my body odour too when passing me in the corridor.

I began to aggressively claw at my shirt and to sniff at my armpits, and quickly understood why she was alarmed. I attempted to explain about the 'guest' in my flat, but Alice struggled to understand what I jabbered at her. I quickly apologised and promised that no one would be 'troubled' in future.

'We all get preoccupied,' Alice had said in a confidential tone, 'and forget about the simplest but most important things at these times.'

> 42. And his flesh will be made stronger with her incense. 43. Indeed, the king in rags, her servant and most dear love, will be robed in divinity that escapes the eyes of men but will leave their other senses in awe of him. 44. And he shall leave his flesh unclean for the passing of eight seasons, drink strong drink and eat rich foods in readiness for his passing into her kingdom. 45. And he may choose companions to follow him, and to follow her,

through him, till they too be granted passage. 46. For lo! Look up all believers and she will be revealed to you in all her magnificence and glory and beauty, and ye shall be nourished and anointed by her incense also.

I left work early and stopped at a supermarket to buy deodorant and a fabric neutralising agent before catching the tube to Julie's flat.

'Did you notice it too?' I asked her upon arrival.

Julie nodded. 'At the weekend. In the cinema.'

'Oh, for Christ's sake!'

'You've got to get rid of him.'

'Don't you think I'm trying?'

'Don't shout at me!'

Julie's roommates fell silent in the lounge outside the dining room.

'I'm sorry.' We finished the remainder of our evening meal in silence. Julie was hurt when I told her that I couldn't sleep over, and that I had to go home and fetch clean clothes for work the next day, if such a thing as clean clothes even existed at my address.

Briefly, we also Googled my legal position and tried to figure out if Ewan qualified as a squatter. I couldn't even lock him out, as Julie suggested, because Ewan had a key. Besides his monumental walk to Peckham while I'd slept, he never left the apartment when I was there. And I no longer believed this was coincidental. If I was at home, I doubt Ewan ventured much further than the 24-hour shop across the road. Even if he did slip outside when I was indoors, there would be no time to call a locksmith and drill out locks. I could only leave the catch on while I was inside the flat. I would have to leave at some point for work, and that would give him ample time to get back inside and to redouble his efforts to remain at the address. The situation was preposterous.

I promised Julie I'd phone the police in the morning. She vowed to speak to a friend who practised family law. But what still perplexed me was how Ewan had managed to find me in the first place. I was certain his 'bumping' into me on the street, a few weeks before, had been no accident. Ewan had been looking for me.

Socially, he had always been on the periphery of the alternative undergraduate crowd at university. Rarely speaking, painfully shy but tolerated by the self-styled bohemians in the Student Union bar. The long hair and beard hadn't changed either. Several times back then, out of curiosity and sympathy, I had spoken to him. At the time I was fooling myself that I was an Expressionist painter and I remember us sharing a passion for Francis Bacon and Hieronymus Bosch. In fact, Ewan was the only other person in my peer group who had heard of Grosz.

Back then, Ewan also drank heavily, fancied himself a poet and was always carrying around a copy of some Arthur Machen short stories. People had shaken their heads at my association with him. Girls were especially hard on him. They thought him creepy, and things like that. He failed his first year and moved on. And that was the extent of my knowledge of Ewan. So what had he been doing for the last ten years? Where had he been living? Estranged from his parents and unemployable, had he been secured in an institution? And if the *Gospels* were in any way autobiographical, he hadn't washed or laundered his clothes in two years.

'That's just disgusting,' Julie said, when I told her.

'He is disgusting,' I said. 'Repellent.'

'I feel sorry for him. He's ill. Maybe I should have a word with him. See if I can get rid of him.'

'No way. My place is out of bounds until he's gone. It's embarrassing.'

'Perhaps you're too soft. And he's so manipulative. Alcoholics are. He's turning you into an enabler.'

'Soft? Physical violence is the only thing that I haven't tried. And, believe me, I've come close.'

'Please, let me have a go at him.'

'Why? He doesn't even like you.'

'What do you mean?'

I mentioned Ewan's complaint about me having guests.

'Bastard. What a bastard.'

'Now you're talking, but look at us. He's all we ever talk about. And I can't sleep. He's affecting my work. He's taking over my life.'

'The bare-faced cheek.' Julie wasn't really listening to me; she was still smouldering because Ewan objected to her visits, which was probably what prompted her to make one the following evening; though that was the last time that Julie ever set foot in my home.

But I still had to go home that night.

Across the road, in front of the Cypriot deli, I looked up and watched the windows of the first floor of my flat – the living-room windows. And immediately I began to wonder what Ewan was watching on television to make the edges of the curtains flicker and flash a blue-white colour, as bright as a magnesium flare. The curtains were thin, but I was still surprised at the effects of the TV's luminosity. Was it always like that when I watched television? Perhaps Ewan had tampered with the contrast.

Slowly, on weary legs, I crossed the road and made my way to the front door, only to have it opened from the inside as my key slid into the lock. I stepped back, my heartbeat thickening inside my throat. But it was only Holly and Michael, my neighbours, coming out and carrying two cat cages with Marmalade and Mr Chivers inside.

'Oh, hi,' Holly said. 'Afraid we've got to take the boys over to my sister's for a sleepover.'

'Hey, mate,' Michael said, joining her on the pavement.

I was compelled to apologise. 'Look, I'm really, really sorry about this. I'm having a spot of trouble with a guest. A visitor. But he'll be gone soon.'

'You know, I'm glad to hear it,' Michael said, smiling. 'That guy in the baseball cap?'

I nodded, my face a mask of shame.

'It's that music,' Michael said. 'We couldn't believe that it was something in your collection. What's he doing, pushing vinyl backwards against a needle? But it's just freaking the cats out. Sorry, mate. I had to come down and knock, but no one is answering.'

'We turned the TV up,' Holly interjected. 'But the boys can still hear that noise. It took us an hour to get them down from the top of the wardrobe. And look at these scratches. They've never scratched me before.' Holly showed me a lined forearm. I apologised again and made my way up the stairs to the front door.

The music thumped about me on the communal staircase of the building. A hammering of drums beneath a squealing of guitars. Why would Ewan have the stereo and television on at the same time? I then thought of his childish affectations for visual things, for sweets and noise, his inability to concentrate on anything that required effort, and so dismissed the query. No wonder he'd only written forty pages in a decade.

As I approached my front door, I was also reminded of his verse, his performance the night before, and the curious and unpleasant dream that I'd suffered. I began to wish that I'd stayed at Julie's. Increasingly, I was afraid of what Ewan might do next. After all, he'd convinced himself that he was a god-man in the service of an all-knowing deity.

Without making much of a sound, I slipped inside the flat.

The smell was all the more potent for my having being away for twelve hours. Sharper, more acrid. Almost living, I felt. But despite the stench and the contained heat, I soon realised that the situation had changed. All of the lights were switched off, though the hallway was intermittently lit by the ghastly phosphorescent light flashing from beneath the door of the living room. With some discomfort, I thought of the dream again.

I crept down the hallway and glanced into the kitchen. The squalor had returned with what I suspected was renewed vigour, and I briefly marvelled at how one man could produce so much filth and waste.

I moved down the hallway to the bathroom. Closed the door and stuffed my ears with wet toilet paper. Under a powerful blast of hot water, I scrubbed and scratched at my flesh in the shower. I felt violated.

When I'd finished in the bathroom, the soundtrack in the living room had changed, and I recalled what Michael had said in the street. Beside the discordant thumping of Ewan's feet on the floor of the living room as he danced about drunkenly, he was now playing a new CD. It wasn't music exactly, unless it was one of those industrial noise outfits like Coil, but I heard a series of elongated sounds, as if recorded backwards in a fuzz of static and played at a slow rotation. An electric cacophony scratching itself around the ceiling of my living room, but all going the wrong way. Yes, it was like a record being pushed backwards against a stylus.

It made me tense, and fragile. The sound was inside my head and it made me writhe inside my skin, as if a chunk of polystyrene was being scraped down a windowpane next to my ear.

I listened outside the door of the living room. Through the swollen and fetid air, I heard Ewan talking to someone. It was hard to make out any words, but the tone of his voice surprised me because he seemed to be pleading with an individual that he was familiar with.

Unable to face another confrontation, or even the sight of his red face and oily dreadlocks, I moved silently into my bedroom. I pulled my dresser against the door to block access, and then changed my bedlinen. Lying in bed, with that insane, menacing noise coming at me through the walls, I thought of calling the police. But it was getting late, and I didn't have the strength, or the presence of mind, to fully articulate all that I was feeling to the authorities. I made another vow to do it in the morning.

Sometime near 3 a.m. I was woken from an unpleasant dream, experienced in sleep that was fitful at best. The dream existed in my memory more as a sense of something unpleasant than as a definite narrative. But I awoke feeling as if I had been tightly bound, within a dark space where gravity had ceased to exist and in which my feet rose above my head towards *something* close to their soles. An aperture that suggested a large, open mouth, one moving in circles above me, while I struggled to keep my body on the mattress.

I could again hear the terrible vortex too, the maelstrom of live current and static in the living room, but it was also horribly mixed with something far worse than anything that I'd heard before. This new sound had yanked me from sleep and lasted for no more than a few minutes, but they were minutes in which every single second stretched itself, until my fear and discomfort became unbearable. I heard what I can only compare to the deep croaking of a bullfrog, as if the amplified sound had been stretched backwards and played in a perverse surround-sound effect, circling the living room, up near the ceiling. Between these amphibian barks was a sound not dissimilar to an old woman in the final stages of emphysema whom I'd once heard coughing in a hospital ward.

Shortly after the coughing or barking ceased, and at the exact instant that one tremendous phosphorescent flash lit up the hallway outside my room and shone beneath my door, I heard Ewan leave the lounge. This was followed by the hurried sound of his bare feet slapping down the hallway to my room. Staring at the door, my every hair on end, I watched the handle snapped up and down from the outside. Ewan was trying to get in.

I sat up in bed and pulled my knees up against my chest. 'What do you want?'

'Let me in,' Ewan demanded, his voice slurred by drink and breathless with excitement.

'No!'

But the door now began to bang against the dresser, which immediately rocked back and forth. He made a gap and threw his shoulder against the door.

'Fuck off!' I roared, but heard nothing besides his laboured breathing. He hurled himself against the wood repeatedly, until the dresser began to inch further away from the door frame.

By the time I had my mobile phone open to call the police, the dresser had slid away from the door and Ewan was inside the room.

He was naked save for his fetid boxer shorts. Face red and covered with a sheen of oily sweat, his eyes full of maniacal excitement but struggling to focus, he tottered back and forth on the spot. 'She's here,' he declared, and waved his hands above his head. 'Fluttering, fluttering all about. She's here. She's so beautiful, it hurts to look at her.'

I said nothing. Completely worn down, even resigned somehow, my fight had fled in the face of Ewan's insanity. I just listened to him rant at me for over ten minutes, endlessly repeating the same jubilant boast about the 'Goddess's arrival and beauty'. Eventually, Ewan's drunkenness and fatigue overwhelmed him and he stalked out of my room to weave his way back to the living room.

I sat still until he turned off the Necrophile Autopsy album at around 4.30 a.m., and fell into a coma of exhaustion with my nose filled with the scent of his soiled white flesh that had polluted my room – belly of a fish, vinegar-sweat of vomit.

It was the last night I would ever spend in the flat.

Julie met me at eight in the evening, at a bar at Notting Hill Gate. We each had a couple of drinks for courage in the beer garden, the indigo sky above us streaked with apricot as dusk set in. We then headed to my place, our intention to introduce the civilising presence of a woman in order to persuade Ewan to leave the flat.

From the distance, when we reached the top of Moscow Road, we saw the brilliant white flashes erupting from around the curtains of the living room. Several other pedestrians had also paused on their way to Queensway, or the Whiteleys Shopping Centre, to stare at the flickering phosphorescence.

Julie giggled nervously. 'What's he doing up there, setting off fireworks?'

I squeezed her hand.

We entered the communal hallway and Julie said, 'Oh, my God, the smell. I think I'm going to be sick.'

I pressed a finger to my lips and swallowed the impulse to cough. Even on the stairs, the miasma clung to our faces before penetrating our mouths and noses in a belligerent, insistent manner.

'What could make a smell like that?' Julie whispered.

'Someone who hasn't washed for two years,' I replied. But this stench, surely, went beyond the bacteria that incubate on an unwashed body and within soiled clothes. Again, I detected what I imagined to be the stench of burning bones, incendiary and sulphurous and cloying.

On the landing outside the front door, Julie shook her head at the noise and pressed her fingertips inside her ears. A painfully distorted and warped sound was in full swing again, but seemingly in the living room and up above our heads too. Inside the unlit hallway, vibrations thrummed through the floor, the walls and the very air. Ewan must have fused the circuits too, because the lights weren't working at all. 'Nothing,' I said, after flicking the light switch in the passage up and down.

'But how…' She didn't need to finish her question. I had also arrived at the same realisation that it could not have been the television or stereo, or any other appliance, making the sounds and incandescent flickers and flashes that had guided us down the passage and deeper inside the thickening bestial stench.

Eyes in a squint, and with one forearm across my nose and mouth, I led the way to the living-room door. Behind me, with both hands clamped over her ears, Julie followed, her face pale and intense in the brief washes of sickly light that almost crackled across the moist curves of our eyeballs. We stopped by the door and dithered, staring at each other.

'Go in,' she said, breathlessly. 'Go in. See what the fuck he's doing.'

Unsteady on my feet, disoriented by the circling noise, I said, 'Stay outside.' And added, 'He's probably naked.'

I don't think Julie heard me. She was just staring at the door of the living room, her face set with a purpose that I recognised and should have tried to deter. Nauseous to the tips of my fingers, I was unable to recover enough courage to do much but vacillate. And Julie pushed herself around me and opened the living-room door.

'No!' I cried out, but it was too late. She stepped through the doorway and into the maelstrom of white strobe and the lurching shadows. The door shut behind her with a force that made me jump. But the scream that followed her entrance into the living room snapped me out of my paralysis.

Before my hand managed to grasp the door handle, the discordant rotation of sound did not so much stop as implode, as if being sucked back through a tiny aperture in the ceiling, on the other side of the door. I yanked the handle down and stumbled into the room.

At first, the scene that confronted me seemed anticlimactic. It was dark; there was no illumination beyond a faint bluish residue of light with no definable source. That faded in seconds, leaving only a yellow glow of street-light that seeped around the curtains. But on seeing the expressions on the faces of the two occupants, I realised that something extraordinary had just occurred within that room.

Standing still, with her arms at her sides, Julie stared fixedly at the far corner where two walls joined the ceiling. Her expression struck me as peculiarly childlike as she gaped, her eyes wide with either shock or wonder or a combination of the two emotions.

The second figure in the room was Ewan, and he was standing where the coffee table had once been. He was completely naked, his beard, hair and body wet and dripping, the moisture adding an ugly prehistoric aspect to his red and grimacing face. The floor was also sodden. Ewan remained motionless but glared at Julie with a look of such antipathy and loathing that my blood slowed. His fists were clenched and stringy muscles corded his sallow forearms.

I snatched Julie's elbow and, although she turned towards me, she did not immediately recognise me, or even where she was. Amidst the distraction of complete shock, she looked through me, or past me, or even inside herself.

I led her, like an obedient, sleepy child pulled from the back seat of a car after a long drive, out of the living room, down the hall, out the front door and away from the reeking darkness of my home. I took her away, as much for her safety as to escape the sight of Ewan's fierce, wet face.

Julie stopped sobbing in the back of the black cab that I'd hailed from Queensway to take us to her flat. Looking peculiarly thin and weak, she leaned against me in the back of the car and refused to speak as I stroked her hair, my own thoughts frantic. What had she just seen? What the hell was Ewan doing in that room, naked? What was the source of the flashing light? Had Julie seen the origin? Was that why she'd been gaping at the ceiling?

By the time we had reached her flat, Julie had fallen asleep on my shoulder. I roused her into a stumbling drowsiness, to get her inside and into bed, still fully dressed. She curled her body around me. I asked her if she was ill, and if I should call a doctor, but she shook her head. 'Tell me, baby,' I pleaded. 'For God's sake, tell me. What did you see?'

'I can't really remember. I just felt so sick and dizzy in that room. The smell. It nearly made me faint. And the lightning. It was like lightning and it blinded me. And I slipped. The floor was all wet. But when I looked at Ewan, I saw something falling onto his face.'

'What? His face?'

'Something wet. A jet of something that was silvery, like mercury. It was coming out of the corner of the ceiling and splashing onto his face. Into his mouth... I'm so tired, baby.' She was asleep in minutes after the short confession. Over the next few days, I managed to get even less out of her.

Although the police called at the flat twice that week, they never raised an answer from inside. Holly and Michael moved out four days after me. Not so much because of the noise – though they claimed that it remained a considerable nuisance – but because of an electrical fault of some kind. They told me that a massive surge of power had melted their fuse box and most of the cables around the mainframe. Their landlord was struggling to repair the extensive damage, or even identify the cause of the fault, so they and the cats were set up with temporary accommodation in Westbourne Grove.

The next day I extracted a promise of financial assistance from my father and then employed a barrister specialising in civil law. He began to prepare my case for a forcible removal of Ewan from my property. Bizarrely, because Ewan hadn't technically forced his way inside, and had a key to the front door, I had to pursue a private prosecution, and these things, I found, took time. It seemed the police had neither the time nor the brief to do much at all. So I stayed at Julie's for the next four weeks, unwilling to even set foot in my own home again until Ewan, the terrible smell that he brought with him, and the sounds were gone.

But every other day during that month of exile, I still made my way back to the flat and stood across the road and watched the flashing lights around the curtains of the living room. Down on the pavement, night after night, I thought to myself: this is how civilisation ends. Standards decline, accountability ends, the rule of law is impotent, the thugs take over and do what they will. And those of us softened by convention, courtesy and all the privileges of post-historical freedom are dispossessed, victimised and turned into refugees in our own neighbourhoods and homes. It was the first time in my life that I'd ever felt tested. Really tested. And I'd proven myself incapable of meeting the challenge. But in my defence, there was no preparation in life for characters like Ewan, or the strange things that they worshipped.

On the Monday of the fourth week, there was no flashing at the windows. Nor on the Wednesday, Thursday or Friday. I could barely contain my excitement and I even dared to think that Ewan had left after reading the summons posted through the door, requesting his appearance in a magistrate's court.

Julie made me promise that I would not enter the flat without the police. My barrister also advised against it. But curiosity and self-righteous anger made the decision for me. This was, after all, my home.

On a Sunday morning, one month after I had abandoned my own sanctuary, I snuck away from Julie's flat on the pretence that I was going for a run in Kensington Palace Gardens, and I went to my flat. My desire to know if Ewan was inside was bolstered by mental images of my smashed record and CD collection. The mere thought of what he might have done to my books could leave me shaking.

But I dithered in the street below for nearly an hour, buying a smoothie and a latte, before quizzing the owners of the Cypriot shop, the Kurdish 24-hour store and the staff of the Greek restaurant about Ewan. All of them claimed they had not seen him for over a week. 'Good customer. He has the sweet tooth, aye,' the Kurdish owner of the grocery said. 'But the smell?' He shrugged his shoulders. 'Maybe not so many Mars Bars, aye? He better off with the soap, aye?' I forced a laugh and hoped that it sounded sincere; for me, Ewan was no laughing matter.

Eventually, in the bright sunlight and under a blue sky, I rang the buzzer, beside the street-level door, to my own apartment. There was no response, but I never really expected one. Encouraged, I entered the communal hallway of the building.

The stench of Ewan's occupation was still present. Very much so, but again something had altered within it. The dreadful burned-bone smell had been overwhelmed by an odour of meat left in a dustbin on a hot day. I pulled the neck of my shirt up and covered my nose. I expected to find Ewan's body; the anticipation filled me with a macabre optimism.

Inside the flat, the curtains were closed and the lights were out. Nothing flickered from beneath the living-room door. Three times I shouted Ewan's name, but there was no answer.

The instinctive awareness of vacancy is a strange extra sense, but one much under-appreciated. My hunch that the flat was empty was reinforced by the sharp scent of stale urine, a penetrating reek of ammonia and phosphate timelessly associated with abandoned places. What had once been a show home for a young West London professional now reeked like a derelict squat, stained by the piss of drunks. The bathroom looked like a nightclub toilet left to dry; I couldn't bear even to look inside the toilet pan, and the entire floor was sticky. As were the veneered floorboards of the hall, all tacky beneath the soles of my running shoes. Briefly, my rage flared at the realisation that Ewan had been urinating on the floors and walls, and potentially for the entire time that I had been absent from the flat. The cream walls had a tidemark. Dust and grime had become ingrained in the dry piss. When a peculiar, numb resignation took hold of me, my rage seeped away.

I inspected my room, where the greatest saturation of his excreta was visible on the bed, the soft furnishings and on clothing. The moment the whole place was cleaned by professionals, I also knew that I would put the flat on the market. I doubted that the most powerful cleaning agents would ever get rid of the smell.

Drawing blinds and curtains and opening windows as I moved from room to room, I let the sunlight illumine the destruction, the filth and the desecration of a place that I had once called home. The worst mess waited for me in the kitchen. Where I had once sautéed mushrooms, drizzled olive oil onto salads, and oven-baked seasoned Mediterranean vegetables, the meaty scent of human excrement dominated. And then I saw the walls.

A bolus of revulsion rose from my already queasy stomach. Was this a warning to intruders, or some hideous parody of religious iconography in a place of worship? Drawn in human shit, the images on the walls resembled something a precocious but deeply disturbed child might finger-paint in a specialist nursery school. Some kind of abhorrent forest had been daubed onto the Pacific Blue of my walls. Lumpy and crusting branches smeared away from the impression of the trunks. But it was the suggestion of what sat in the highest branches of this faecal arboretum that made me turn away, more in fear than in disgust. A sophisticated level of detail had been applied to the depiction of a group of figures with tatty heads and large mouths, all huddled into themselves. The mouths were filled with tilting spikes.

I kicked the door of the living room open and let it slam against the wall. Briefly wishing Ewan was still inside, so that I could deal with him in hand-to-hand combat,

I stepped into the gloom. And then stepped straight back out again, choking on the carrion smell of rotten flesh – in the place where it was most powerful, the origin, where everything began. And where it seemed to have ended.

Leaning through the doorway, I peered into the room with my hand clamped over my mouth, but failed to see the immobile lump of a body. Unless his corpse was crammed behind the settee, he was not inside the room. So the smell of decomposing meat must have been issuing from one of the many bags littered about the floor, or it wafted from somewhere else within that meadow of garbage. A chicken wing in a heated and unventilated flat could produce the stench of a charnel house within days. And I thought it not unlikely that a box of fried chicken had been left out to ripen in my absence, in honour of the Goddess, because this was no longer my home, but a temple of filth dedicated to *her*.

The floor was strewn with food wrappers and screwed-up sheets of newspaper, crisp and yellow with urine. The strange order of the original garbage pyramids had gone, though, or been kicked into oblivion by a pair of dancing, dirty feet. But my visions of a destroyed music collection were not unjustified; Ewan had smashed every CD and record against the walls or snapped them between his long fingers.

I quickly noted that my books appeared strangely undisturbed; perhaps Ewan had discovered some residual respect for what had once been important in his life. A small mercy, but one that failed to give me much comfort. The sheer stench of their pages would now prevent their further use.

Hauling the curtains wide open and throwing the two big sash windows up as far as they would go, I begged the fresh air and sunlight to come inside the room. I then turned around to better survey the destruction in proper light. Like the victims of hurricanes, you just have to walk through the wreckage and see what's left. And it was then that I saw Ewan.

I'd not seen his remains from the doorway, nor as I walked through the room, because my focus had been solely directed at the floor. But now, with my back to the glare of the open windows, I discovered what was left of him. On the ceiling.

Unthinking, I walked toward the opposite corner of the room. Unable to blink or take a breath through the cloth of my shirt, I moved on legs that I could not fully feel, while looking up at that terrible smear.

Within the dark, brownish stain of an entire human skin, turned inside out, I saw the unmistakable evidence of the long, oily strands of Ewan's hair that had previously drooped from beneath a baseball cap. Where the bones and innards and eyes were, to this day I will never know, but I was struck with an impression that he'd shed his skin while departing the room through the ceiling, at considerable haste, and in the most uncomfortable manner imaginable.

> 1. For she doth declare that when all is done, the god-man shall be given passage into the light of a hidden sun. 2. And lo, he will be stripped of all earthly things to enter her kingdom, where such beauty and riches beyond the dreams of lowly men will await him, her chosen love. 3. Yea, the god-man shall lie down with her, as does the proud groom with his sweet bride, and they shall be joined for all time. 4. And as a babe doth enter the low world, without raiment or hair, and wet with a mother's red blessings, so will ye come unto me. 5. And pure and clean ye shall be embraced.

On the floor, directly beneath the large, circular blemish on a ceiling once coloured a shade of porcelain satin, I spotted Ewan's teeth. His yellow teeth, with dark matter still attached at the root. They were no longer grinning at me, though, but were now scattered amongst the litter, like seashells broken from a leather thong.

Pig Thing

The end of light seemed to rise from the land rather than descend from the sinking sun, and a darkness that they seemed to feel upon their skin entered the bungalow. Day's end came with its own taste and smell too, was peaty, and dewy with sodden ferns, and seeped inside to make the air as damp as the garden's black earth. The skeletal branches of the mighty Kauri trees surrounding the bungalow vanished into the void of the moonless country night and made the children feel a strange dread that was much older than they were.

Had they still been living in England, this would have been an evening when bonfires were lit. And to the three children, although these nights were frightening, they had a tinge of enchantment too and were never as unsettling when their parents were inside the house. But tonight, neither their mother nor their father had returned from the rear garden that was enclosed by a vast wilderness of bush, ever intent on reclaiming their home, or so it seemed. Whenever the sun shone after the heavy showers of rain and made their world sparkle, their dad often remarked that he could hear the plants growing.

Dad had ventured out first, to try and get the car started in a hurry, shortly after nine o'clock. Twenty minutes later, her face long with worry, Mom had gone outside to find him, and they had not heard from her since either.

Before their mom and dad had left the house, the three children remembered seeing these same expressions of concern on their parents' faces when Mom's younger sister caught cancer and when Dad's work closed down. That wasn't long before the family travelled to New Zealand in the big ship for a fresh start on the day after the Queen's Silver Jubilee. Tonight their parents had done their best to hide their anxiety, but the two brothers, Jack, who was nine, and Hector, who was ten, knew that the family was in trouble.

Together with Lozzy, their four-year-old sister, Jack and Hector sat in the laundry room of the bungalow with the door shut, where Mom had told them to stay before she went outside to find their father.

Jack and Lozzy sat with their backs against the freezer. Hector sat closest to the door by the bottles and buckets that Dad used for making wine. And they had been in the laundry for so long now that they could no longer smell the detergent and cloves. Only in Lozzy's eyes existed an assurance that the situation might become an adventure with a happy ending. They were large brown eyes too, and prone to awe when she was told a story. And these eyes now searched Jack's face. Sandwiched between his sister's vulnerability, and the innocence that he recognised in himself, and his older brother's courage, that he admired and tried to copy, Jack's task was to stop Lozzy crying.

'What d'ya reckon, Hector?' Jack said, as he peered at his brother while trying to stop the quiver in his bottom lip.

Hector's face was white. 'We were told to stay here. They are coming back.'

Both Jack and Lozzy felt better for hearing Hector say that, although the younger brother suspected that his elder sibling would always refuse to believe that their mom and dad were not coming back. Like Dad, Hector could deny things. Jack was more like his mom, and by making their voices go soft he and his mother could sometimes get Dad and Hector to listen to their ideas.

But no matter how determined anyone's voice had been earlier that evening, their dad had not been persuaded to stay inside the house. He had always rubbished their stories about the bush not being right; about there being something living inside it; about them seeing something peer in, through the windows of the two end bedrooms of the bungalow that overlooked the garden and the deserted chicken coop. When their dog, Schnapps, disappeared, their dad had said they were all 'soft' and needed to 'acclimatise' to the new country. And even when all of the chickens vanished one night, and only a few feathers and a single yellow foot were left behind, he still didn't believe his children about the bush not being safe. But he took them seriously that night, because he had seen it too. Tonight, the whole family had seen *it*, together.

For months now, the children had been calling the intruder the *pig thing*. That was Lozzy's name for the face at the windows. She'd seen the pig thing first when she had been playing with Schnapps at the bottom of the garden, amongst the dank shadows where the orchard stopped and the wall of silver ferns and flax began. Pig thing had suddenly reared up between the dinosaur legs of two Kauri trees. And never had their mother heard Lozzy make such a fuss. 'Oh, Jesus, Bill. I thought she was being murdered,' she had said to their dad, once Lozzy had been taken inside the house and quieted. Up on the hill, east of the bungalow, even the boys, who were putting a better roof on their den, had heard their sister's cries. Frantic with excitement and fear, they had run home, each carrying a spear made from a bamboo beanpole. And that was the day the idea of pig thing established itself more formally in their lives. But pig thing had returned and was no longer a children's story.

That evening had played host to pig thing's worst visit, because earlier that evening, as they had all sat in the lounge watching television, pig thing had come up and onto the sundeck, and had stood by the barbecue filled with rainwater, to look through the glass of the sliding doors, like it was no longer afraid of their dad. The pig thing had come out of the darkness beyond their bright windows and reared onto its hind legs to display itself like an angry bear, before dropping to all four trotters and moving back into the shadows of the Ponga trees at the side of their property. Pig thing could not have been visible for more than a few seconds, but the power in the thin limbs and the human intelligence in the eyes had frightened Jack far more than the large Longfin eel that had once swum over his boot in the creek.

'Don't. Oh, Bill, don't. Let's go together, Bill, with the torch,' their mom had said to their dad, once he'd said he was going out to get the car started.

They were so far from Auckland, and, had either of the police officers based at the nearest station been available that evening, it would have taken them over an hour to reach the bungalow. Their dad had told their mother what the police operator had told him, after he called the police and reported an 'intruder', some kind of 'large animal or something' that was trying to get into their house. He couldn't bring himself to say 'pig thing' to the operator, though that's what it had been. Lozzy had described it perfectly. Maybe it took a four-year-old to *see* it properly. Pig thing wasn't quite an animal, and was certainly not human, but it seemed to have the most dangerous qualities of each when it had risen out of the darkness, bumped the glass and then vanished.

The two police officers had been called away to a big fight between rival chapters of bikers on the distant outskirts of the city. And with pig thing so close and perhaps eager to get inside the bungalow, waiting for help to arrive was not an option that their father even entertained.

Their nearest neighbours, the Pitchfords, lived on their farm two miles away and hadn't answered their phone when the children's dad had called them. They were old too. They had lived in the national reserve since they were both children, and had spent the best part of seven decades within the vast cool depths of the bush, before much of the area was cleared for the new migrants. Mr Pitchford still owned hunting rifles that were as old as the Great War. He'd once shown the guns to Jack and Hector, and let them hold the heavy and cumbersome weapons that stank of oil.

After the children's father ended his phone calls, he and their mother had exchanged a look that communicated to Jack a suspicion that the pig thing might have already visited their neighbours that night.

Going cold and shuddery, Jack believed that he had been close to fainting with fear. And all that repeated inside his mind was the vision of the creature's long torso pressed against the window, so that its brown teats, inside that black, doggy belly hair, had squished like a baby's fingers on the surface of the glass. Pig thing's trottery hands had merely touched the pane, but that had been sufficient to make the glass shake in the door-frame.

There was nothing inside the house, not a door or piece of furniture, that could be used as a barricade. Their dad knew it, and Jack had imagined the splintering of wood and the shattering of glass, followed by his sister's whimpers, his dad shouting and his mom's screams, as pig thing came grunting with hunger and squealing with excitement into their home. He had groaned to himself and kept his eyes shut for a while after the form had disappeared into the lightless trees corralling the sundeck; had tried to banish the images of that snouty face and the thin girlish hair that fell about its leathery shoulders.

And then their mother had said, 'Bill, *please*. Please don't go outside.' The children had guessed that their mom had put her hand on their dad's elbow as she'd said this. They didn't see her do it because, by that time, they had been herded into the laundry room, where they had stayed ever since, but they had known by the tone of her voice that she had touched dad's arm.

'Ssh, Jan. Just ssh now. Stay with the kids,' their dad had said to their mom. He'd gone outside but no one had heard the car engine start. The Morris Marina was parked at the bottom of the drive, under the wattle tree where Hector had once found a funny-looking bone that might have come from a cow skeleton. Inside the laundry, the children had all huddled together and silently strained their ears and prayed for the sound of the car engine, but they were left disappointed. And since he'd gone for the car they had heard nothing more from Dad at all.

The new and sudden gravity introduced into their evening had increased with every passing minute as a stillness inside the house, and a heaviness that had made them all aware of the ticking of the clock in the hall; it was the very thickening of suspense around their bodies.

Their mother had eventually opened the laundry door to report to the kids. She was trying to smile but her lips were too tight. On her cheeks were the red lines made by her fingers when she held her face in her hands. Sometimes she did that at night, sitting alone at the kitchen table. She did it a lot when Dad was out looking for Schnapps, day after day. And Mom had never liked the new house, or the surrounding countryside. She didn't like the whistles and shrieks of the birds, or the yelps in the night that sounded like frightened children, or the animal tracks in the soil beneath her washing line that spun around in the fierce winds, or the fat, long eel that they had seen by the creek with a lamb gripped between its jaws, or the large sticky red flowers that nodded at you as you walked past, or the missing dog, or the stolen chickens… Their mother didn't like any of it, and she had said that she doubted she would ever become a Kiwi. She had moved to this place for their dad; Hector and Jack knew that. And now she was missing too.

Holding Lozzy's Wonder Woman torch, because their dad had taken the big rubber flashlight from the kitchen drawer where the matches were kept, they had heard their mother calling, 'Bill. Bill. *Bill*!' and trying to smother the tremble in her voice as she went out the front door and then walked past the side of the house towards the car. Her voice had gone faint and then stopped. Just stopped.

And the fact that both of their parents had vanished without a fuss – no shout or cry or scuffle had been heard – had made the two boys hopeful that their mom and dad would soon come back inside. But as the silence lengthened, their heads had become busy with some dreadful ideas, including one that suggested that whatever had taken their parents had been so quick and so silent that they'd never had a chance to escape. Not a hope out there in the dark with *it*.

Lozzy had sobbed herself into a weary silence after seeing the pig thing on the sundeck, and had then begun whimpering after her mother's departure. For the moment, she had been placated by each of her older brothers' reassurances, lies and brave faces. But her silence would not last for long.

Lozzy stood up. She was wearing pyjamas. They were yellow and had pictures of Piglet and Winnie the Pooh printed on the cotton. Her hair was tousled and her feet were grubby with dust. Her slippers were still in the lounge; Mom had taken them off earlier to remove a splinter from her foot with the tweezers from the sewing box. Although the soles of the children's feet were getting harder, from running around barefoot all day outside, they still picked up prickles from the lawn and splinters from the sundeck. 'Where's Mummy, boys?'

Immediately, Jack patted the floor next to him. 'Ssh, Lozzy. Come and sit down.'

Frowning, she pushed her stomach out. 'No.'

'I'll get you a Tip Top from the freezer.'

Lozzy sat down. The freezer hummed and its lemon glow emitted a vague sense of comfort and familiarity when Jack raised the cabinet lid. Hector approved of the ice-cream trick, and, after a deep breath, he returned his stare to the laundry door. He sat with his chin resting on his knee, both hands gripping the ankle of that leg, listening.

Committed of face, Lozzy tucked into the cone loaded with Neapolitan ice-cream.

Jack shuffled to sit next to Hector. 'What d'ya reckon?' He used the same tone of voice before he and his brother crossed a waterfall in the creek, or explored the dark reeking caves up in the hills that Mr Pitchford had told them to 'steer clear of, lads', or shinned across a tree fallen over a deep gorge in the steamy tropical bush surrounding their house. The forest stretched all the way to the crazy beaches of black volcanic sand, where the blowholes and riptides prevented them from swimming.

Hector was the eldest and in charge, but he had no answer for his brother about what to do. But he was thinking hard. His eyes were a bit wild and watery too, so Jack knew that his brother was about to *do* something. And that frightened him. Already he imagined himself holding Lozzy when there were only the two of them left inside the laundry room.

'I'm gonna run to the Pitchfords,' Hector said.

'But it's dark.'

'I know the way.'

'But…' They looked at each other and each of them swallowed. Even though Jack hadn't mentioned the pig thing, they had thought of it at the same time.

Hector stood up, but he looked smaller than he usually did.

Peering between his knees, Jack kept his face lowered until the creases disappeared from the sides of his mouth and from around his eyes. He couldn't let Lozzy see him cry.

Before his brother left the laundry room, and then the house too, Jack had longed to hold him for a while but couldn't do it, and Hector wouldn't have wanted that anyway, because it would have made his leaving even harder. Instead, Jack just stared at his own flat toes spread out on the lino.

'Where's Hegder going?' Lozzy asked, as a bubble popped on her shiny lips.

'To get the Pitchfords.'

'They have a cat,' she said.

Jack nodded. 'That's right.' But Jack knew where Hector would have to go first before he even got close to the

Pitchfords' place; Hector was going into the forest with the clacking branches and ocean sounds, and along the earthen paths and over slippery tree roots, exposed like bones; these places that they had run and mapped together. And Hector would leap across the thin creek with the rowing-boat smells, race across the field of long grass that was darker than English grass and always felt wet and where they had found two whole sheep skeletons and brought them home in a wheelbarrow to reassemble on the front lawn. Hector was going to run a long way through the lightless night until he reached the Pitchfords' house with the high fence and the horseshoes fixed around the gate. 'To keep things out,' Mrs Pitchford had once told them in a quiet voice when Hector asked why they were nailed to the dark planks.

'No. Don't. No,' Jack had whispered, unable to hold back, when Hector turned the door handle. Everything had slowed thick and cold inside Jack's chest. Welling up to the back of his throat, this feeling spilled inside his mouth, tasting of rain. Inside Jack's head sang urgent, desperate sounds that were prayers trying to find words, and he squeezed his eyes shut to try and push the thoughts down, to squash them down like he was forcing the lid back onto a tin of paint. He did everything that he could to stop the hysterics from storming out of his entire body.

'Got to,' Hector said, his eyes wild inside a stiff face.

Lozzy stood up and tried to follow Hector. Jack snatched her hand but gripped it too hard. She winced, tearing up, and stamped a foot.

'Jack, don't open the door after I'm gone.' They were Hector's final words, and the laundry door clicked shut behind him.

Jack heard his brother's feet patter across the floorboards of the hall, and the catch being turned on the front door. When that door closed too, the wind chimes in the porch clinked and made an inappropriate spacey sound. There was a brief creak from the bottom step of the porch stairs, and then Lozzy's sobs made an unwelcome return into the laundry room.

After comforting her with a second ice-cream cone, Jack unplugged the freezer. Quickly but carefully, so as to make less noise, he removed the rustling bags of frozen peas, the steaks, stewed apple and fish fingers. He put the food in the big laundry sink that smelled like the back of Gran's house in England. Then he stacked the white baskets from inside the freezer against the side of the sink. Around the rim of the freezer cabinet, he placed plastic clothes pegs at intervals, so that there would be a gap between the grey rubber seal of the freezer lid and the cabinet, otherwise they would run out of air when he shut them both inside the freezer.

'Come on, Lozzy,' he said, hearing some of his mom inside his voice, and he felt a bit better for doing something that wasn't just waiting. He picked Lozzy up and lowered her into the freezer, and together they spread Schnapps's old blanket over the wet floor of the cabinet so they wouldn't get cold bottoms and feet.

'This smells. His fur is on it. Look.' Lozzy held up a tuft of the brown fur that the dog used to get stuck between his claws after riffing his neck. Their mom and dad had been unable to throw the dog's blanket away, in case Schnapps ever came home, so the blanket had stayed in the laundry where Schnapps had ended up sleeping at night. Their dad's idea of dogs sleeping outside had become a bad one after Schnapps had begun barking, whimpering and finally scratching at the front door every night. 'He's soft,' their dad had said. But tonight, their memories of Schnapps's distress had made more sense.

After handing the tub of ice-cream and the box of cones to Lozzy, Jack climbed inside the freezer and sat beside his sister. She reached for his hand with her sticky fingers.

As Jack pulled the lid down over their huddled bodies, he secretly hoped that the cold, wet freezer would stop the pig thing from smelling them. He also wondered, if it stood upright on those hairy back legs, as it had done out on the sundeck, if those trotter things on the ends of its front legs would be able to push the lid up. But he also took another small comfort into the dark with him: the pig thing had never come inside their house. Not yet, anyway.

Mrs Pitchford entered the bungalow through the empty aluminium frame of the sliding door; the glass had been smashed inwards and had collected within the mess of the curtains that had been torn down during the forced entry. Mrs Pitchford favoured net curtains behind the windows of her own home; she didn't like the sense of exposure that the large windows gave to the new homes that the government had started delivering on truck-beds for the migrants who were settling all over the area. She'd found it hard to even look at the red earth exposed beneath the felled trees. The appearance of these long rectangular bungalows, with tin cladding on their walls, never failed to choke her with fury and grief that was no good for her heart. And who could now say what kind of eyes would be drawn to these great glassy doors if you didn't use nets? *You couldn't then go blaming them who was already here.*

All of the lights were still on inside the bungalow. She looked at the brown carpets and the orange fabric on the furniture, and was startled again by what the English did with their homes: all Formica and white plastic and patterned carpets and big garish swirls in wallpaper the colour of coffee. Shiny, new, fragile, and she didn't care for any of it. There was a television too and a new radio, coloured silver and black, and both made in Japan. They mesmerised her, the things that these pale-skinned Poms brought from faraway places and surrounded themselves with. But anyone could see that the Poms and their things didn't sit right with the old bush. The bush had ways that not even the Maoris liked, because there were *things* here before them too.

Glass crunched under her boots as Mrs Pitchford made her way further inside the house.

The kitchen and dining room were open-plan, divided from the living room by the rear of the sofa. Unable to resist the lure of the kitchen, she went inside and touched the extractor fan above the stove. It was like a big hopper on a petrol lawnmower, and she marvelled again at what young mothers considered necessary for the running of a household. And here was the food mixer Jan had once showed her. Orange and white plastic with *Kenwood Chevette* printed along one side. A silver coffee pot with a wooden handle, what Jan had called a percolator, beside the casserole dishes with their orange flower patterns.

Mrs Pitchford ran her hard fingertips across the smooth sides of the Tupperware boxes that Jan had lined up on the counter; they were filled with cereal, rice, something called spaghetti, bran and sugar. You could see the contents as murky shadows through the sides. Everything in her own home was wood, pottery, steel or iron. And she remembered seeing the very same implements in use when she was a little girl and had helped her mother prepare food. Hardwoods and metals lasted. Plastic and carpet and 'stereos' hadn't been much use to this family tonight, had they?

The sound of the car engine idling outside returned her sense of purpose; Harold had told her not to get distracted. She turned and waddled out of the kitchen, but her eyes were drawn to the sideboard beside the dining table; at all of the silver and ceramic trinkets behind the sliding glass doors: little sherry glasses; small mugs with ruddy faces on the front; China thimbles; teaspoons with patterns on the handles.

There was a washing machine in the little laundry room beside the 'dining area', and a freezer too. Jan had been horrified to learn that Mrs Pitchford still washed clothes in a tin bath, used a larder for food and still preserved fruit in jars. *The bloody cheek.*

The laundry room smelled of wine, soap powder and urine. All of the food from the freezer was melting and softening inside the sink. The lid of the freezer was raised and there was an old blanket inside the white metal cabinet. It was still cold inside the freezer when she leaned over to look inside, puzzled why the food was stacked in the sink. They had no mutton, no venison, no sweet potatoes that she could see. She looked under her foot and saw that she was standing on a yellow clothes peg.

Inside the unlit hallway that led down to the four bedrooms, she paused for a few moments to get herself accustomed to the darkness. It was a relief to be out of the bright living area, but she would need more light to conduct a proper search in the bedrooms. Ordinarily, she could have found a sewing pin on the floor by the thinnest moonlight, because around here there were plenty who could see better at night than others. But tonight there was no moon or starlight at all, and the curtains in the bedrooms were drawn, and it would be terrible if she missed something important. She found the light switch for the hallway.

The family had no rugs; they had laid carpet all the way down the passage and even inside the bedrooms. How did Jan get the dust out of them, or air them in the spring like she did with her rugs? Shaking her head in disapproval, she went into the first room: Jan and Bill's room. Two suitcases were open on the bed and had been filled with clothes. The headboard was softened with padded white plastic. Mrs Pitchford reached out and pressed it.

The next room was for the little girl with all of the lovely thick hair. Dear little Charlotte. The light from the hall revealed the dim outlines of her dolls and toys, the books on all of the shelves, the bears in the wallpaper pattern. 'Darlin',' she said, quietly, into the darkness.

No one answered.

Some of the teddy bears and stuffed rabbits were on the floor; they had been pulled off the shelves. Mrs Pitchford had a hunch a few would be missing too.

She carried on, down the passageway to the two end bedrooms: Jack and Hector's rooms. Hector was safe at their home. How he had managed to scuttle all the way to their farm, in the dark, had surprised her and her husband. But little Hector had come and banged on their door, then fallen inside, panting and as pale as a sheet. She and Harold hadn't wasted a moment and had swept him into their arms, before spiriting him across the yard to Harold's workshop.

'That kid was as slippery as an eel and quick as a fox,' Harold had said, his eyes smiling, after he returned to the kitchen from his workshop, and had removed his sheep-shearing gloves and leather apron. He'd then yanked their coats off the pegs. 'Come on, mother, we better get our skates on.'

And when he'd arrived at their farm, Hector had been so concerned for his younger brother and his sister, that she and Harold had sped to the bungalow in the old black Rover that someone else had once brought over with them from England. Harold had taught himself to drive the car too, not long after acquiring it from an elderly couple with those Pommy accents that miss the *H* in every word.

Harold would dress Hector when they returned with the other two children, if they were still around, though that seemed unlikely to Mrs Pitchford.

The family's bungalow was looking like it was completely deserted, like all of the bungalows on the Rangatera Road that were waiting for new Pommy families, or Pacific Islanders, or even more of those bloody Dutch Dike-Duckies. Poles were supposed to be coming too. *What next?*

The two end bedrooms were empty, but she smelled what all life leaves behind, and then found the spoor on the floor of one of the boys' rooms that overlooked the wattle tree. It was ruddy in colour and smelled strong; the fresh stool of excitement, the stool of too much fresh blood gulped down by a very greedy girl.

Kneeling down, Mrs Pitchford tried to scoop it into her handkerchief, but there was too much of it. She stripped a pillow case off the bed. 'You've been at it here, my little joker,' Mrs Pitchford said with a rueful smile. Her errant daughter must have hunted right through the house until she'd found the other two kiddiewinks hiding; under the beds maybe, or in that hardboard wardrobe with the sliding doors on the little plastic runners. 'What a rumble you've had, my girl.' This kind of house couldn't possibly make a family feel safe either; it was like cardboard covered in tin. But her daughter must have, at the very least, had the sense to take Jack and little Charlotte outside the house first, like Harold had shown her how to do with the other Poms. Otherwise, they'd have to burn out another of these bungalows to incinerate the leavings, and that always made a flaming mess. 'One more and it'll smell funny,' Harold had warned after the last bungalow that they'd lit up.

Mrs Pitchford went back to the laundry room and found a scrubbing brush, detergent and a bucket. She filled the bucket with hot water from the tap in the laundry, then went back to the boy's room and scrubbed the rest of the muck out of the carpet. While she was doing this, Harold had become impatient and had sounded the car horn. '*Hold* your bloody horses,' she'd called out, but Harold couldn't have heard her.

When Mrs Pitchford was finally back inside the car and seated beside her husband with a pillow case in her lap, the contents wet and heavy, and with three Tupperware containers inside a brown paper bag clutched in her other hand, she asked Harold, 'You want to check the creek?'

'Nah. *She'll* be right. Long gone. *She'll* be up in them caves by now, mother.'

'She got carried away again, my love.'

Smiling with a father's pride, Harold said, 'She's a big girl, mother. You've got to let them suss their own way in this world. Be there for them from time to time, but still, we've done what we can for her. She has her own family now. She's just providing for them the best way she knows how.'

'We've been very lucky with her, Harold. To think of all them sheep that Len and Audrey lost last year with their girl.'

'You're not wrong, mother. But when you let a child run that wild...' Harold rolled his eyes behind the thick lenses in the tortoiseshell frames of his glasses, which he'd taken off the old Maori boy whom they'd found fishing too far downstream last summer. 'It's all about pace, mother. We showed our girl how to pace herself. A chook or two. A dog. A cat. And if dags like these Poms are still around after that, well, it comes down to who was here first. And who was here first, mother?'

'We was, dear. We was.'

What God Hath Wrought?

1848. Utah.

And in the darkness the soldier came upon the old man.

Five miles out the dragoon had seen the red spark of the campfire, down in the desert, like it was the last ember in hell yet to wink out and leave only the abyss behind; the black void that was there before all of this, and before hell too.

And the soldier came upon that old man as silently as a Comanche upon his pony comes with ease into an enemy's camp to leave more widows in this world than it ever wanted. Came out of nothing with not so much as a jingle of spurs or a jangle of sabre against his saddle, just like he'd been showed by the Apache scouts down on the Rio Grande, when he rode for 'Old Rough and Ready' General Zachary Taylor against the Mexican Army of the North.

When the old man saw the dragoon come out of the night air, he might have been some kind of avenging angel with an hourglass and scythe in each celestial hand, and it was too late to reach for the musket that he had laid out on his bedroll.

Around the fire the soldier spied a mule, a pick, a shovel, some pans. Smelled coffee, a mess of beans in a skillet. A prospector, heading for the Barbary Coast of San Francisco. Another fool.

Since the news broke in New York about the gold out

west, the soldier had been coming across these men and their desperate dreams all along the trails through Iowa, Nebraska, Wyoming. Men would suffer for their greed more than they would suffer for anything else. Give them snow and road agents and Indians and starvation and every disease that rolled your eyes up inside your head, and all the privations of hell on top of that, and they would still suffer and make others suffer for a mere rumour of gold.

'Easy,' he said to the old man, who was just sat on his ass, all wide of eye and open of mouth before his skillet, and whose skittery, honking mule now seemed to be transmitting a crazy terror into its owner; a man who might yet reach for the musket, or snatch at the Bowie knife stuck in the sand, and end up getting himself shot dead.

From up high in his dragoon saddle, in plain sight, the soldier holstered the pistol. Then flashed all 44 inches and six pounds of his sabre through the reaching red light of the campfire, before sinking Old Wristbreaker back into its scabbard, real smooth. 'You ain't the one,' he said.

The soldier dismounted.

'Well, I sho' is pleased to hear it, sir,' the old man said. 'Had all the fear a man can git for one day.'

'Mind sharin' that fire a time?'

Out of an instinct for self-preservation, and a relief that he'd live a little longer, maybe even long enough to see some of that gold up near San Francisco, the old man said, 'Sure. Got a mess of beans and some biscuit I'm willing to part with.' The old man would refuse him nothing; the soldier knew that. There was a time when he'd have felt bad for scaring an old boy in the night, but that time was hard to even remember now.

'Coffee be appreciated. Few words. Then I be pulling out.'

The old man nodded back at him. His beard was filthy with tobacco juice; his face creased like dried fruit in a store jar, the skin brown as molasses. He smelled of mule, years of sweat, bear grease, pipe tobacco and shit.

The soldier fed his horse; talked to her in a soft voice, touched her ears. She nuzzled him like an obedient daughter. Then he pulled his cape of navy-blue wool round his neck and squatted opposite the prospector.

The fire snapped between them, blinded them to the greater darkness of the desert, a whole universe with no edges out there.

'Where ye headed, fella?' the old man asked, jittery in his hands that were busy with the pouring of his guest's coffee, black as oil, into a tin cup from the jug sat among the embers.

The soldier never answered or moved his pale-blue eyes from staring into the fire, right into the red ashes. 'Yer beans burnin'. Go ahead. Eat,' he eventually said.

The old man complied. Straight from the hissing skillet and piled onto a long spoon, he shovelled beans into the dark hole within that dirty beard; all the time wary of moving his big veiny eyes from the soldier, who removed his leather gloves and held the metal mug of coffee between both hands.

They sat in silence for a while, until the soldier broke his stare from the fire and looked at the old man's meagre provisions: a few sacks tied with rope, two large canteens, probably already empty first day out of the mountains. He'd seen others, footsore and half mad with thirst, carrying twice as much. 'You still got five hundred miles of desert to ride. Think you can make it?'

The old man laid aside the skillet. He took a pipe from a shirt pocket as dark and greasy as the flakes that he stuffed into the little clay bowl, using fingers thick as corn cobs and nails so dirty he might have just been blacking boots. 'Aimin' to resupply from them Saints.'

The soldier's face tensed; his blue eyes narrowed and hardened and the old man couldn't look into them for long. 'Don't call 'em that. Saints. They ain't no such thing.'

The old boy nodded. 'Them sons a bitches with Brigham Young been shakin' everyone down passes through here, I hears,' the old man said, wary all over again, but eager to be conspiratorial. 'But there ain't nowhere else to get feed. Supplies. Not this far out.'

The soldier stayed quiet. Remembered the cup in his hand, sipped at the coffee, winced. 'You come across any of them today?'

The old man looked down. 'Ain't rightly sure.'

'Either you come across them or you ain't. Which is it?'

'Easy, fella. I see all kinds. Mind my own business. I got no beef with no one. Them Mormon Saints neither.' He looked at the insignia on the soldier's cap, swallowed. 'You one of them Grey's militia, from Missouri way? If you are, I ain't no Mormon. I swear on the Lord, sir. Just aimin' to buy some vittles from them so I can get to the ocean. I –'

'I ain't ridin' with no militia.'

The prospector relaxed again, sucked on his unlit pipe. 'Them Mormons all out at the dead water. Timpanogos. Since '47, I heard. New settlement. God's own kingdom they callin' it. The Saints Zion. You got a beef with them, then that's where they is at.'

The dragoon spat. 'They ain't all out there with Brigham Young. There's others of a similar creed. Settin' up on their own. Nearby.'

The old man sucked too hard at the pipe stem; a shake had come into his shoulders. The soldier looked hard at the old man. 'You ain't never asked my name.'

The prospector's hands shook too now. He cleared his throat and his voice wasn't much when it came out. 'I learned a long time ago to mind my own.'

'You never asked on account of you just guessing at who I am. That right?'

'Man hears things.'

'What they calling me now?'

The prospector started to look like his skin was full of sand. He lowered his eyes and spoke into his lap. 'Look, sir. I'd as soon share a pipe with you and get my head down –'

'I ain't gonna hurt you. Long as you're straight with me.'

'Yessir.' The old man dared to look up at the dragoon again. 'Some talk about a man out here. Cavalry. The Devil's right hand, they been sayin'. Man I hear about's goin' to chase Brigham Young and his polygamist sinners right back into hell. Others be callin' him the Destroying Angel, like it's the Lord's work he be doin'.' The prospector finished with a swipe of one grubby hand across his appalling beard.

The soldier smiled. 'They's work to be done. Whether it be the Devil's or the Lord's, who can say? But looks like I been chosen for it. And it ain't Brigham Young and his congregation I'm here for. It's them others that came this way too, and the preacher they follow.'

The fire seemed to shrink then, all on its own, and take away its glare and heat from them, as if the mere mention of a certain man was enough to put out the light of the stars. And all the blood suddenly seemed to flow out of the old man, leaving his tanned face pale as a dressmaker's dummy.

'Have you seen the black horse? Have you seen the black carriage?' the soldier asked.

The old man started to shake again, like the night-time cold suddenly dropped a few degrees further at the mention of these things of black. He pulled his bedroll around his shoulders. It had once been grey, but was now just grubby with no particular colour around the holes in it. The old man nodded. 'And I'm fixin' to forget it.'

The soldier leaned his face further into the firelight. 'To have seen it and still be breathin' is somethin'.'

'I never got close enough to parlay. No, sir. That be who you lookin' for?'

The soldier said nothing.

The old man reached out a hand, pointed a finger at the dragoon. 'They say an angel put a curse on them, and only an angel can take it off again. You an angel, soldier?'

'Who I was and who I am ain't the same things no more. One time, I was Sergeant Ephraim Lisle. Dragoon. US Cavalry. Now, you could say I truly am an instrument of vengeance. But I ain't no angel.'

'He took yer wife?' the old man said, his voice not yet put back together, but curiosity had piqued over his fear.

The soldier mused that the story of their meeting and what passed between them would be told again, by other old men at the foot of mountains older than them, older than time, and the tale would change with every telling, until no one would ever know who that soldier had been. It mattered little what he said. The only truth in the world was what you saw with your own eyes, and that truth never came from another man's fool mouth. But maybe some of his purpose, which had its business with death, should be put in the wind. Tonight. Here. He was close; and this might be his last night on earth. Ought to be, considering the odds that would be stacked high against him in the morning. Maybe a last testament was called for at these times.

'Sister.' And just that word in his mouth and in the air around him seized him up inside and he had to dip his head so that the old man could not see the tears that shone in his eyes; eyes that had been open for twenty-five years but had seen things that no man should ever see in all of ten thousand years.

And so the dragoon spoke for himself as much as he spoke for the old bearded fool in the desert, so that there was a chance that it might be known that when all of the black blood was let, it had been shed for a purpose pure and righteous. And the dragoon, Ephraim Lisle, began by telling the old prospector that the thing that rode the black horse, with the black carriage rolling behind it, was no longer a man.

'Sho' didn't look much like one neither,' the old man said to himself, and he now seemed uncertain about his appetite for such stories in this lonesome part of the earth. 'I ain't sure they's any damn thing a man can do to hurt them more than they is already sufferin'. I heard they all had the black pox and was out here to do some dyin'. Sure looked like it this mornin'.'

'You heard of the Second Great Awakening?' the soldier asked the night. 'And of the con man known as Joseph Smith?'

'The martyr.'

'He weren't no martyr. He was a bum. A trickster who sold himself as a seer and a prophet to them with shit for brains in Missouri, and then Illinois once Missouri come to its senses. A dabbler in peep stones, scrying, witchery. Plenty a fool and his money were soon parted, old man, when Joseph Smith was around. As they was soon parted from their wives and daughters and… sisters too.'

The prospector nodded. 'They say he got gold tablets straight from the Lord by way of the angel Moroni in a cave, on the Hill Cumorah.'

'Horseshit.'

'No doubt.'

'But Smith got something he weren't bargaining for, sho' enough, and in an old Indian cave in the hill they call Cumorah. He and his friend in black you saw out ridin'. Fella that went inside that cave with Joseph Smith was a man named Lemuel Hawkins. Man just as crooked as Smith. Was a time old Lemuel Hawkins and Joseph Smith claimed they could find treasure with their black magic and peep stones. But it weren't no angel of the Lord who they mixed it with inside that cave in Cumorah.'

'How you come by way of this?'

'When I come back from the war in Mexico, my sister was missing from home, as well as the damn fool aunt and uncle I left her with. And most every other woman an' girl in my home town was gone too. Cuz they were all wedded to the Prophet and on the great Exodus to find the Kingdom of God, out in this desert. Following the man once known as Lemuel Hawkins. Who claimed he was given instructions like Moses, in some cave, by the angel Moroni.

'But before I lit out to fetch my sister back, I went and stood in that cave, looking for the divine message. And all I saw was drawin's up on them walls. What the Indians and them before the Indians had put up there. A warning. Any fool could see it. Ain't no angel of the Lord was ever in that place before or since. I reckon that cave went all the way down to hell. Sure smelled like it. I seen brigs, I seen jails plenty. And that's what that cave was. A prison with no bars. Made to keep something inside it for a long time, old man, with something stronger than bars. What them fools found in that cave was nothing I reckon they were bargaining to find neither. But those fools broke it out of there.'

And the soldier remembered the place because he could not ever forget the terrible black fear that frosted his wits, like he was walking in the Devil's own footprints. It could have been a child that had made those markings on the brown stone of the long, low cave in the Hill Cumorah. But the pictures in the damp and the dark were all the worse to look upon because of their rough nature; and what the unschooled style of the artists had scratched on stone, when viewed by lamplight, a mind given to figuring would not easily forget.

The soldier guessed it was the thing that traded under the name of the angel Moroni. So tall and thin and tatty about the head. Etched over and over again, onto the walls and the ceiling. Striding at the little figures of the Indian braves who pointed their bows upwards. In its talons it held the bodies of men. Into its spiky mouth it shoved them too, like they were corn dollies to a dog. It was able to fly like an eagle in some of the drawings too, and all the animals and men of the earth fled beneath it.

And the longer the soldier stood in that cave and moved his lantern here and there, he got to figuring that the thing the Indians had taken to drawing with such frequency and desperation, might nary have been a single deity after all; it had been drawn many times by them because there had been more than one.

In one corner of the low, dark cave that still stank of sulphur and the meat of a dead man left in the sun, he determined another clear message being imparted to him, as if those warriors of old were telling another warrior in another time that such things that preyed upon the flesh of men, and had to be shut up in caves, could be beaten. Because the little figures of the braves on the far walls of the long, low cave were using bone and flint axes to take off the angels' heads, one by one.

But why the Indians had left one behind, alive, sealed inside a cave in the dark, was still a mystery. Because judging by the way it had dug at that floor, and thrown itself against the walls with stones in its long fingers, and then just ended up waiting and dreaming and reaching out for the minds of the men who came nearest to it, the soldier guessed it had been inside the cave for a very long time. And it had left its bones behind. Because no man walked upright on legs like that. But whatever black spirit those legs and bones had once carried must have still been deep inside that Hill Cumorah when Joseph Smith and Lemuel Hawkins found the cave and opened it up like two greedy lecherin' fools all out of better ideas.

The dragoon sighed. 'I reckon what folks say was the angel Moroni promised ole Smith and Hawkins it could make them gods among men. God men. And that they could take as many wives as there were cattle in the field, and as much wealth as was in all the world. So them pair of hustlers with nothing left to lose, who wanted to clean up in the Second Great Awakening, made some kind of bargain.'

The soldier paused, spat into the fire. 'Seems they had it all too, for a while. Over twenty wives each and a parish of six thousand fools, who handed over all their worldly goods, victuals and assets to them. People who were ready to die for their prophets.

'But when Smith was murdered in Carthage by the militia, Brigham Young took up Smith's believers and lit out here from Illinois. Seen his own opportunity there, I reckon. But the other one who was in that cave with Smith, Lemuel Hawkins, goes by the name of Brother Lehi now. And Lehi broke away from Smith early. Started sayin' he was the true leader of a lost Hebrew tribe, not Joseph Smith. Pronounced himself true king of the Fair-skinned Nephites. Maybe he thinks he is, but whatever he is, it sure ain't Lemuel Hawkins no more. I reckon whatever was in that cave got hisself into old Hawkins. And it was Hawkins that took my sister, and took the whole damn town too. Aimed to bring his congregation out here. One hundred and forty men, women and children, ever' one, came with Hawkins. Ain't but a few left breathin' now. I been finding and dealing with them… all the way in here from Illinois.'

''Bout your sister?'

'Ain't seen her since '46. My guess, she's still followin' the black carriage, and the black horse.'

'I sho' hope she ain't, soldier,' the old man said, and looked into the palms of old hands as worn and beaten as boot leather.

The soldier swallowed another mouthful of the bitter coffee. 'Woulda been a mercy for me to find her back a ways with the others. She was not yet fourteen years old when Lehi took her for his bride. What she is now only the Lord can say.'

'They's sayin' you's shootin' Saints dead soon as you look at 'em. Running them to ground. Burnin' farms.'

The soldier nodded. 'Some. Sure. Them that used to be neighbours. Family too. Killt my old schoolteacher last week in Bear Creek. But it's only them that Lehi made into Nephites that I got dealin's with.' The soldier looked hard at the old man. 'I be doing them a favour, and this world too. You truly seen Lehi and his tribe of Fair-skinned Nephites, you'd know it too, old man. Devil in that cave already took 'em for his own.'

The old man wiped his mouth. Produced a small metal flask. Uncapped it, offered it. 'They was down yonder. South of the Dead Sea.'

The soldier shook his head at the offer. 'It truly there, the Great Dead Sea?' he asked.

The old prospector nodded. 'Seen it with my own eyes

jus' this mornin' while lookin' for Brigham Young's place. I heard of Timpanagos back east. Nary believed a word of it. But it's right there, just as sho' as you is, sir. White sand of salt. A dead ocean in the middle of it. Godforsaken. A place damned in the Lord's eyes, where the damned will surely congregate with impious ways.'

'Where was Lehi's place?'

'Half a day's ride due south. They got up a few buildings. Some tents too. I took it for Brigham Young's Zion. Thought I was lost and all turned around from the Wasatch mountains. But I never was, and it weren't Brigham Young's new town I found neither. That's north o' here. This place must be Lehi's. It ain't on any map. Nor should it be. But I sees a bunch of his people comin' through the desert this morning, out of them buildings they got up like I told you. I saw 'em through a spyglass from back aways, then lit out up here, real quick.'

'What you see?'

'Was like you said. Black horse. Black carriage.'

'How they lookin' to you?'

The old prospector looked at the embers. Studied his pipe like he was surprised to suddenly find it in his hand. Then looked at the soldier, and shrank further down inside his blanket. 'What's the worse thing you ever seen?'

In the shadows under the peak of his cap, the dragoon's eyes narrowed. 'Same thing as you, I'm bettin'.'

The old man nodded. 'Seen my young'uns get took by cholera in '35. Wife a year later. But hard as that was to see, leastways doctors say it's the way of things. But them Nephites down there ain't part of any way of things I ever seen afore this mornin'.'

The soldier nodded. Took out his tobacco pouch and a thin sheet of paper. Spat into the fire once he had the cigarette rolled and lit. 'At Palo Alto a gunner in Ringgold's artillery fired a single shell, full with shot, and it took down a whole Mexican band. They was playing to rally their side against our artillery. Nary one of them stood up agin. Not even the saviour coulda put all them pieces back together.' He shook his head. 'Never thought I'd see a thing as bad as that agin. But I was wrong. How many you see out yonder this mornin'?'

'Didn't look long enough to count. But there was him, Preacher Lehi, on his horse. And… and his wives in the carriage behind. Some chillun too. Six, seven maybe. Maybe more. An' all lookin' like the dead that rise on Judgement Day, but what's come early.'

The trooper nodded. 'That's them.'

'If they the Devil's own, soldier, how can a man cut them down?'

Thumbing a hand back at his horse, the soldier said, 'Eighteen-forty-three breech-loading carbine do some mean work at distance. That's how I started the cullin'. Take 'em down, then get in close for the disarticulatin'. Afore they's got wise anyway, and started hidin' like Injuns. Waitin' for me. When things get close, I got a smoothbore pistol back there too. Fires a 230-grain ball. Clusters up twelve inches wide on fifty yards. Long as it's about they's heads, she be fine.' He nodded at his sabre. 'Wristbreaker comes out swift when we get eye-to-eye. The head on a Fair-skinned Nephite got to come away from the shoulders, so Old Wristbreaker done most of them so far.'

The old man was impressed and afraid; his dark mouth hung open like he was some kind of imbecile. 'Shee-it.' He snapped out of his gaping. 'You gonna do 'em all, soldier?'

'Ever' last one.'

The old man swallowed and his eyes went wide again. 'What about your sister?'

The soldier stared right into the black heavens. 'She ain't my sister no more. She ain't like you and me. No, she ain't. When the time comes, the time comes.' He pinched his fingers into his eyes sockets and the old man looked away to let him have his moment.

'Aw heck,' the dragoon said, shaking his head. 'That's how

it spread. Folk wanted to hold onto their own, even though they was bit by Lehi. Then they got bit too by their own folks. Pretty soon, the whole town was on its way out here. All bit. Converted. All of them Fair-skinned Nephites.'

And when the soldier rode away from the old man, whom he left with a gift of three hundred Yankee dollars, and his campaign medal, and his story, he remembered too the time that he rode away from his sister. All white in the face with her bottom lip trembling she was, as the last person she knew enough to love rode away. He remembered every moment of their parting. Not only because it was the last time that he saw her, but he remembered every moment of their parting because it was wrong of him to have left her alone in the world at his uncle's dirt farm. Consumption took their daddy and smallpox killed their ma. And they was all each other ever had after. Two orphans with a dour aunt who knew more scripture than she did kindness, and an uncle who thought the young should get whipped like mules. And he left little Mercy Lisle with them because she wasn't old enough to light-out and run herself, like he did by joining the army to get into the scrape down in Texas. He left her cryin' on that porch. And only after he was gone from sight did he let himself feel the cold unbearable anguish that he had left behind in that child's little heart. And it burst inside him like canister round and the hurting never faded like the scars of old wounds are supposed to do.

But he kept himself alive through every charge at the Mexican lines, and kept his head down and under every one of General Mariano Arista's cannonballs, which pounded out of those big brass guns and came down at the dragoons like the fists of giants thumping the earth all about their mounts. He kept his head and his blood all in one place through that war, because his memory of the abandoned child on that porch kept him eaten by guilt so strong that not even his remorse for what his sabre did to the hatless heads of routed Mexican infantry could ever equal it.

There was nothing left of her when he returned from the war to his uncle's patch in Illinois; none of her trinkets, or any of the three little grey dresses that she wore, or the dolly his pa had made her. Nothing of her was left in a bare room in that ramshackle house that sat at a slouch on a few acres of miserable dust. Every farmhouse was the same for ten miles; left dismal and swept empty of life on account of the little settlement's vigour to be part of Prophet Lehi's lost Hebrew tribe of Fair-skinned Nephites.

Some Gentiles across the wash told him of the town's exodus following their suffering a plague that past winter, from which many of them miraculously arose from their sickbeds, but changed. Ravaged bone-thin by disease, but somehow brighter of eye and quicker on foot than any survivor of the black pox had a right to be.

And the Nephites had organised themselves but four months before his return from war, to travel in a long wagon train to the Promised Land as the Day of Judgement was all but nigh. Because Lehi's congregation needed to be in place at the Great Dead Sea to escape the persecution of the apostates, the Gentiles and the already damned, who comprised a multitude so vast that it included anyone who was not a devoted and servile follower of the Prophet Lehi.

And the soldier learned from the first few Fair-skinned Nephites that he came across, as they snapped up at him with their dry mouths, around the sole of his boot that pressed their necks into the dust, that his sister had been wed to his uncle soon as he left for the war. Then taken from his uncle, along with his aunt, and married to Lehi after the Prophet's final engagement with the angel Moroni on the Hill Cumorah.

Lehi had branded his uncle an apostate, the fate of many simple men in that town; men who atoned for their lack of faith by parting company with their wives and children and goods and chattels, and finally with the very blood in their veins if the prophet so wished. It was the only favour the Prophet Lehi had ever done him: saving him the trouble of shooting down the dog that was his uncle.

But as for this act of mass witlessness and self-trickery perpetrated by an entire community, the soldier began to see it as an act of the most grievous wrongdoing against his sister, the little girl he had left behind, defenceless and alone, for safekeeping. An act of dereliction that demanded retribution. A swift and violent end to any and all who had stood by and watched as his sister was married to those two sons of bitches, so full of low animal cunning that they might as well have been prairie dogs and run to the Great Dead Sea on all fours.

After he left the old prospector, his first opportunity to settle matters, or to find the very end of his own dealings on this earth, came in a long, thin ravine made of red rock and floored with shadows and dust, south of the Great Dead Sea.

The soldier rode slowly through it, his carbine resting across the saddle. His eyes moved beneath the peak of his cap, from his horse's ears to the steep sides of the ravine. He'd ridden all morning on the prospector's directions, and guessed this was the last of the canyons before he came across the settlement that the Nephites had hidden here. And he could see that this place was a strategic location. It was far enough away from Brigham's Mormon Saints not to compete, but close enough to lay the blame on them for its nefarious actions in attracting a share of the sun-beaten, thirsty, California gold-rush traffic, that could be waylaid in these ravines and gathered like rich pickings.

Toward the end of the ravine, the dragoon's horse began to pull her head away from whatever scent she'd caught on a cool morning breeze. The soldier calmed her by whispering into her ear like he always did and stroking her fine chestnut neck with one hand. She cantered to one side of the ravine and they waited until her master could also hear the squeak of the axles and the rolling creak of the carriage's wheels across the rocky floor.

The dragoon dismounted and crouched, not more than two feet from the stirrup of his saddle, aiming the carbine straight ahead. When the carriage came rattling and shaking around the bend in the ravine, he was disappointed to see that Prophet Lehi was not out front on his black horse, leading this gathering party. With the soldier despatching every one of his assassins that the Prophet sent back east to stop him culling the stragglers and feed-gatherers and convert-hunters of the Fair-skinned Nephite tribe, it seemed that it had become too dangerous for their leader to range far from Zion. The soldier had cut, shot or smashed down some thirty-three Nephites to date. Another thirty he'd found dead, killed by other hands, including their leader's. Over forty more he'd found withered to husks from starvation along the trail upon which he'd tracked them to Utah. He doubted there could be more than forty left in the congregation that had reached the Great Dead Sea.

The man who sat up front in the wagon was not Lehi, whom he had seen only three times and at a distance. The Prophet was taller and more horribly thin than any man he had ever seen. He always wore a black suit, gold watch chain, short preacher's cape and a hat of good quality wool felt, with a tall crown, curved brim and matching hatband ribbon around the base of the crown.

Behind the figure driving the carriage through the ravine, the soldier saw a collection of whitish hair and dowdy bonnets. He waited for the preacher to appear, because he had always been near the wagon on previous sightings. Cursing under his breath, he waited until the black carriage with those big narrow wheels was fifty yards away from him and the driver had seen him plainly. As the driver pulled up on the reins of his train, the soldier shot him back into the bucket seat. Caught him up high in the chest and punched him sideways in his seat, where he sat with his papery maw just snatching at the air.

The sound of the carbine bullet echoing through that ravine set off the passengers into a terrible shrieking, accompanied by the throwing of their long arms up and into the early red sunlight.

As the dragoon reloaded the carbine, he heard Lehi, further back and out of sight, issue an order. And the passengers, three women and one man naked from the waist down, stood up and tottered in the carriage like they were in a rowing boat that was sinking fast. They disembarked over the sides quickly and scuttled away to either side of the ravine.

When he'd reloaded the carbine, besides the shot driver, who was still swallowing at the air and holding his throat, all that was left to see of the Nephites was suggestions of sprightly dark shapes, crawling upwards. There was no clear shot to be had. The trooper swore and holstered the carbine. Then swung up and into his saddle. He drew his sabre and kicked his horse forward, to a canter that she knew preceded a charge.

And down that valley he thundered, his sabre forward, angled down so he could see the slotted throat, level with his charger's bit. He passed that carriage in a slipstream of dust. His sabre flashed but once, before returning to position. And as the trooper was passing by, the head and forearms of the driver came asunder from his brittle body.

Above him the soldier received the sense that four dark figures had gone scratching like ocean crabs in flight from a sea bird's sharp beak. They were unarmed save for one Mississippi musket that he saw the male drag off behind its wasted legs. But as this was the closest he'd ever come to Lehi, the soldier kept on the charge like it was those Mexican gunners that he was riding down at Palo Alto. The Prophet dropped from his thin horse and ran to the right side of the ravine as the cavalry dragoon rode upon him.

The Prophet's black horse reared and shook a terrible yellow mouth from which no spittle would ever froth again. The dragoon aimed his mount right at it. Then cleaved its bone muzzle and skull in two great parts with Old Wristbreaker as he passed its shuddering, angry shape.

The dragoon inclined his charger to chase the scrabbling Prophet into the rocks, but his horse buckled, and then slid sideways, before he even heard the shot from somewhere behind his right ear.

In the rushing cold of the dawn, the crimson world of dust and stone was all a blur about him, and he jumped from his horse before she bumped and skidded across the valley floor.

He rolled and came to his feet with his sabre up high like the French Hussar taught them back east. He hobbled back to his horse, who was shot bad through the neck by two balls from one barrel. Took from the saddle his carbine, and he ran to the closest side of the ravine opposite from where he'd been shot at.

He went up the ravine twenty feet and no more, in case the shooter had reloaded and could sight him in the open. The soldier dropped down behind a big red boulder that showed him the way in and out of the valley from each side. Three Nephites were somewhere up above him. Another two, one of them Lehi, were on the other side. 'Son of a bitch,' he said.

'That you, Trooper Ephraim Lisle?' It was Lehi calling out from where he hid like some black spider amongst the rocks.

'You know it.' The trooper peered across the ravine to see if the Prophet had poked up his white face.

'Little Mercy Lisle I keep close, Ephraim. I think you know that. Real close out here on those cold, cold nights. Your uncle may have made her a woman, but I been ploughin' her like a dry field, soldier. You hear me?'

The soldier gritted his teeth and two of them broke their tips clean off at the back of his mouth.

'But I'm a generous man, Ephraim. I might be willin' to let you stud little Mercy yourself. Now, how about that, soldier blue?'

'You tryin' to get a move out of me, preacher? Well, it nearly workin',' the soldier said, and had to bite down hard on his sleeve and fill his mouth with wool to stifle his sobs of such rage that all he could see was hot red blood pumping through his eyes. And it was all he could do to keep himself nailed to the earth and not rise up with his pistol and sword and run at the Nephites across the wash.

'God in heaven,' he prayed. 'Lord who has walked beside me through the valley of the shadow of death, I ask you now, just one more favour. That you keep me strong and breathin' long enough to send these devils back to the mouth of the hell that they come crawlin' right out of… After that, my Lord, I am happy to come home and to take good care of my sister like I never did that last time.'

And on the last word of his prayer, he saw the long shadow of the first Nephite come crawlin' through the dawn for him. Like the long shanks of a scarecrow put up in a Missouri cornfield, and about as well put together as some bird-frighter too, it was coming down the wall of the ravine. Head first, body after. Hopping and jerking quick, like a bat he'd once seen moving across some dirt.

The soldier used the instincts that only a man accustomed to having been under plenty of gunfire can call upon, and he stayed put. Never twitched a muscle, even when the raggedy thing's shadow covered him up completely. They rarely made a sound, the Nephites, when stalking. Unless a man saw them coming, or got some sign from a shadow, it was all over for that man, and he had no choice but to convert right there and then as their dirty teeth baptised his flesh. But the soldier had learned from the Indian scouts in the army, as he had learned from the Indians who made those drawings in that cave on the Hill Cumorah; he had learned how to follow signs in the dirt and to move without leaving any himself; he'd learned too how to be still and to wait, as all the killers on the plains and in the desert wait. Before he struck.

He saw *it* as he turned and lengthened the arm holding Old Wristbreaker; saw it readying to leap like a starving man upon the carcase of a horse in a famine. And before the black eyes in the paper-dry face had a chance to blink and adjust to the sudden whirl of dust and sunlight on steel before it, the Nephite was looking up at the indigo sky. And three feet away from the workings of its jaw in the dirt, and the attempts to twist that terrible head on a scrawny neck severed, lay its long body, so thin and hard among the loose folds of clothes that it no longer filled so well.

The soldier looked up the wall of the ravine, and saw two more, hanging like black shadows upon the red rocks. They paused, then reached down their yellowy faces, snake-like, with threadbare heads pushed forward like geese with no feathers, as if to sniff at the sudden commotion they had just witnessed below and not yet fully understood.

Their hesitation gave the soldier time to raise his pistol and shoot the closest one clean off the rock. It came out of the air shrieking, but thumped so hard against a boulder next to him that he heard its back break like a tomato cane. He saw that it had once been a woman. The ball from his pistol had shot most of its black bonnet away, and half of the skull along with it. The washed-out eyes were rolled up. A small sigh, like a hiss escaping from a kitten, came out of the pale, lipless muzzle. It never moved again.

Up on one knee, carbine butt packed into the familiar embrace of his shoulder, just like a cavalry trooper down off his horse and ready to fire in battle, he sighted the other one. It turned and skittered like a long rat, back up the red rock wall. Strands of white hair had come loose from the bun on the back of its head, and streamed down the dusty cloth of its dress. He'd seen this one before, a long time ago, eating a snake in a valley in Wyoming. Maybe she'd been the wife of a miller back home, but he couldn't be certain.

It was hard work crawling upwards on that sandy rock

this second time, and the Nephite struggled. It made a pitiful keening sound in its throat too, like a goat, because it must have known that the tables had been turned on its sneaking approach down that dawn-lightened rock. The trooper shot out its back in a great puff of dust.

She hung on for a few seconds before dropping straight down, close to the face of the cliff, hitting a promontory and bouncing away, over his head, and further down towards the valley floor.

There was a terrible strangled cry of rage and anguish from across the ravine, and he heard the pounding of thin, hard feet over the rocks and through the dust. Another voice cried out, and it was Lehi's. 'Brother, be still!' the Prophet commanded, but the last of his congregation still standing was so driven by fury and grief, there was no delaying its desire for immediate retribution.

Calmly, the soldier reloaded the carbine, working quietly with steady hands. Then peeked over the ridge of his position and saw the female Nephite that he'd just shot from the cliff-face, crawling slowly back towards either the black carriage or the other side of the ravine where Lehi had been taunting him. One of its stick arms was twisted backwards and flopped across the ruin of its exposed spine. The legs were useless. Even if it made it back to the Prophet, Lehi would not let it live. The soldier had often found the bodies of those Lehi had saved him the trouble of despatching; whatever the insult caused to bring about apostasy the soldier could but guess, but mad Lehi often killed his own by bludgeoning their skulls with something blunt, probably his boot heel.

The soldier guessed the husband of the broken-backed female was the thing now racing across to him. He smiled when he saw that it carried the musket the Nephites had in the wagon. The soldier remembered the sudden sideways fall of his horse, shot out from under him, and he stopped smiling.

Leaning up and onto his toes, with one blue knee pressed into the rock, he sighted the carbine at the hopping fright that came at him through the rocks. Its long arms were thrown into the air and it carried the musket like a club. The sleeves of its black jacket and the hair shirt beneath it appeared too short for the length of its pale forearms. Its trousers were long gone too, as was its underwear. A pelvis papered with mottled skin topped two shanks thin as oars, and they strode those clawed, yellowish feet through the dust towards him.

At fifteen feet the soldier shot off the bereaved husband's face, along with the top of his head, leaving just the jaw hanging down beneath the spray of black juice, pinkish drops and dusty skull that pattered amongst the dry rocks like an unexpected rain.

As he reloaded the pistol and carbine, without once looking at his hands, the soldier peered over his cover and watched the other side of the ravine. He holstered the pistol, sheathed the sword and leaped over the rock; he followed the scratching that the female Nephite had made in the dust as she crawled.

The trooper stamped on the back of the wounded female's head to stop its mutterings, and felt the skull give way like a cabbage underfoot in a farmer's field. Then he cut the head free with two sawing swipes of Old Wristbreaker, before mounting the greyish ruin of the head upon the point of the sabre and holding it aloft.

'Lehi! See what comes to the Fair-skinned Nephites. Nary one of your flock will see another night. By the Lord and all that is righteous, you will be smote down. And you will see your flock cut like wheat afore you go. I promise you that, you son of a whore's cunt!'

There was no answer from across the ravine. No movement, save a trickle of pebbles and sand from somewhere up high. The Prophet had been making his retreat while the trooper despatched his congregation, who had unwittingly gathered here that morning for a cleansing by steel and iron ball. Lehi would be gone now, the soldier guessed, retreating on foot to his ramshackle Kingdom of God.

The two mares that pulled the black carriage were nothing more than bone heads covered in dusty hide, with rotten manes and ribs sticking through skin so thin and cluttered with moving blowflies that they looked like they'd been dead for months. Their eyes were sightless milky orbs, hung with bunches of white ticks. Their smell was of graves freshly interned in the eternal black fields of Hades. Their distended bellies were peppered with tooth marks, from where the faithful had bled them down to these sorry tired husks.

The soldier cut through each long neck with one stroke of Old Wristbreaker and they fell swiftly, with a clatter of old bones within their bridles. The black carriage would roll no more across God's earth.

There was little inside the bed of the wagon. Some metatarsals; three Bibles that had been chewed down to the bindings by dirty teeth; a child's bonnet, stamped into the dust; and two long thighbones from either a man or a steer, he couldn't be sure, but they had been whittled by a fastidious gnawing to thin flutes of scratched bone, bleached white.

The dragoon looked at the sky; indigo turned to blue cut with pink striations. In the west a great yolk of hot sun seemed to be peeking beneath the horizon like a fire at the hem of a tent's skirt. The Nephites would be inside when the sun burned this desert white. He'd rather fight them in the open and it would now be a race on foot between him and the Prophet to the promised land.

He went back to his horse, where she lay so quiet and solemn in the dust. She licked his hands and looked up at him with more love than he'd received from any living thing, save his sister, in this sorry unfeeling life he oft wished that he'd never been born into. He kissed her warm forehead and trickled water into her open mouth. Then he shot her still with the pistol.

The soldier wiped his eyes and slung the saddlebags over his shoulders. The bottles of kerosene bumped together inside their oilcloth wrappings. The rest of his ammunition was inside the bags too. He took two canteens and tied them to his belt; threw his dragoon's cape over the saddlebags. And started walking toward Zion.

They had kept slaves, captured along the trail through three states, and had used them to erect the hopeless wooden buildings of the Prophet Lehi's Zion, on the shores of the Great Dead Sea. Once their labours were complete, the Nephites had eaten the slaves alive, right where they had sat exhausted in their chains. Amongst the dozen sets of dirty bones, the soldier moved a few greyish heads with the toe of one boot. The slaves were not *the chosen* and had never been converted. He moved out of the black barn and onto Main Street.

Beside the barn, where they'd been keeping the black carriage and the three hell mares, they had another three wooden shacks barely upright and facing the shimmering white sand that stretched to the ravines that he'd passed through that morning. At the end of the row of wooden buildings were a dozen tents, their dirty canvas sides billowing from the wind that came off the long, salty water behind.

The settlement appeared empty. Desolate. Damned.

The soldier had made good time out here though, and was sure that he'd beaten that long-legged Prophet back. Nephites tired easy; were always hungry; their salvation as the chosen seemed to amount to nothing more than scratching in the dust to gobble down any living thing that had blood inside it. He'd once found one buried waist-deep inside a skinned bear carcase, and feeding hard.

He guessed the population of Zion would rest inside the broken-down buildings and loose tents until their Prophet returned with something warm and squealing in the back of that black carriage. The soldier smiled. Laid down his bags outside the building beside the barn. 'I will be avenged sevenfold. Yes sir.' He sprinkled the kerosene oil around the wooden foundations of the building, and peppered the liquid with gunpowder. Nary a sound from within, not even a whisper, and he'd burned three Nephite infestations out of farms they'd occupied in Wyoming the exact same way. Nephites did not like fire; must have reminded them of home, he often mused.

He lit a cigarette and dropped the match into the oil, which lit off in a trail of blackish smoke, the flames invisible in the sunlight. The timber they'd used for the buildings was so worm-eaten and dry, and mostly cobbled together from wagon beds, that it took fire quickly and with a furious relish.

Outside the front entrance that was covered with a dirty muslin sheet, the soldier laid down his carbine and drew Old Wristbreaker. And waited.

But not for long. Deep inside, back someways in the darkness that they had all been lying inside, he heard the rustlings of thin limbs. Then a bumping of bony feet and a chattering of dry teeth sounded, and all getting nearer to the entrance as they came through that house of rotten wood, not yet warmed by the bright sunlight, but roused by the thick smoke.

They came out into the light of dawn, blinking and coughing and whimpering: three raggedy females. The one in the round dress – once a tan check, but now filthy and hard with black blood down the front – came out first, its whited-out eyes blinking within the tatty bonnet. It paused momentarily to fight another behind it, a thing wearing a stained nightgown, which was trying to push around the wide skirts of the other female. They snarled at each other and there was a brief raking of long yellowy nails against leathery faces, until they became aware of the dragoon close by.

With two swift downward strokes, as if striking from the saddle, he caved in their skulls like he was breaking crockery pots with a hammer. The third one he skewered back against a wall, where it kicked out with sharp feet, and whipped a wispy skull back and forth, and showed him a black tongue, before he shot it full in the face with his pistol from two feet out.

At the next building, he worked faster with the kerosene on account of the gunshot. Smashed three bottles in the first room by throwing them against the far wall. Upstairs, on the next level, and just after he lit the place up, he saw a parched face grin down from a window without glass. Looked like the townsfolk were stirring. But the lower floor of the building went off blazing with them all still inside it, and nervous about coming out to face him; and he prayed to God that if his sister were inside, she would be taken by the smoke so that he would not have to see her in this morning's white light.

Through the dance and beat of the flames inside the building, he eventually saw insubstantial outlines of partly haired heads, bobbing in the smoke, before they rushed at the front door. Two females came out coughing and he slew them swift because their heads were practically bowed for the task set before him. Another, without a hair on its patchwork skull, came through on all fours in petticoats and a filthy shawl, and he took from its narrow shoulders its foul head.

Two children, not yet twelve, he reckoned, when they were bit, tottered out blind from the heat and heavy black smoke that they'd woken into. He took each one down from behind with quick cross-body-cuts, then stepped away to the carbine.

He looked back at the great white desert that shimmered into the far hills, and then looked again when he thought he saw the lope of a thin black figure coming hither. But once he'd shielded his eyes and squinted hard again, he saw nothing out there but the flat, hard salt that could hide not so much as a coyote upon it.

From the third building, a nervous evacuation was in progress, and he scanned the starved upright devils for weapons. A gangly male in braces and a top hat held what looked like a flintlock the French had left behind from when they fought the English. Using the carbine, the soldier shot three parts of its head away; in the smoke-blinded confusion another ragged figure trod on the top hat with a clawed foot.

Taking advantage of the two neighbouring fires, the thick black smoke that dropped onto the tented area, and the litter of wasted, head-smashed bodies about the ground, the soldier calmly reloaded, both pistol and carbine. And he came up from kneeling, firing steady at those that, sighting their nemesis, took it upon themselves to race at him. Two crones, dust as much as bone, came apart like sticks and straw in their bonnets and pinafores. And then Old Wristbreaker cut down the two teenage girls that tried to scatter before him like hens.

He lit up the third building from the inside, keeping his sabre ready and up high. It was dark in there and under his feet the chewed bones and hollowish skulls of the unfortunates that had been fed upon snapped and rolled away as he stamped into the godforsaken dark and dust.

He came out coughing and looked towards the tents. A weary line of dark silhouettes, he counted no more than five, tottered in the bright sun. Two of them wept, which made the other three females take up a wailing like they knew the time of the Great Awakening was all but done. One of them struck her naked head with long hands and pulled from her skull the last straws of colourless hair.

At his back the three temples of Zion, a New Jerusalem to the congregation of Lehi's Fair-skinned Nephites, burned red and black and high into the deep-blue sky.

The soldier walked toward the tents and reloaded as he went. There was little fight left in those that remained, and though they snarled like guard dogs they seemed reluctant to move far from whatever was under the canvass.

One finally came out to him, low on all fours, its bone legs kicking up the dust, and the soldier shot most of its neck and cheek away on the right side. It set up a howling that only ceased when he crunched a boot heel down upon its forehead. Of the remaining four, he shot down one, right where it stood, hollerin' at him, hitting it full in the bark-crinkled face from ten yards. The other three scattered into the tents.

The soldier turned about, Old Wristbreaker out before him. Something with little cold feet had run up the back of his neck and given him a tingle that he knew he could trust. Something low to the soil, wearing a tall-crowned hat, had scampered behind the barn like a stray dog. Prophet Lehi must have circled Zion and come in due west across the desert; a slower and more indirect route, but better for evading the eyes of the dragoon.

The soldier knelt down and reloaded the carbine, the pistol. Holstered the pistol, stood up and trotted to the barn in search of the Prophet.

'Lehi! You cocksucker –'

Out of the smoke and fire in the building beside the barn came a sharp orange crack of light and something like a fist punched the trooper from his feet. He felt three ribs snap like wheel spokes, lost all the air from his lungs and knew that he was hit, and hit wet-through his right side. When he tried to drag in a breath, the pain was so bad that it would not even let him scream.

He scrabbled about in the dust to get at the carbine that he had thrown away as he fell.

From behind the burning buildings, the Prophet let out a cry of triumph and fury, and called his decimated congregation to perform a service long overdue. 'And he will atone, my brothers, my sisters. And he will atone with his blood that we shall let on this holy shore!'

Up popped a trio of dreadful raggedy heads from among the tents. They weaved from side to side as they tried to sight the wounded soldier with their dim eyes, and then they dropped and scurried to where the soldier lay blind and sick-white with pain.

He snapped his head up twice, when the black swoops came into his burning eyes and tried to put him down and to sleep. He checked the sopping hand that clutched his right side. The bullet had ripped away the skin and muscle below his nipple and smashed some bones. He prayed the ball had not fragmented down and into his belly because he could feel a hundred little brands burning inside a stomach that he might never eat with again.

The Nephites came at him quickly too, seeing as he was down and winged bad. They hopped madly at him from out of the tents. They could also scent his hot blood in the dust and all over his white skin, and that made them prance and skip and yowl like hungry cats, and cry stark like starving black crows.

On his other side he heard the preacher's boots in the dirt.

The dragoon clenched his teeth, drew his pistol and looked back at the blaze beside the barn, but Lehi was using the smoke as cover while reloading. The trooper turned and shot out the face of something on all fours that was the first to the feast. The other two broke around him, and shrieked at the sound of his gun.

He got up to his knees and then his feet. Unsheathed Old Wristbreaker with his left hand. The ground swooped and swooned around him.

Something landed on his back and bit deep through his hat, and he felt his scalp come up and off his bones in a whole mess of dirty chewing teeth. He threw the Nephite over his shoulders and stamped on its head to smash it still in the dirt. The second one leaped up at him, long fingers going for his eyes, but he ran Old Wristbreaker through its grubby bodice and held it away from his body, and watched it writhe like a serpent. Put it down and stamped it still and off his sabre with one quick boot, like he was trampling dry kindling flat.

Lehi showed himself then. All teeth under a black hat and one long arm out front with a long pistol waving in his white hand. An old cavalry pistol and not accurate; as likely to blow a man's hand off as to hit a target at no more than twenty yards. The Prophet had been lucky with that first shot from out by the barn. He aimed to make certain with the second and came in close to do it.

'Looks like I need to start up a new congregation here, Ephraim.' A few wisps of hair moved gently as Lehi came up closer on him. One knee that was mostly bone stuck through the preacher's trouser leg.

The soldier tottered, sweat-soaked and bleeding. He held his sabre up, but doubted he had the strength to use it again, or even the strength to curse himself for getting so far but failing to behead this false prophet, this corrupt messiah, before his last breath. But deep down, beneath the burning pain and flooding away of his life, the soldier still found an ember of hatred so hot for this devil, that he managed to spit at it.

The devil grinned from under the brim of its black hat. Its voice was soft and gentle and near feminine. 'Soldier, I might jus' start a new followin' with you. You'd make a fine fightin' apostle. Whaddya say, trooper? I bit your sister good on our weddin' night, in your uncle's bed. She tasted sweet. Bet her brother done taste like milk and honey. She bore me two, soldier. And your nephews lie out yonder, waitin' for the sweet red milk o' life.'

The soldier shook his head, his eyes blurred by tears, his heart burned to a husk by the unceasing horrors that confronted his weary eyes and scorched his ears.

The Prophet aimed the long, heavy barrel of the pistol between the dragoon's eyes. 'Or maybe I should jus' cut you down here and swallow you like the fish and loaves that our saviour put out for the five thousand. Yes, I do believe I may rightly –'

The Prophet was jerked off his feet.

Twisted in the air.

Hit the sand with a great dusty thump.

And then the soldier heard the musket break the desert air further out.

Down in the sand, the Prophet wrenched himself about like a man having a fit; his gun arm was twisted out and away from his body.

His eyes mostly closed, the soldier turned about, his sword dragging through the dirt. And he saw the small, old prospector with the filthy beard coming across the white sand slowly, his musket longer even than he was.

The soldier turned back to the Prophet Lehi, who had turned round and got to its thin knees. Was trying to take the pistol from its right hand with the left. The musket ball had hit its chest and smitten through the back of its jacket and cape, which smoked whitish around a dry hole.

Using both hands, holding the weight of the sword with his left and guiding with his right, the soldier raised Old Wristbreaker, but it made him cry out and then drop the sabre's point. The pain in his side was too great for vengeance to have its way and he cried out in his despair, and his wretchedness, and for the blood that fell from him and for the sister that was took from him. He bent double and held himself up on his feet with the sword as a crutch. Then rose with the last of himself and let that sword fall hard into the Prophet's scrawny neck.

It knocked Lehi flat down in the dirt, but did not sever his head.

The old man came up to him. 'Easy. Easy. Easy,' he said. Then looked at the preacher and spat a long stream of tobacco and saliva across the back of that white skull. Trod a foot in a dirty moccasin onto the Prophet's gun hand. 'Shee-it. I'll be. Man ain't alive nor dead. How can that be? Sweet Jesus.'

'My pistol. Load it,' the soldier said.

'Yessir.' The old prospector took the pistol and loaded it with powder and ball and handed it to the dragoon.

'Lehi. My sister. Where is she?'

The Prophet spat and gasped, his mouth wet with black

blood. And his face twisted and every tendon stretched inside that long neck and sharp jaw, and the jabbering that came out of that mouth and into the air in the thin, high voice of a child was words that no old prospector and soldier would ever make sense of. So the soldier terminated the interview. He was close to fainting and needed to know, before he left the world, that the Prophet was truly dead. So he put the dragoon pistol against the back of that pale, cold skull and shot it all apart like a pumpkin off a fencepost.

'Them tents yonder, old man,' the soldier said.

The old man got his self under the dragoon's left arm and walked him across to the tents. And once there the old man dragged the sagging dragoon from one yellowy interior of flapping canvas to another.

'What God hath wrought this, soldier? What God?' the old man asked him in the final tent. But by then the soldier who had fallen into him had already closed his tired eyes and left the foul tent and the foul world, and gone far from what lay grey and dry and mewling in the filthy bedding in the dirt beneath their feet. The dragoon had gone to another place to look for his sister whom he never did find among the Fair-skinned Nephites on the shore of the Great Dead Sea. The dragoon's last words were: 'Use my sabre.'

The old man took the young soldier outside the stench of death, which was soon to be heated by the white desert sun, and laid him at peace upon the dust. He closed the dragoon's eyes and said three lines from the only prayer he could remember. Or was it a hymn? He didn't know, but he did what he could for the man. And then he sawed the dragoon's head clean off with his own sword, which was so heavy and long that the prospector marvelled at the arm that had wielded it like a switch about the godless.

The prospector walked back to the twelve tents, and went in to finish the cavalryman's dreadful work.

In the last tent, as he carved off the tiny shrivelled heads of what was already dead or mostly dead – at those that had rustled from out of the dead wombs of Nephite mothers – the sabre's keen edge scraped at stone. Again and again, as if these birthing tents had been laid upon a stone floor in all of this sand.

Curious, the prospector kicked aside the tatty bundles of the headless young, and then scraped his foot through the dust. What lay beneath the sand in the tent was smooth, undulating, like a water-smoothed boulder in a clear mountain stream.

Accustomed to digging in the dust for wonders to behold, the old man dropped the sword and wrapped some foul swaddling raiment about his left moccasin and began to sweep his leg back and forth across the hard rock.

After a few minutes, he uncovered a great eye, curved like an almond, and shielded by a heavy lid. Ten minutes later, he had swept the desert sand and grit away from what was an entire face.

By the end of the day, the Nephite remains of young and old were all burned to ash within the burning buildings of Zion, on the shore of the Great Dead Sea, and their tents were all cut down from the ground and dragged away from the campsite and left like a pile of dirty rags; also soon to be ignited, for the prospector felt that was what the solider would have wanted. And as the sun set across the glittering ocean of lifeless water, and the buildings were nothing more than blackened smoking bones upon its damned shore, the old man stared down at what he had uncovered beneath seven of the tents; at what had been hidden under the weightless husks of dead babes in the plague hospital, and under the sand.

He looked at the six colossal basalt heads, each measuring eight to nine feet in height and weighing, he reckoned, about forty tons. Stared searching into their great open eyes that, in turn, watched the sky darken and fill with bright stars. And when he eventually walked away, carrying his musket and the dragoon's pistol, carbine and sabre, not wanting to linger at these ruins in the darkness, he wondered if they were the faces of Gods. The Gods that had wrought all of this.

Doll Hands

I am the one with the big white head and the doll hands. I work behind the desk in the west block of Gruut Huis. When I'm not taking delivered medicines upstairs to the residents who slowly die in their beds, I watch the greenish screens of the security monitors. Security cameras cover every inch of Gruut Huis's red-brick walls and empty tarmac forecourt.

I watch out for deliveries and for intruders. Deliveries come every day. Intruders not so much any more. They have mostly died out there in the draughty buildings of the dead city, or are lying still on the dark stones before the Church of Our Lady. In Bruges, the dying shuffle and crawl to the church. It's like they have lost everything but a memory of where to go.

Last Christmas I was sent out with two porters to find the baboon child of Mr Hussain who lives in the east wing. The baboon boy had escaped from his cage and blinded his carer. And as I searched for the boy in Guido Gezelleplein, I saw all of the wet stiff bodies beneath the tower, lying down in the mist.

One of the day porters, Vinegar Irish, beat the baboon boy when we found him feeding among the bodies. Like the residents, the baboon boy had grown tired of the yeast from the tanks in the basement. He wanted meat.

At ten in the morning, there is movement on the monitor

screens. Someone has arrived at the Goods and Services entrance of Gruut Huis. Out of the mist the squarish front of a white truck appears and waits by the roller gate. It is the caterers. Inside my stomach I feel a sickish skitter.

With my teeny fingers I press the buttons on the security console and open Door Eight. On the screen I watch the metal grille rise. The truck passes into the central court of Gruut Huis and parks with its rear doors before the utility door of the service area. Behind this utility door are the storage cages for the residents' old possessions, as well as the porters' dormitory, the staff room, the stock cupboards, the boiler room, the workshop, the staff washroom and the yeast tanks that feed us with their yellow softness. Today, the caterers will need to use the staff washroom for their work.

Yesterday, we were told a delivery of food was arriving for the Head Residents' Annual Banquet. Mrs Van den Broeck, the Head Resident of the building, also informed us that our showers were to be cancelled and that we were not allowed into the staff room during the day because the caterers needed to use these areas to prepare the banquet. But none of the staff ever want to go into the washroom if the caterers are onsite. Despite the sleepiness of the white ape, who is nightwatchman, and the drunkenness of Vinegar Irish, and the slow movements of Les Spider, handyman, and the merry giggles of the two cleaning girls, we can all remember the other times when the little white truck came to Gruut Huis for the banquets. None of the staff talk about the days of the General Meetings and Annual Banquets. We all pretend that they are normal days, but Vinegar Irish drinks more cleaning fluid than usual.

Using the desk phone, I call Vinegar Irish, who is the porter on duty in the east wing. He takes a long time to answer the phone. On the security console, I switch to the camera above his reception desk to see what he is doing. Slowly, like his pants are full of shit and he can't walk straight, he stumbles into the green underwater world of the monitor screen. Even on camera I can see the bulgy veins under his strawberry face. He's been in the key cupboard drinking fluids and not beside his monitors like he is supposed to be at all times. If he was behind his desk he would have heard the alarm sound when I opened the outer gate, and he would have known that a delivery had arrived. His barking voice is slurred. 'What you want?'

'Delivery,' I say. 'Watch my side. I'm going down.'

'Aye. Aye. Trucks come. What you need to do –' I put the phone down while he is speaking. It will make him go shaky with rage in the east wing. He'll call me a bastard and swear to punch his trembly hands at my big head, while spit flies out of his vinegar mouth. But he won't remember the altercation tonight when we finish the day shift, and I have no time right now for a slurred lecture about all the things that I already know about our duties, that he cannot manage to do.

As I walk across the lobby to the porters' door, with my sackcloth mask in my doll hands, the phone rings behind my desk. I know it is Vinegar Irish in a spitting rage. All the residents are still asleep. Those that can still walk never come down before noon.

Smiling to myself at this little way I get revenge on Vinegar Irish, I stretch the brownish mask over my head. Then I open the airlock and duck through the escape hatch to the metal staircase outside. As I trot down the stairs, the mist rushes in to cover my little shiny shoes. Even with the mask pulled over my fat octopus head, I can smell the sulphur-rust of the chemical air.

At the bottom of the staircase, I enter the courtyard. The courtyard is right in the middle of all four blocks of flats. The residents can look down and into the courtyard from their kitchen windows. I bet their mouths fill with water when they see the white van parked by the utility door. What the head residents don't eat, we porters deliver to their flats in white plastic bags.

Seeing the caterers' white truck makes my stomach turn over with a wallop. The two caterers who came in it are standing by the driver's door, talking, and waiting for me to open the utility area. Both of them are wearing rubber hoods shaped into pig faces. The pig faces are supposed to be smiling, but they look like the faces in dreams that wake you up with a scream.

The caterers are wearing rubber boots to their knees too, with stripy trousers tucked into the tops of them. Over their stripy trousers and white smocks they wear long, black rubber aprons. They are both putting on gloves made from wire mesh.

'Christ. Would you look at the cunt's head,' the older caterer says. His son giggles inside his rubber pig mask.

I clench my tiny hands into marble hammers.

'Awright?' the father says to me. Under the mask I know he is laughing at my big white head and stick body. The father gives me a clipboard. There is a plastic pen under the metal clasp that holds the pink delivery note to the clipboard. With my doll hands I take the pen and sign and print my name, then date the slip: 10/04/2152. They watch my hands in silence. The world goes quiet when my hands go to work because no one can believe that they have any use.

On the *Grote and Sons Fine Foods and Gourmet Catering* sales slip, I see I am signing for *2 livestock. Extra lean, premium fresh. 120 kilos.*

The caterers go into the cabin of their truck and drag their equipment out. 'Let's get set up. Give us a hand,' the father says to me. Up close, his clothes smell of old blood.

From behind the two seats in the dirty cabin that smells of metal and floor bleach, they pass two big grey sacks to me. They are heavy with dark stains at the bottom and around the top are little brass holes for chains to pass through. Touching the sacks makes my legs shake. I tuck them under my arm. They give me a metal box to carry in my other hand. The container has little red numbers beside the lock. The box is cold and is patterned with black and yellow stripes.

'Careful with that,' the fat father says as I take the cold box in my small hand. 'It's for the hearts and livers. We sell them, see. They is worth more than you are.'

The son hangs heavy chains over one arm and grabs a black cloth bag. As he walks, the black cloth sack makes a hollow knocking sound as the wooden clubs inside bang together. The father carries two steel cases in one hand, and two plastic buckets in the other that are reddish-grubby inside. 'Same place as before?' he asks me.

'Follow me,' I say, and walk to the utility door of the basement. We go inside and between the iron storage cages and are watched by the rocking horse with the big blue eyes and lady lashes. We pass the white door with the Staff Only sign on it, and the floor changes from cement to tiles. I take them through the white tiled corridor to the washroom where they will work. In here it always smells of the bleach used by the whispering cleaners. The cleaners sleep in the cupboard with all the bottles, mops and cloths and are not allowed to use the staff room. When the nightwatchman, the white ape, catches them in there smiling at the television, he roars.

I take the caterers into the big washroom that is tiled to the ceiling and divided in two by a metal rail and shower curtain. There is a sink and toilet on one side and the other half has a floor that slopes to the plug grate under the big round shower head. Against the wall in the shower section is a wooden bench, bolted to the wall. The father drops his cases and mask onto the bench. His head is round and pink as the flavoured yeast that the residents eat from square ration tins.

The son coils his chains on the bench and removes his hood too. He has a weasel face with many pimples among the scruffy whiskers on his chin. His tiny black eyes flit about and his thin lips curl away from long gums and two sharp teeth like he is about to laugh.

'Luvverly,' the father says, looking around the washroom. I notice the father has no neck.

'Perfek,' the weasel son adds, grinning and sniffing.

'Your night boy asleep?' the father asks. His fat body sweats under his smock and apron. His sweat smells of beef powder. Small and yellow and sharp, his two snaggle teeth are the same as the son's. When he squints, his tiny red eyes sink into his face.

I nod.

'Not for long,' the weasel says, and then shuffles about, giggling.

I move towards the door.

'Hang on. Hang on,' the father says. 'We need you to open that friggin' door when we bring the meat in.'

'Yeah,' Weasel agrees, while he threads the chains through the brass eyes in the top of the sacks.

The father opens his cases on the bench. Stainless steel gleams under the yellow lights. His tools are carefully fitted into little trays. In his world of dirty trucks, old sacks, rusty chains and snaggle teeth, it surprises me to see his fat fingers become gentle on the steel of his tools.

With eyes full of glee, the weasel son watches his father remove the two biggest knives from a metal case. Weasel then unties the ribbon of the last sack with the hollow wooden sounds inside, and pulls out two thick clubs. He stands with a club in each hand, staring at me. He is pleased to see the horror on my little face. At the bottom of the clubs the wood is stained a dark colour and some bits have chipped off.

'Go fetch 'em in,' the father says, while he lays two cleavers with black handles on an oily cloth.

'Right,' the weasel son says.

We go back down the tiled corridor. I walk slowly because I am in no hurry to see the livestock. When Mrs Van den Broeck, the Head Resident, announced the banquet, I decided that I would show the livestock a friendly face before it was taken into the washroom; otherwise, the fat father and the weasel son would be the last people that it would see in this world, before it was stuffed inside the sacks and chained up.

When we reach the courtyard, I remember what the fat father told me last time, about how the meat tastes better with bruises under the skin. That's why they use the clubs. To tenderise the meat and get blood into the flesh. When he told me that, I wanted to escape from Gruut Huis and keep running into the poisonous mist until no one in the building would ever find me again. The residents don't need to eat the fresh meats. Like the staff, they can eat the soft yellow yeast from the tanks, but the residents are rich and can afford variety.

We go back into the courtyard. Above us, some lights have come on in the flats. I can see the dark lumps of the residents' heads watching from their kitchen windows. And suddenly, from the east wing, the baboon child of Mr Hussain screams. It rips the smoky air apart. Weasel Boy flinches. You never get used to the sound of the baboon child in the cage.

The weasel son rattles keys in his chain-mail hand. 'We done a wedding last week. St Jan in de Meers.'

I can't speak with all the churning in my tummy.

'We done eight livestock for the barbecue. Da girl's farver was loaded. Had a tent built and everything. Ya know, a marquee. All in this garden, under a glass roof. Me and Dad was up at five. They had fifty guests, like. We filled four ice-chests with fillets. Done the sausages the day before. For the kids, like.'

He finds the correct key and unlocks the back doors of the truck. Under his pig mask I know he is smiling. 'We made a few shillings. There's a few shillings to be made at weddings in this part of town.'

When Weasel opens the back doors, I feel the hot air puff out of the truck. With it comes the smell of pee and sweat to mix with the chemical stink of the swirly air. Two small shapes are huddled at the far end of the truck, near the engine where it is warmer.

I walk away from the open doors of the truck and look up at the vapours. They drift and show little pieces of grey sky. There is a smudgy yellow stain where the sun must be. But you can never tell with the cloud so low. I wish I was in heaven.

'C'mon, ya shit-brains,' Weasel shouts from inside the truck. He's climbed in to get the livestock out. They never want to come out.

I cringe as if he is about to pull a lion out of the back. Through the white sides of the truck comes a bumping of bare feet on metal and then the *chinka, chinka, chinka* of a chain.

Weasel Boy jumps out of the truck, holding a rope in both hands. 'They as dumb as shit, but it's like they know when this day is coming. Get outta there. Git! Git!'

Out of the back of the truck two pale, yellowish figures stumble and then drop onto the misty slabs of the courtyard. They fall down and are yanked back to their feet by the weasel.

The livestock is skinny and completely shaven. Their elbows are tied together and their hands are tucked under their chins. They are young males with big eyes. They look like each other. Like angels with pretty faces and slender bodies. They start to cough in the acid-stinging air.

Shivering against each other, the smaller one starts to cry and hides behind the taller one, who is too frightened to cry, but pees instead, down the inside of his thighs. It steams in the cold air.

'Dirty bastards. They'll piss anywhere. Truck's full of it. Yous'll have to wash that corridor down after we're gone.' Weasel Boy pulls the rope taut. Each male wears a thick iron collar that looks loose on his sallow neck. A rope is attached to the short chains welded to the collars. In his metal hands Weasel Boy holds the slack rope.

As Weasel Boy pulls them across the courtyard, the livestock jogs and jostles together for warmth in the cold air. I run ahead to open the utility door, but can't feel my legs properly, even when my knees bang together.

Inside the corridor I take off my mask and walk behind

the livestock. Weasel Boy leads the way to the washroom. The livestock peers about at the storage cages. The small one stops crying, distracted by the paintings and furniture and boxes inside the cages. The taller one looks over his shoulder at me. He smiles. His eyes are full of water. I try to smile back at him, but my jaw is numb. So I just stare at him. His face is scared, but trusting and wanting a friend who smiles on this day when he is frightened. I think what I think each time the caterers come to Gruut Huis: that there must be some kind of mistake. Livestock is supposed to be dumb. It has no feelings, we're told. But in these eyes I can see a frightened boy.

'No,' I say, before I even know I am speaking.

Weasel Boy turns around and stares at me. 'You what?'

'This can't be right.'

Weasel Boy laughs under his pig mask. 'Don't you believe it. They got human faces, but they is shit-brains. Pretty as pitchers, but dead in the head. They ain't like us.'

There is so much that I want to say, but all the words vanish off my tongue and my head is filled with wind. A big lump chokes my sparrow throat shut.

'Git! Git!' Weasel snarls at the livestock, which cringes at the sound of his voice. On the back of each livestock-boy I see the scars. Long pinkish scars with little holes around the slits, where the stitches once were, after things had been taken out of their thin bodies for the sick. 'Best meat in town,' Weasel says to me, grinning. 'They cook up lovely, like. Thousand euro a kilo they cost. More than fruit in them tins, like. Think of that. *More than fruit in tins.*'

Weasel Boy is pleased that he has made me feel dizzy and sick. And, like most people in this building, he likes to tell me things that I don't want to hear. 'These two, we been feeding for months. Shut it!' He straps the smaller one, who has started to cry again, on the backside with the end of the rope. The little one suddenly stops crying when the rope makes a wet sound on his yellow buttock. The mark goes white, then back to yellow again. The force of the blow makes him trip over the feet of the taller boy too, who is still looking at me with watery eyes, wanting a smile from me. They have long toenails.

'Where…'

Weasel Boy stops dragging the livestock and looks at me. 'Aye?'

I clear my throat. 'Where they from?'

'Nuns.'

'What?'

'Nuns. Them old nuns up in Brussels who all died of the milk-leg. So all their shit-brains went to auction. These two were like strips of piss when me and me dad looked at them. No meat on them. All they got fed from them nuns was yeast and water. No good for the meat, see. So we been feeding them for months. Who's they for, like?'

'One is for the head residents.' My voice is a whisper.

'Aye?'

'The head residents of the building. For the annual banquet. The other one is for the residents in the top-floor penthouses.'

'They gonna love them.' Weasel Boy rips his mask off and points his septic muzzle at the livestock in a grimace to frighten them. They both try and hide behind each other, but get tangled.

The weasel's bristle hair is wet with sweat. I wondered if the salt stings his pimples. They go down his neck and onto his back.

'Are… are… are you sure it's OK?' I know the answers to all of my stupid questions, asked in my stupid voice, but I have to keep speaking to hold my panic back. The livestock starts to giggle.

'Like I said, don't be fooled. They's useless. Was nothing but pets to them nuns. Only me and me dad make them worth anything. They is worth more than the organs in you and me put together.' He tugs the rope hard so that the livestock makes chokey noises and their naked bodies slap against his rubber apron. Their eyes are watering. The little one looks up into the Weasel Boy's rat eyes and tries to hug him.

But the livestock goes quiet when the washroom door is opened. Weasel Boy shoves them inside. Through the gap in the door, I can see his fat dad holding a sack open. 'Get in here,' he growls at the big one. The livestock starts to cry.

'I have to get back to my desk,' I manage to say, even though I can no longer feel my jaw.

'Fair enough,' Weasel says, with a smirk. 'We need you to open the doors when we finished the first one. Me mam is coming at three. She's the cook. Me dad'll bring her later. We'll *do* the second one in the morning.'

He closes the door. Behind me the livestock is crying in the washroom. The fat dad is shouting and the weasel son is laughing. I can hear them through the white tiled walls. I put my fingers inside my ears as I run away.

Follow me through the dark house. Watch me kill the old lady. It won't take long.

My little brass clock says it's three in the morning, so I'll go and put a pillow over Mrs Van den Broeck's bird mouth until she stops breathing. It'll be all right as long as I pretend that it's just an ordinary thing that I'm doing. I know because I've done this before.

Above my bunk, Vinegar Irish is asleep and snoring in his bed. He won't see me leave the dormitory room. After drinking so much this evening – the cleaning liquid with the wet-paint smell that I stole from the stores for him – he climbed into his bunk on his hands and knees with eyes looking at nothing in particular. Most mornings it takes me over twenty minutes to wake him for our work upstairs behind the reception desks. He drinks all day, can remember nothing, and needs his sleep. His face is purple with veins and his lumpy nose smells of bad yeast.

I go out of the dormitory with the bunk beds and I follow the cement path through the big storeroom. There are no lights on in the store because we are forbidden to come here at night, but I know my way around in the dark. Sometimes at night I go into the cages with a torch and the master keys to poke around boxes, trunks and the cases that are full of things that used to matter in the world. But nothing that you can eat or sell for food is kept in storage, so these old things have no value now. Sometimes, as I walk through the store, I feel that I'm being watched from inside the cages.

Slowly, I unlock the air-tight door that opens into the courtyard. Already, since I have worked here, five residents have jumped from the sixth floor and smashed themselves onto the tarmac below. They had the lunger disease and were choking on red brine. At night I used to hear their voices in the cold courtyard, drifting out of windows and spanking off all of the brick walls as they drowned in bed. *Whuff, whuff, whuff* they went.

I go out from the store and step into the mist. The door shuts behind me with a wheeze. Cold out here and the rain sizzles through the fog to sting the thin skin over my skull. Then the air gets inside my nose and mouth too and it feels like I am sucking a battery. No one is permitted to go outdoors without a mask because of the poison in the air, but the porters' masks are only sacks with plastic cups sewn over the mouth-part. My face stings just as much with a mask on and I sweat too much inside the linen, so when no one is watching I go out without a mask over my big white head. I'm not too worried about dying. At the boys' home that I came from, the nurses told me, 'People in your condition never see their teens.' I'm eighteen so I should be dead soon. Inside my see-through chest, one of those little blackish pumps or lumps will just stop working and that'll be the end for me. Maybe I'll go greyish first like most of the residents dying upstairs inside the flats.

Crouching down, my shoulder in the nightgown slides against the red-brick walls. A special coating to stop the air dissolving the whole place has made the bricks smooth. Taking shallow stinging breaths, I look up. Most of the apartments are dark, but a few yellowy kitchens shine like little boxes, high up in the vapours that fill the world outside our airlocks and sealed doors.

I go up the giant black metal fire escape to the airlock that will get me into the west wing reception. If there was a fire here, and the thought of it makes me grin, where could the residents be evacuated to? They would stand in the courtyard and watch the building blaze around them until the air in their masks ran out. This is the last place they can retreat to in the city. There's nowhere left to hide from the mist in the world. At night, when I stand on the roof by the big satellite dishes, I see fewer lights out there in the city. Like the people, the lights are all being turned off one by one.

Outside the little back door of the west wing, I wait for the dizzies in my head to stop. I'm so scared now that my dolly hands and puppet legs have gone all shaky. Closing my eyes, I tell myself that this job is going to be easy; it's just an ordinary thing that I'm about to do.

I think of the two little boys that came here inside the white truck too. I will always see their frightened faces as they were pulled by the caterers' ropes. Mrs Van den Broeck wanted them. She brought them here. So now I am going to her.

Feeling stronger after the attack of the dizzies has passed, I tap the code into the steel number pad on the wall beside the little back door: 1, 2, 3, 4. An easy sequence to remember so that Vinegar Irish can always get inside. The door unlocks with a click and hiss. I push it open.

Yellow corridor light, the smell of cleaned carpets and polished wood comes out through the door to die in the mist. Ducking my head, I climb through quickly. If any of the doors of the building are open for longer than five seconds a buzzer will go off behind the reception desk and will wake the night porter.

Blinking my black-button eyes, I get rid of the outside mist with my tears. The corridor becomes clear. It's empty. Only thing I can hear is the sound of the ceiling lights as they buzz inside their glass shades. My thin feet go warm on the red carpet. This corridor will take me down to reception.

Creeping and sneaking, I go grinning down the passage and stop at the end where it opens into the reception. Listening hard with my eyes closed, I try to hear the squeak of the porter's chair. But there is only silence down there behind the reception desk. Good.

I drop to my hands and knees, put the top half of my head around the corner, peek and smile. Leaning back in his chair, with his red face pointed at the ceiling, the white ape sleeps tonight. Big purple tongue and one brown tooth, hot with shit-breath, swallowing the clean air. He is supposed to be watching the monitor screens on his desk, but he has even taken his glasses and shoes off to sleep. On top of the desk he has placed his feet; his black socks are full of white hair and yellow claws.

I go into reception on my dolly hands and bony knees and I crawl to the staircase that will take me up to *her*. Even if the white ape's eyes open now, he won't see me because of the desk's high front. He would have to stand up and put his glasses on to catch sight of my thin bones in the nightgown, and my swollen skull, going up the stairs like a spider.

I climb the stairs to the second floor and stand outside the door marked number five. And her smell is strong up here, perfume and medicine. When I think of Mrs Van den Broeck's grey bird head on a fat silk pillow, sleeping somewhere on the other side of this wooden door, my slit-mouth trembles.

All day long I run up and down these stairs on errands for the residents, who cannot be argued with at any time. But now I am up here, in a flappy nightshirt with a stolen key in my teeny hand, because I mean to drown one of them in pillow softness. A big part of me wants to run back down the stairs, through the building and across the courtyard to my little warm bunk in the dormitory where Vinegar Irish snores and wheezes above me.

Resting on my ankles, I put my head between my knees and screw my eyes shut. All of this – the building of old brick, the shiny wooden doors, the marble skirting boards, the wall mirrors and brass lights, the rich people and Mrs Van den Broeck with her white gloves and pecking face – are so much bigger than me. I am a grain of seed that cannot escape her yellow teeth. In my left doll hand I squeeze the key until it hurts.

Today, two pale boys with pee on their hairless legs stepped about on cold toes in the back of the caterers' truck. They held each other with small hands, crying and smiling and making throaty sounds to each other. They were marched by the caterers to the washroom with the white tiles and the big plug in the middle. And then the smaller one had to watch his brother put inside a sack…

Inside my slit-mouth my squarish milk teeth grind together. Inside my fists my long nails make red half-moons on my palms. She brought them here. Mrs Van den Broeck called for the white truck that had the bumping sounds of boys inside. My stomach makes squirly sounds as the rage makes me shake and go the pink colour of the blind things that no chemicals can kill, who flit deep in the hot oceans, so far down that they cannot be caught and eaten.

With a snarl, I stand up. Into the brass lock of her front door goes the key. The *thunk* of the lock opening feels good within the china bones of my dollish hand. My fingers look so small against the brown wood. I push the heavy door. A sigh of air escapes. The whisper of her apartment's air runs over my face: medicine, dusty silk, old-lady sour smell.

Inside it is dark. The door closes behind me with a tired sound.

As I wait for my eyes to get used to the place, the outlines of vases, dry flowers, picture frames, a hat-stand and mirror appear out of the gloom. Then I notice a faint bluish light spilling from the kitchen. It comes from the electric panel with the warning lights about leaks and gases and fires; all of the flats have them. In the kitchen is where I usually take yeast tins and put them on the blue table for the maid Gemima to unpack. Gemima is the tiny woman who wears rubber sandals and never speaks. But after tonight, Gemima will also be free of Mrs Van den Broeck, and there will be no more journeys up here for me, with the wet meats inside the plastic bags. No more feeling like my body is made of glass that will shatter when she shouts. No more poking from her bird claws. No more squinting from her tiny pink eyes when she teeters out of the elevator in the afternoon, and sees my big head behind the reception desk.

I look down the hallway and see her bedroom door at the end. I pass the living room where she sits in the long silk gown and scolds us porters down the house phone. Then I tiptoe past the bathroom where Gemima scrubs Mrs Van den Broeck's spiny back and rinses her shrunken chest.

I stand outside the two bedrooms. Gemima sleeps in the left one. Now she will be resting for a few hours until her mistress's sharp voice begins another day for her. But part of Gemima never sleeps. The part of Gemima that must listen for the sound of Mrs Van den Broeck's bird feet on the marble tiles, and the scratch of her voice in her room, calling out for attention from amidst the crystals and china cups and photos of smiling men with big teeth and thick hair. This part of Gemima I must be careful of.

Mrs Van den Broeck sleeps behind the right door in a big bed. I enter the master bedroom. In here there is no light; the curtains are thick and fall to the floor. There is complete darkness… and a voice that crackles inside my ears. 'Who's there?'

I stop moving and feel like I am underwater and trying to gulp a breath that will never come. I want to run from here. Then I am about to say my own name automatically, like I do on the house phone, when the residents call down from upstairs. *Hello, Bobby speaking. How may I help?* I stop myself before my lips form the shape of the first word.

'Is that you, Gemima?'

Has my heart stopped beating inside its cage of thin bone and see-through skin?

'What's the time?' Mrs Van den Broeck says. 'Where are my glasses?'

I listen out for Gemima and I imagine her rising without thought, or choice, from her cot next door. The other room stays silent, but it won't for long if Van den Broeck keeps talking. Somewhere in front of me I also hear a rustling. Out there in the dark, I know a birdie claw is reaching for the switch of a table lamp. It the light comes on there might be a scream.

I cannot move.

'Who is there?' she says, her voice deeper. I can imagine the squinty eyes and pointy mouth with no lips. Again, I hear her long claws rake across the wooden surface of the side-table by the bed. The light cannot come on or I am finished. I race to the sound of her voice.

Something hard and cold hits my shinbones and blue streaks of pain enter my head. It is the end of her metal bed-frame that I have run into, so I am not in the part of the room that I thought I was.

Greenish light explodes through the glass shade of the table lamp and makes me flinch. Propped up among fat pillows with shiny cases is Mrs Van den Broeck. I can see her pointy shoulders and satin nightgown where the bedclothes have slipped down. Collarbones stick through skin. She must sleep with her head raised and ready to snap at Gemima when she comes in with the breakfast.

Her small red eyes watch me. Her face is surprised, but

not afraid. And for a while she cannot speak and I stand there, dizzy before her, with pinpricks of sweat growing out of my whole head.

'What are you doing in my room?' There is no sleepiness in her voice; she has been awake for a long time. Not even her hair is mussed-up or flat at the back. Her voice gets sharper and fills the room. 'I knew it was you. I always knew you were not to be trusted. You've been taking things. Jewellery. I suspected you from the start.'

'No. It wasn't me.' I feel like I'm five again, before the desk of the director at the boys' home.

'I'll have you executed in the morning. You disgust me.' Her face has begun to shake. She pulls her bed sheets up to her chin, as if to stop me looking at her bird body in the shiny nightie. 'People will thank me for having you put down. You should have been smothered in the cradle. Why do they let things like you live?' All this I have heard before, when she is in a spiteful mood. But the thing that makes me so angry is her suspicion that I want to look at her skeleton body in the silk gown.

At any moment I expect Gemima to come in and to start wailing. Then the white ape will be up here too and I will only have a few hours to live.

I stare at the bird-face with the plume of grey hair. Never have I hated anything so much. A little gargle comes out of my throat and I am at her bedside before she can say another word.

She looks at me with surprise in her eyes. Neither of us can believe that we are facing each other like this in her bedroom. This is not how I imagined it would be: the light on, me in my nightgown, and Mrs Van den Broeck's dry-stick body sitting upright and supported by pillows.

She opens her mouth to speak, but no spiky words come out to hurt my ears. It is my time to speak. 'You,' I say. 'The boys. The boys in the truck. You brought them here.'

'What are you talking about? Have you lost your mind?'

I take one of the pillows from behind her back. Mrs Van den Broeck never liked to see my china-doll hands poking from the sleeves of my uniform, so it is only right that they are the last things that she sees before I put the pillow over her face.

'Oh,' she says in a little-girl voice. Her frown is still asking me a question when I put her into the dark and take away the thin streams of air that must whistle through her beak holes. I grin the wild grin that I cannot control when I am killing, that makes my whole face shake. This bully-bird can't peck me now!

Her pigeon skull fidgets under the pressing pillow. Twiggish legs, with brown spots on the skin, kick out inside the sheets, but only make whispers like mice behind the skirting boards. Claws open, claws close, claws open, claws stop moving.

I put my big onion skull against the pillow to add weight to my late-night pressings. Now our faces are closer together than they have ever been before, but we can't see each other. A few feathers and some silk are all that is between us. The pillow smells of perfume and old lady. Squalls and squirts of excitement start in my belly. Triumph makes me want to take a shit.

I whisper words through the veil between us. I send her on her way with mutterings. 'The little boys from the truck were crying when they were taken into the tiled room' – flicker of talon on the mattress – 'They were scared, but didn't know why they were going to be hurt. They didn't understand' – stretching of a single bony leg under the sheets – 'What did the big boy look like on your plate?' – final kick of twisted foot, and a yellow nail snags on silk – 'There was laughter in the boardroom during dinner. I heard you. I was outside and I heard you all' – all the thin bones relax and go soft underneath me – 'Then you made me bring the leftovers up here in white bags. They banged against my legs on the stairs. They felt heavy. The bags were wet inside.'

Now she's still. Nothing under me but bird bones, fossils wrapped in silk and some hair, but not much else.

I stay on top of her for a while.

When it's done I feel warm inside. Milky sweat cools on the skin under my nightgown. I take the pillow off Mrs Van den Broeck's face and step back from the bed. I pad out the part that was over her beak. Leaning across her, I put the pillow back behind her warm body.

Underneath my body, one of her chicken-bone arms moves, quicker than I thought something so old and skinny could move. Yellow claws curl around my elbow.

I look down. An eggshell brow wrinkles. Pink eyes open and make me gasp. I try to pull away.

Bird snarl. A pinched mouth opens wide. Two rows of tiny yellow teeth sink into my wrist.

Now I'm drowning. Pain and panic fills my balloon skull like hot water. I pull, and tug, and then yanky-shake at her biting beak that wants to saw off my dolly hand. Grunting, she holds on. How can an old thing like Mrs Van den Broeck, made from such tiny bones and paper skin, make so deep a noise?

Digging my heels into the rug, I push backwards with all my strength, but her body comes forward in a tangle of sheets, pulled across the mattress by her mouth. Snarly and spitting, she shakes her head from side to side and I think that my wrist must be broken. I should have guessed that 170 years of her evil life could not be stoppered by a soft pillow in the night.

Mad from the pain, I swat my free hand around in the air and it hits something solid. Now there are stabbing pains in the knuckles of that hand too, from where it struck the heavy lamp. Strength leaks out of my feet and into the rug. Black dots float in front of my eyes. I might faint. It feels like her serrated beak has gone through a nerve.

I fall backwards and pull her whole body off the bed. Her stick-body hits the floor but makes no sound. I stand up and try to shake her off like I'm trying to pull off a tight shirt that has gone inside-out over my face. Tears blur my eyes.

I reach for the lamp on the bedside table. My little hand circles the hot smooth neck below the bulb. I pull it off the table and watch the thick marble base drop to the biting head on the rug. There is a *thock* sound as the sharp corner strikes the side of her head by the small ear. She stops biting.

I twist my wrist free of the loose beak and step away. I look down and can't believe that so much liquid could spill from the broken head of a very old bird. The liquid is black. It's been going through her thin pipes and tubes for 170 years, and now it is soaking into a rug.

Working fast, I wrap the white cord of the lamp around her claw and make it go tight. Maybe they will think that she fell from her pillows and pulled the lamp down on top of her bird head. With the tail of my nightshirt I then wipe all the things that my dollish fingers have touched around the bed.

I flit from her room like a ghost. Go down the long hall and close the front door behind me. In the light of the landing, I inspect the circle of bruises and cuts that her beak has made on my stiff wrist. Not as bad as it felt.

I find it hard to believe that Gemima is not screaming and that doors are not opening and that phones are not ringing and that residents are not shuffling down the stairs, wrapped in their dressing gowns. But there is only silence in the west wing.

Then the shaking starts.

Down the stairs I go on my hands and knees like a spider with four legs torn off. Back to my bunk.

Curled up in the warm place that I have made in the middle of my bed, with the thin sheet and itchy grey blanket pulled over my head, I try to stop the shakes and wipe away all of the pictures that swirl around my pumpkin skull. There is so much room inside my big head-space, so I guess it can hold more memories than a smaller head. Over and over I see the chewing bird that was Mrs Van den Broeck, with her beak fastened onto my wrist. And then I see the heavy lamp land with a *thock... thock... thock...* It's all I can hear: the sharp marble corner breaking the wafer of her veiny temple.

What have I done in this giant house? What will become of me? They will know that my dolly hands got busy with a pillow and bedside-lamp to crush that flightless vulture in its own nest. I wonder if turning back the hands on my little brass clock will take me back to the time before I went sneaking and creeping into her room.

An impulse makes my face scrunch up to cry and my body shivers under the blankets. Then I stand up beside the bunk and peer into the top bed where Vinegar Irish snores. I wish I was him. With no killing pictures inside his head, only thoughts of clear liquid to sup from plastic containers, flowing through his twitchy sleep.

The cold in the porters' dormitory makes my shaking worse. My wrist throbs. I want to get back into my bed and curl into a ball. Like the baby in a tummy before I was cut out and made my momma die.

I leave the dormitory and look down to the washroom door.

No one is shouting, there are no alarms or lights being turned on. All is quiet in the building. No one knows that Mrs Van den Broeck is dead. No one knows that it was me who did it, not yet.

Inside I feel better. No one saw me. No one heard me. Gemima was asleep the whole time, dreaming of the hot green place across the oceans where she was born. I just have to stay calm. Maybe no one will suspect me, the big-headed boy with the doll hands. What can he do with those puppet legs and pencil arms? That big bulb-head, with the baby face stuck on the front, is not capable of thinking of such things:

maybe that is what they will think. That's what they thought at the orphanage too. That's how I got away with it before. They never even thought of me at the same time as they thought about the nasty, smacking carers who were all found dead in their beds. I did three of them carers with these small china hands.

I grin with joy. My little grey heart slows down its pumping. Pebbles of sweat dry across my skin. Warmth spreads through every teeny toe and twig finger, and goes up my see-through body to my roundish head, until I am glowing with the happiness of escaping and of tricking them. All of *them* who don't know about the power in my tiny hands.

And in my head now I see the boy who came in the white truck. The one they ate yesterday. He is dancing in heaven. Up there, the sky is totally blue. He likes the long grass that is soft between his toes, and he enjoys how the yellow sun warms his jumping, running body. It was for him and his brother that I dropped the heavy lamp. *Thock*. What happened to him must always be remembered. I see it again now. I see it all behind my squeezed-shut, black-button eyes.

But what of the other one?

And then I go down to the washroom and I unlock the door. Behind the wood of the door, before it is even open, I hear the skitter of dry feet retreating into a corner. And a whimper.

No, they shall not have you too.

I open the door and walk past the dark, wet bench beside the white wall. And I go to the huddled yellowish boy in the corner. I smile. He takes my small outstretched hand and blinks wet eyes.

I think of the Church of Our Lady and of the mist. We'll need a blanket.

'Your brother's waiting for us,' I say, and he stands up.

To Forget and Be Forgotten

Even in the most populous cities on earth a multitude of people exist in solitude. And yet, after a sufficient period of time has been endured while feeling awkward, or being neglected socially and professionally, it is my experience that individuals can yet make themselves moderately comfortable in the role of the excluded, or the barely tolerated.

I was never really cast out, but manoeuvred toward the edges of human affairs by the herd. And it was only after considerable experience within this role of the outcast that I finally accepted my own fate. It was liberating.

I considered myself a true outsider, because my loneliness itself became a purpose. My new vocation was to avoid all of those things that drew people together and could be termed a shared experience, for I developed a desire to create a silence and stillness around myself, and a space within my head, in which to think and to read. For the rarest aspiration for any individual to pursue, in this solipsistic age of *me*, is to be ordinary. Just ordinary. Unexceptional and invisible. And this was a goal that I would take to the mountain.

I would take the last seat at the back of a tram and remain so still as not to attract scrutiny; I would stand in shadow at the edge of a crowd if a crowd could not be avoided; I would not court fad or fashion; I suppressed any feature or attribute that could be termed distinguishing; I lived in unremarkable lodgings without cohabitants in unfashionable districts; I took no part in any community or subculture; I never stuck my hand up, or spoke out loud. I shuffled away from the party and breathed a sigh of relief. I would be courteous and civil if contact was unavoidable, but if it could be avoided then it would be. Every time.

And I began to come to life in a way that few could imagine, because much can be seen and understood when the mind is not clamouring for attention and approval or acceptance from those around it.

Fade to grey. It became my motto, my release, my peace. And my mission led me to Dulle Griet Huis in Zurenborg, Antwerp.

The very idea of work is an incongruous proposition for the self-excluded who want no truck with team-players or professional advancement. But funds for the basic needs of lodging and food were still required. A modicum of security was necessary because I did not want my new mental space troubled by gnawing financial anxiety. And what was required, I realised quickly, was an *occupation* as opposed to a career, and an occupation that could be performed alone. Such positions without colleagues and supervision do exist. In fact, there are plenty of openings available because few want to fill them.

Where I was going to commit myself, even the poorest imagination could envisage a profound isolation, a lack of opportunity for progress, inhuman working hours and a slide down a slippery slope that could remove me so far from society that I might never find my way back. 'When do I start?' I said to the agency manager who had interviewed me for the job of nightwatchman. 'Sounds perfect.' My new job title was the fastest track in Antwerp to nowhere, and I stepped onto it with glee.

The only qualifications required were a clean criminal record, the ability to be punctual and the willingness to stay awake for twelve hours. My duties were described as 'light' by the agency that employed such odd individuals as myself, by placing us in the old but well-maintained apartment buildings in Antwerp's chi-chi zones.

I would relieve a concierge at 6 p.m., and he would then relieve me at 6 a.m. the following day. I would work four nights in a row, and then take four nights off. While on duty, I was required to monitor the monitors that monitored the nine-storey exterior of Dulle Griet Huis, patrol the internal communal areas every four hours, and assist the residents when required. The rest of the twelve-hour shift was my own.

The last duty on my job description did set off bells and buzzers, as I imagined perpetual interaction with the affluent residents and their guests, going on through the night as they entertained and swaggered and brayed as the privileged seem keen to do. But not so, according to Pieter, who ran the employment agency. There were only forty flats in Dulle Griet Huis and most of them were empty; all owned by overseas companies, or belonging to private residents who lived abroad and hardly ever used their properties. The building had a strictly enforced rule that forbade children under the age of fourteen, so there were no families, and the only permanent residents were very elderly and rarely left their apartments. At night, in Pieter's own words, 'It's dead. You'll never see them. So I'm afraid you'll have to amuse yourself.'

'Not a problem,' I assured him, and could barely contain my elation at what sounded like a bespoke position for a gentleman of absence like myself. 'Is it OK to read?' I asked. 'I like to read.'

Pieter nodded quickly, as if he was as pleased at filling the post as I was at taking it. 'Of course. I have a lot of students working nights, so they can get some work done without distractions.'

'And who can blame them? This sounds ideal, Pieter.'

'It might well be. Terry, your predecessor, worked that building for thirty-five years.'

'Thirty-five years?'

Pieter nodded.

I will confess, that detail alarmed me, as if by taking the job I was signing a guarantee that I would stay for an indefinite period of service, and it felt akin to making a final decision about something that would change my life, and there would be no going back.

Pieter closed our interview quickly by handing me a background-check form and reminded me, 'Take a look at the monitors now and again.'

I quelled my last vague doubts and left the agency whistling. And I could not remember being more excited about starting a job. In fact, I could not remember being excited about beginning any job before, because I never had been. I dreaded them all. But now, at last, I would finally be free of the manipulative, and so far beyond the hunting grounds of the pathological who delight in a colleague's downfall in conventional employment, that they would never pick up my scent again. I would have no colleagues at Dulle Griet Huis who could deride, contradict, undermine or discredit me. And no one would ever take ownership of another one of my ideas, because this was no place for ideas, or competition, or ambition. It was no place for anyone but me. I didn't even have a supervisor. My employers were the residents, who left the business of paying me to an offsite management company. Finally, I could forget and be forgotten.

Dulle Griet Huis cast a long shadow through the back streets of Zurenborg and instilled a strange hush on the square below. Looking up at the ten floors of imperious red brick and white stone balcony from the street, the first time I saw the building I was tempted to lower my eyes, and even to bow my head in deference to the aura of exclusivity that the building projected. *Run along, my good man. Nothing for you here.*

The interior had been renovated in the 1920s and not since. It had the eerie grandeur of a luxury passenger liner. There were antique elevators panelled in brass and mahogany, stairwells and corridors papered with silk, and ornamental light fittings of patterned glass that created a brownish haze in the communal areas. I even imagined myself wearing a top hat and tails and roaming between decks on some giant floating ballroom. And the entire interior had that peculiar smell of traditional importance. Not quite ecclesiastic, but not far from it: a scent of old things preserved and of poor ventilation, of wood and metal polish.

On each floor a square landing contained the elevator entrance and two veneered front doors, with brass knockers, which led into penthouse apartments. Ornate marble radiator covers, reminiscent of late-nineteenth-century tombs for children, stood beneath the gigantic gilt-framed mirrors, fitted at eye-level opposite the elevator doors. Between each floor, a staircase turned once.

Manuel, the day porter, was so tired each morning when he arrived to relieve me, and so eager to get out of the building at the end of each day shift, that contact between us was minimal. And we both liked it that way. No gossip, no intrigue, no Machiavellian tactics, just a nod and we were out of each other's space. We changed our little guard without fuss or spectacle.

The front desk was quaint and efficiently positioned opposite the elevator doors in the ground-floor reception. Below the top of the desk were six tiny monitors showing greenish exterior views of Dulle Griet Huis, as if the square outside the building were at the bottom of some silty ocean.

The remainder of the reception sparkled. It was all very quiet and civilised. Not a bad little environment in which to pass twelve hours while reading the great books under a good overhead light in a comfortable leather chair that could be reclined. The three nightly patrols could be done in fifteen minutes each, and who was watching to say that I even did them? Though it was always my intention to complete the patrols; it would be good to stretch my legs after sitting still for hours, and it was also one of my duties, and what little I was being paid to do, I would do. I am a recluse, but that is no screen for laziness.

And during my first four weeks, I often eased backwards in the recliner and congratulated myself on discovering a successful escape route from life and its responsibilities. I had pulled it off. I was actually free, at last, of *them*. Free to reverse my absolute ignorance of most subjects too, because I had created an opportunity to re-educate myself with what I thought significant. I began reading the historians, the philosophers, the popular scientists. I made lists of all the things that I wanted to know. I spent my days, between shifts, in bookshops and public libraries, making careful choices. I took a broadsheet newspaper in with me each night and subscribed to two literary journals as insurance. And if I liked, which I often did, I would just sit and stare into the rain. A much derided and underrated pastime, though one that must be meted out or the mind can turn against itself.

My new position was showing so much promise that I even began to prefer a night shift to the days that I spent in my dim lodgings. Though only until my second month, when Dulle Griet Huis decided to show its true self to me.

At first the alterations within the building were barely perceptible: minor alterations in temperature and lighting that I easily shrugged off. But these atmospheric changes soon intensified to command my full attention and discourage me from making the second patrol at 2 a.m., when the activity reached its peak.

I began to feel uncomfortable using the staircases. And it took time to define exactly what was making me feel peculiar. But I reduced it to an unaccountable manifestation of enclosure. After midnight, when a silence fell over the world outside, my chest would tighten from more than exertion, the air would feel unnaturally cold about me, and I would struggle to catch my breath, while all the time something pushed at my thoughts. Squeezed them into sudden frenzies of recollection and paranoia and fear that seemed unaccountable when I returned to my desk downstairs.

The sudden claustrophobic feeling was accompanied by shadows. In every case, at the edge of my sight, I would catch sudden flits of movement. Movement loaded with the expectation of an appearance behind it. Only no one ever came into view. The shadows seemed to come down the stairs after me, as if their owners were closely following my descent to the ground. Or at times, as I walked to a lower floor, a shadow, that was not my own, would rush around a corner on the stairwell ahead of me.

A few times I even called out, 'Hello there?' But no one answered or showed themselves. When I stood still and applied a steady and careful scrutiny to my surroundings there was no longer any evidence of these moving shadows at all. But the lights on the walls, and the ceiling lights on each landing, would dim. It gave me the impression that either my sight was failing or the environment in which I stood was gradually disappearing into darkness.

Or *did* the lights dim? Was all this merely a result of my tired eyes? These were only vague and peripheral hallucinations and I was unaccustomed to night work. I was not, after all, a nocturnal animal and was only becoming one by design. Who could say how it would affect me? So I passed the phenomenon off as the early signs of sleep deprivation, as it always happened at around two in the morning when my need for rest was at its peak.

The noises were more alarming because of their unaccountability. They came after the beginning of the shadows. Joined them, in fact. And I knew after checking the duty roster that the sounds were originating from inside empty apartments.

It was as if a tremendous wind could gust through an open window on the outside of the building and narrow its way through the rooms and corridors of the penthouse apartments, before striking the front doors, from the inside, with terrific force. A blow that made the doors bang, then shake in their frames.

Perhaps, I'd thought, this might have been caused by strong air currents, or updraughts from the air-risers. I knew nothing of the physics of air circulation in these old buildings and there was, of course, no one to ask. But the sudden boom and tremble of a door beside me, at the precise moment of my passing across the landing, began to do strange things to my nerves, and to my imagination. I suffered the unsettling notion that someone had thrown their full weight against the inner surface of a front door, as a disturbed guard dog will hurl its body at a door at the sound of a postman. My increasing paranoia suggested that something inside the empty apartments was demanding my attention.

'Excuse me?' I would say to the closed doors. 'It's me. Jack. The nightwatchman. Everything OK?' But there was never an answer and I realised there was no one to answer because, when I checked the desk ledger, the affected flats were clearly marked Vacant. But the noises occurred even if it was a windless and calm night. And on both sides of the building too.

Still, this was a dream job and by the middle of my third month I convinced myself that I could live with the malfunctioning lights, the strange inner winds and the odd mental side-effects of working nights. But no sooner had I renewed my vow to stay than my tolerance of Dulle Griet Huis was challenged again, though by a more tangible threat.

What began to introduce itself to me from the occupied apartments was more alarming than any tricks that the lights or air currents were playing on my senses. And I had never seen such a collection of the aged assembled under one roof. A community at the height of dysfunction and eccentricity too, and one that had kept itself completely hidden from me for the first ten weeks of my employment. I suspected that it was my stubborn presence within the building that had awoken them.

The first residents that I saw were the Al Farez Hussein sisters, of number 22, who were both over one hundred years of age. Or so Manuel told me once the sisters began to make an occasional appearance during my shift. And I had no reason to disbelieve him.

Upon entering the building (though Manuel had no recollection of them leaving during his day shift), they would walk at an impossibly slow pace across reception, as if they were performing an odd Regency dance that had been slowed down to such a degree that they didn't appear to move anywhere but slowly up and down, from one foot to the other.

After offering a customary smile and wave, I would return my eyes to my book, only to then be fooled by the illusion of the sisters making quicker progress across reception. And their speedier movements, glimpsed in my peripheral vision, were aided by them dropping to all fours and scurrying.

Impossible and no doubt another strange quirk of sleep deprivation. Because the two figures, swaddled in robes, one in white and the other in black, were so shrunken and hunched that it would have been impossible for them to move with any rapidity, let alone ease.

They never spoke a word to me in any language, but their eyes were always fixed upon me as they made their way to the elevator doors. One small face, treacle-brown and wrinkled like a raisin, would turn to me, so that the two small glints of obsidian within the collapsed flesh of the eye sockets could study me. The other wore a mask. A golden beaked mask, attached to her face by a series of chains that disappeared inside her burka. I believe it was supposed to represent the face of a hawk.

But there were unappealing curiosities within that building far graver than the sisters.

The first thing I noticed about Mrs Goldstein from number 30 was her extraordinary hairstyle: a perfect bulb of silver wisps. But completely transparent from any angle. And through the illusory lustre of this spherical creation, her birdlike skull, bleached between the liver spots, would present itself horribly. Her nose was a papery blade, while the flesh of her avian features was as transparent as boiled chicken skin in the places where her make-up had rubbed away. At the age of 98 her body had also wizened to such an extent that the top of her head only reached the bottom of my ribcage. But she moved quickly, in a spidery manner, from the front entrance to the lift doors in reception, aided by two black sticks that moved like quick chopsticks. I never saw her wear anything but high heels and the ancient black suits that her maid, Olive, hung from her skeletal body. She made me think of a marionette with a papier mâché devil face. She was no sight for the faint-hearted, certainly not at night.

Mrs Goldstein and Olive resided in a palatial three-bedroom penthouse. And Mrs Goldstein did not care for me at all. Olive told me. Whispered it to me with a smile as her round Filipino face passed my desk one evening. 'She think you too young to be porter. Not married. No children. He up to no good, she say.' Olive soon became fond of reporting to me all of her mistress's disparaging remarks about me.

I began to see the pair once each night at eight. Olive would bring her mistress downstairs for a short walk around the square outside the front of the building. Or so they said. Again, as with the Hussein sisters, I was stricken with the uncomfortable notion that they had only come inside reception to stare at me.

According to the desk ledger, all of the other permanent residents were female too, but bedridden so I never saw them.

Though I would sometimes hear their nurses talking in the stairwells.

But it was number 18 on the eighth floor that housed not only the building's longest-standing resident but also its most sinister occupants: Mrs Van den Bergh and her full-time nurse, Helma.

My first brush with Helma and Mrs Van den Bergh created such a powerful impression upon me that I suffered a nightmare the following day while I slept at home. A long, random and tortuous dream scenario in which I was wed to ancient Mrs Van den Bergh in a meadow, while my parents and two sisters were slaughtered with Halal knives in a pen nearby to the accompanying sound of clapping children and excited young women; a crowd that I was unable to see clearly, but which circled the corral in a strange slow dance.

Inexplicable, or, after all that has happened since, perhaps not.

Mrs Van den Bergh was a long, skeletal individual who bore little resemblance to the living, and was confined to a wheelchair as ancient as its occupant. The first time we were introduced, I was reminded of the minor royal of an Egyptian dynasty who had been unwrapped and displayed in a case in the British Museum, in London, where I had once seen it as a teenager during a school trip. Mrs Van den Bergh's skin was so mottled with liverish discolourations she appeared brown-skinned in any light. Her gender was indistinguishable too, and the black capillaries visible beneath the translucent skin of her bald head and her hands reminded me of the baby birds that fall from nests and that I sometimes found as a child.

Always dressed in a leisure suit, faded like a candlewick bedspread in a Schipperskwartier squat and stained down the front, the heiress was contained in her chair by canvas ankle and wrist straps as if she were a danger to the public. And yet her eyes were as clear and blue as the arctic waters that lap around an iceberg.

Despite her shocking appearance, Mrs Van den Bergh had once been a great beauty, in possession of a brilliant mind. She had laid waste to three husbands and was worth over one hundred million euros from property ownership. She had also been a notorious high-society nymphomaniac. 'A tart! Dreadful!' Helma told me, with one of her conspiratorial asides, on our very first meeting. Mrs Van den Bergh then apparently entered a kleptomaniac phase before finally becoming a pyromaniac. In short, a maniac. 'She brought the dark man here.'

Helma's comment about the 'dark man' confused me – was this a racial slur? – and when I tried to question her about it, Helma only smiled enigmatically. Helma would never answer any direct questions; Helma liked to talk *at* me. I was only there to listen; it was the role that she had assigned to me. But she could tell that I was curious about her ward and she would occasionally elaborate when I frowned at some provocative remark or suggestive detail.

According to Helma, a trauma in the 1930s had transformed Mrs Van den Bergh into a deeply disturbed young woman. It was the birth of her 'gaga child' that caused the breakdown; an incident she never recovered from. 'Gaga child' was an infantile expression that I had never heard before, but Helma was referring to children born with both mental and physical disabilities that were unacceptable in high society, or as heirs. Children that were shipped off and contained within a private sanatorium in Carlsbad, along with several Habsburg princes of which the world still knows nothing, according to Helma.

It was an odd revelation to confide in the uniformed security guard, and as a result it was a story that I disbelieved.

Apparently, Mrs Van den Bergh's two equally glittering and talented sisters then spent the next seventy years containing their damaged and errant elder sister at Dulle Griet Huis. Having spent small fortunes both on hush money to extinguish scandals and for treatment at the best Swiss facilities, it seemed they had finally settled on an expensive method of security combined with sedation that Helma excelled at. Though Helma never presented the treatment to me in that way.

In this part of the world, I also quickly learned that it was not unusual for an employee, with a live-in position, to make themselves indispensable to an elderly resident who had hired them, or for whom they were recruited as guardians by trustees. It was grotesque in the tradition of the Gothic, and redolent of the age when hysterical wives were secured in locked attics. If people had seen how Mrs Van den Bergh had lived under the occupation of Helma, they would have taken their chances in a Romanian nursing home.

Helma was a garrulous, paranoid and profoundly manipulative woman in her fifties, but still almost half a century younger than her patient. In my third month, the frequency of Helma's visitations to my desk increased to at least once each night that I was on duty. Sometimes, to my chagrin, she would stay an hour and talk at me.

Helma also slipped into the habit of wheeling Mrs Van den Bergh down to reception and leaving her beside my desk, while she 'popped out' to fetch nick-nacks from the store open late on Kleine Hondstraat. Why these items were not procured during the day remained a mystery, but I began to suspect that Helma wanted me and the heiress to become acquainted. Though how we would form a connection was doubly mystifying.

Mrs Van den Bergh's mind was long gone. During these short but uncomfortable periods when she sat beside my desk, there were odd moments of lucidity from her, in which an impeccable voice would rise from the chair and wish me 'Good morning'. But most of the time, there were only streams of gibberish about someone called 'Florine', before

Helma returned to the building and reclaimed her ward from beside my desk.

It wasn't until my fifteenth week as the nightwatchman of Dulle Griet Huis that I was reluctantly drawn across the threshold of their penthouse and plunged into the insane world that the apartment enclosed.

During my second patrol, at midnight, one Sunday evening, the front door to flat 18 was open before I completed the final set of stairs to the landing of the eighth floor. And Helma was waiting for me, wearing a pair of Jimmy Choo shoes, silk fishnet tights, a pink Chanel suit and more make-up than a drag queen's eyelids could support. 'Oh, Jack. I need to ask you a big favour. Would you watch Mrs Van den Bergh for an hour? I have to pop out. Something's come up and it's very important. An emergency.'

Emergency, my ass, I had thought. 'Afraid I can't. I have to watch the cameras downstairs.'

Helma's eyes both brightened and hardened and they held me still. This was not a woman who would be defied. 'It'll be all right for a little while. Now, she's been fed and had her medicine, so she won't be any trouble at all. This is for you.' Helma's lacquered claws stuffed two twenty-Euro notes into one of my hands, and then squashed my fingers shut over my paper-filled palm.

I tried again to refuse, then attempted to give the money back, but I found myself swiftly 'shoo-shoo'd', as if Helma were talking to a house cat, and then manoeuvred inside the flat. Upon entrance, I wondered if I was now on some kind of illegal payroll and complicit in the imprisonment and extortion of Dulle Griet Huis's equivalent of Howard Hughes.

Then, from the living room, before I could get my bearings in the dingy hallway of the penthouse, a familiar voice began to shriek. 'Florine! Florine! Florine! Let them out! Please God, let them out! *Florine!*' It was Mrs Van den Bergh, and no doubt disturbed from some drugged nap by the volume of Helma's voice in the hallway as she ushered me deeper into the dark and cluttered interior of the apartment. Helma had been guiding me toward the kitchen, but stopped to shout through an open door on the right-hand side of the hallway. 'Stop it! You're just showing off because Jack's here! You only want attention!'

It didn't sound like showing off to me, and I cringed inside my skin at the awkwardness of the whole situation. I had come to Dulle Griet Huis to avoid interaction with other people, as well as the predictable conflicts that would result.

'Florine! Florine! Florine! She's hitting me!' from Mrs Van den Bergh.

'Enough! Enough of that!' Helma screamed.

From the hall, I peered into the living room while Helma and Mrs Van den Bergh screeched at each other like two vultures in a nest fighting over a vole.

Around the room, sealed boxes marked fragile competed for space with sloping heaps of documents and printed receipts. Letters piled up in drifts against mimsy porcelain figures and silver utensils. It looked like someone was running a business, or a racket. Every other door in the hall was secured by a deadlock. I never found out why, though, after what Helma and Mrs Van den Bergh revealed to me, any further curiosity about their living arrangements was short-lived.

Amongst the debris, Mrs Van den Bergh and her chair were walled into a corner by a large television set. Her hairless, shrieking head looked ghastly when lit up by the greens and whites of the flickering screen.

'Now, darling! Now, now, sugar plum! Shush, shush, darling!' Helma shouted at Mrs Van den Bergh to calm the outbursts.

My eyes then moved to the enormous oil painting hanging between the balcony doors and the dining table. It was a full-length portrait of Mrs Van den Bergh in her prime. An intolerably beautiful, regal face stared down, unimpressed with the detritus and disgrace inflicted upon her final years. Ice-blonde hair was pulled back beneath a diamond tiara; the forehead was porcelain-smooth; the nose perfect beneath the thin arches of haughty brows; full red lips smiled, faintly; white satin gloves shone to the elbows; a glittering necklace pulled my stare to the princess's neck; below the jewellery, a long white dress hugged her embraceable lines and curves. But it was the astonishing arctic eyes that really enchanted and also withered me. It hurt to look into those eyes, but it was impossible not to. They possessed an expression of piercing curiosity, and they revealed the fevered thoughts of the inspired, and the vulnerability of the passionate.

But the sense of impending doom in the painting, the tragedy of these qualities that were soon to flounder into madness, stopped my breath. It was as if the painter had been commissioned, just in time, to capture the last of the subject's allure, before she became something else entirely.

A lump formed in my throat. She had been an angel, I remember thinking. An angel. As close as anyone would ever come to being an angel.

Mrs Van den Bergh and Helma fell silent too, and they had turned to stare at me. From her chair, Mrs Van den Bergh smiled as she acknowledged her admirer.

And then the spell was broken. The moment had upstaged Helma. On her clattering pink heels, she muscled across the stage to obscure the great beauty once more. 'She gets so disturbed! It's the new medication! The doctors are useless! Four hundred euros for a call-out and they're useless!' Now she was talking about money, and reasserting herself as a dreadful painted parody of her mistress's beauty that she might have long despised. Helma vulgarised the very space in which that picture hung.

I felt sick and longed to get back downstairs to my chair. Especially as Helma was now eyeing me with a combination of suspicion and bemusement, a look peculiar in my experience to those who were fond of underestimating me. Helma then brushed passed me on her way to the front door, and slid one hand across my chest, provocatively. 'Goodbye, darling!' She called out to Mrs Van den Bergh.

'Florine! Florine! Florine!' the ancient creature cried out from the wheelchair.

'But… but what do I do?' I implored Helma, following her.

'Just watch her.'

'But what if she needs something? The toilet?'

'You don't need to worry about that. She'll just watch her programmes.'

'She could fall.'

'How? She hasn't walked in twenty years. You took the money easily enough, and I'm not asking you for much. You can keep your eyes open, can't you? *Vaarwel*, my love!' She closed the front door on her way out and was gone.

Alone with Mrs Van den Bergh, I hid myself inside the kitchen, directly across the hall from the living room. Surrounded by soiled dishes and cutlery, old newspapers and plastic carrier bags that were filled with yellowing catalogues and rubbish, I decided to wait out my sentence. If there were any sounds of distress, I could look in on Mrs Van den Bergh. Otherwise I would stay outside her line of sight, because the moment she caught a glimpse of me – and she was always looking for me from her chair – she would begin that dreadful shrieking for Florine.

In the dim brownish pall of the apartment, I then suffered the unhealthiest thoughts about age and ageing. These black impressions and notions extended to my own life and to all of humanity. I felt that despair and immobility were the only natural outcomes of the miserable struggle that is life. At one point I even buried my face in my hands. I desperately wanted to weep, but somehow held that back, though I don't think it did me any good.

In the distance I could hear the chatter of the television, a whooshing sound of what could have been fireworks, and the clang of bells. It was some appalling quiz show that she had been sitting before. A programme that produced whitish flashes that briefly illumined the living room.

It seemed my dream-life of seclusion and contemplation was coming to an end. Even here, at night, while the world slept, there were still parts of it, these obscure quarters, that would give me no peace. Places that would seek me out and torment me in the same insidious manner that caused my former misery working for a corporation, where I was overrun by the will-to-power of baboons with silver tongues.

Was it so much to ask for? To be just left alone?

I thought the world mad. Desperate and cruel and stupid, endlessly repeating the same mistakes with terrible consequences. The world's refusal to leave me out of its activities made me consider its destruction. Bring on the wave. Please, the asteroid. Anything. Just take it away. And then Mrs Van den Bergh stood up. And she ran from the living room on those long brownish bones that served her for legs.

She appeared at the corner of my sight, impossibly tall and thin with that little dry skull grinning above her narrow shoulders. I turned, at once shocked out of my morbid stupor. And I watched her flee, bandy-legged, with both chicken-bone arms thrown upwards at the ceiling. Her hands had looked strangely masculine, atop wrists as thin as woodwind instruments. Her long feet had slapped down the hallway toward the front door.

'No,' I said. Or I whispered it. Perhaps it was just a thought that never made it out of my mind. But I moved into the hallway, unsteadily, where the amber lights were caged within such dirty glass that they gave me the impression that I was trapped inside an old photograph. But I could still make out the figure of Mrs Van den Bergh scrabbling at the latch of the door, and a keening sound issued from her mottled head. The noise transformed into a growl, before it broke into a bellow. 'Florine! Florine! Dear God, let them out! *Florine!* I can hear them!'

I approached her, but I made it no further than the threadbare mat in the hall before she had the front door open and was *out*. Outside. Suddenly. On the landing, under brighter lights, naked, and racing across the landing at speed and on limbs so spindly the sight of them striding like that made me want to crouch in a dark corner and never move again. And as she skittered at the top of the stairs before making her rickety descent, my eyes locked onto something even more dreadful. Folded flat against her prominent scapulae were two brown flaps. Like wings, but hairless, and shrivelled in the manner of dried fish.

What could I do but follow? Below me in the building, I heard Mrs Van den Bergh shouting as she fled from floor to floor, 'Florine! I can hear them! Florine! Florine!' Though whether she was crying out with elation or with grief, it was impossible for me to decide.

I leaped three stairs at a time. My tie flapped about my face. My hand clutched at the brass railings as I pursued the sounds of her flight.

Somewhere below, a door opened quickly. Followed by another, and another.

The other residents must have been disturbed. What would they think, coming to their doors in nightwear, only to see the emaciated form of Mrs Van den Bergh racing past, shrieking for Florine? Had she not looked such a fright, I might have been tempted to add my own hysterical laughter to the commotion. The entire episode was as absurd as it was disturbing. And my reason tried desperately to assert itself, telling me that all of this was not possible: the woman was over a hundred years of age and had not walked in twenty, allegedly. But then maybe Helma was behind this. Helma must have known this would happen. She had deliberately left her ward unsecured in that chair and I had been set up.

And now it was my task to catch an infirm and half-crazed resident. Oh, how they would all laugh: Mrs Goldstein, those mute Husseins, little Manuel and half-smiling Olive. I would be reported. I would be fired.

But so be it; I wasn't being paid enough for this. Any of it. It was not in my job description either to enter flat 17, flat 15 or flat 14. I was not to enter any of the apartments unaccompanied by the owners. But the doors to these apartments were now gaping. Wide open.

I saw the open doorways as soon as I staggered off the stairs on the relevant floors. So why were they open, as if they had so recently released occupants into the communal areas? Had I been misinformed? Was the information in the desk ledger not up to date? I then thought of the desperate winds and the bangs from inside these dark and empty spaces, and for a few seconds I wondered if this was now my last chance to flee the building and to never return.

I called out for Mrs Van den Bergh, my voice disappearing into the darkness of every open flat I passed. But I received no answer.

Flat 12 on the fifth floor, where I came to a stop, was also supposed to be a sealed and empty property. The other flats with open doors were unlit and they issued an air of vacancy, but not flat 12. That one was different.

Hovering on the threshold, biting my bottom lip until it bled, my chest rising and falling too quickly, I could hear *them* inside. *Them?* Mrs Van den Bergh perhaps. And others. I heard a muffled voice, or voices, over the sound of weeping, coming out of the dark hallway, and from somewhere deep inside the apartment. Yes, there was a thin light seeping under a door at the end of the hallway. The master bedroom, if this floor plan followed the graphic in the desk ledger of how these apartments were arranged on this side of the building. But why then were the remainder of the lights out in the apartment?

I dithered. I vacillated. I did not want to see, or to know, where I was being led. It was as if my involvement in this madness had somehow been assumed. But out of some deluded sense of duty I went down to that bruised orange light, faintly washing from under the door at the far end of the hall. And as I went down, I turned on the ancient lights in the hallway by flicking down the heavy porcelain switches in fixtures the size of butter dishes. It was like walking through a museum, with its telephone table, coat-rack made from antlers, and the dusty oil paintings of peasants and beggars engaged in what appeared to be odd and unpleasant gatherings. I glanced into the kitchen and saw enamelled appliances and yellow lino that could not have been changed since the Second World War, and wooden cupboards painted buttercup yellow with little glass doors that protected thin china sets. The dining room was mostly draped in white sheets tarnished with dust, but the chandelier, above a table fit for a boardroom, glittered in what little light seeped inside from the hallway. This place had not been lived in for decades; I knew that at once. Though part of it was occupied that night.

I listened outside the far door. Heard the low murmur of voices again, and something else. Something rhythmic. Like clapping. Gently clapping hands. There were several people inside the room. People who were also cooing in the way that adults make noises around infants. I cleared my throat. I knocked.

No one answered. Was I trespassing? About to intrude on some strange but private gathering that had nothing to do with my search for Mrs Van den Bergh? I feared I was, and experienced far more anxiety than curiosity about what was on the other side of the door.

I turned around and began to creep back down the hallway in a way that made my every footstep resemble the absurd mime of a man trying to withdraw quietly.

'Florine! Florine! Florine!'

After that, there was no mistaking the presence of Mrs

Van den Bergh within that room of dirty light and soft clapping and the incongruous cooing. And her utterances suggested that she was in a state of excitement not yet matched in my experience of her. I was instantly tempted to believe that Florine herself had made an appearance within that room.

'Enough of this,' I said. It could not go on. I had to remove the resident from this place and take her back to her chair and strap her in. Without another thought, I acted. I opened the door.

Round and round they went in the large bedroom. In the slow up and down dance, one foot after the other, the residents staggered in their ungainly circle.

I did not know where to look at first, and saw everything in a jittering panorama because my eyes would not allow themselves to settle for long on any single detail. Not on the diminutive Hussein sisters, naked as cadavers and shrivelled as figs; or the worm-white Mrs Goldstein prancing with those sticks, her hair extending wildly from her scalp as if she had been hit by a gale, and her empty paps with black nipples flapping; or the long and dry Mrs Van den Bergh, with her eyes rolled back white, and the gurgling from her stringy throat and the big hands thrown up to the ceiling. I didn't look long at the others either, whom I had never seen before, but immediately understood them to be the bedridden residents who had somehow made it down here for this occasion. Some *thing* with skin like a plucked bird went up and down, up and down, from heel to toe, heel to toe, and shook its wisps of hair about in delirium. Others tottered like undraped wooden puppets with their strings cut, or the fossils of birds suddenly reanimated out of stone, and they must have been even older than the figures that I recognised. But all did their very best to hop and teeter in that circle. And all of them carried the shrunken flaps behind their shoulders with the skin that looked like the salted cod, rolled into sheets, that I had once seen in Norway. Flightless birds, I thought. Not extinct, but nearly.

And it was an elegant drinks trolley that the bony procession was moving about in this grotesque whirlpool of brittle limbs and gargles and skin like the parchment of dusty scrolls. And upon the top tier of the old and highly polished silver trolley was arranged a set of pickling jars, made from thick glass, with heavy wooden plugs rammed into the necks to keep the occupants safe from exposure to the air. The small figures inside the jars were adrift in a thick but semi-transparent fluid. Their limbs were as pale and delicate as cartilage, but their heads were enlarged and bulbous, thin as eggshell, with tiny faces at rest. On the back of one small body I saw appendages no bigger than thumbs, or unformed wings.

A second sedentary circle had formed around the skipping residents. It was the nurses and carers, and they were responsible for the clapping and the cooing sounds. They wore little crowns of golden paper on their heads and had all dressed in their finest clothes for the occasion. And they encouraged their wards to hop and stagger like that, round and round and round.

No one even looked at me, agape in that doorway. Though I thought at one point that Mrs Goldstein hissed at me from the side of her mouth, as she skittered past.

The first one to break ranks was Helma. Shaking with excitement, she ran to the head of the room, and then padded her hands along the wall until she reached the middle. It was not a wall, but a wooden screen. I had seen the same arrangement in a studio flat, and also in a hotel; an attempt to give one room the potential of becoming two, for privacy. Something I thought odd on every occasion, including this one.

I was sure, with every molecule in my being, that I did not want to see what was on the other side of the screen.

But before I could wrench myself away, Helma had the screen opening along its ancient brass runners, the wooden panels folding flat like a concertina.

In my strengthless delirium of disgust and fear and shock, I then stared across the bobbing of the stained skulls and the thin arms of the prancing circle, and I caught a glimpse of the father of this extended family. Bedridden, mercifully, but still keen enough to raise his great horned head from the enormous bed, in order to smile on what must have been his wives, their staff and the bottled offspring who would bear him no heirs.

The Ancestors

It never stops raining at the new house. When you are upstairs it sounds like hundreds of pebbles thrown by as many little hands onto the pointy roof. We can't go outside to play so we stay indoors and amuse ourselves with the toys. They belong to Maho, but she is happy to share them with me. My parents never knew about Maho, but she is my best friend and she lives in the house too. Maho has been here a long time.

When Mama used to come upstairs to put clean clothes in my drawers, or Papa knocked on the door to tell me that dinner was ready, Maho would hide and wait in my room until I could play with the toys again. Maho sleeps in my bed too, every night. I wish I had hair like her. Maho's hair is long and silky. When she puts her arms around me and hugs me, I am covered by her hair. Tucking itself under my arms and winding around my neck, her hair is so warm that I never need the blankets on my bed. I think her hair feels like black fur too, and like big curtains she pulls her hair across her face so all that I can see is her little square teeth. 'How can you see through your hair, Maho?' I once asked her. 'It looks so funny.' She just giggled. And with their teeny fingers the toys like to touch her hair too. They stand and sway on the bed and stroke it.

In the daytimes the toys never do much, but we still go looking for them in the empty rooms and in the secret places that Mama and Papa never knew about. When we find a toy sitting upright in a corner, or standing still after stopping dancing on those tiny fast feet, we talk to them. The toys just listen. They can hear everything you say. Sometimes they smile.

But at night the toys do most of the playing. They always have things to show us. New tricks and dances all around the bed. I'll be fast asleep but their little hard fingers will touch my face. Cold breath will brush my ears as they say, 'Hello. Hello,' until I wake up. At first I was scared of the tiny figures on the bed, all climbing and tugging at the sheets, and I would run and get into bed with Mama and Papa. But Maho told me that the toys just want to be my friends and play. Maho says you don't need a mama and papa when you have so many friends and I guess she is right. Parents don't understand. Most of the time they think about other things. That's why they weren't needed for the playing.

Maho told me that when the other children who lived here grew up and left the house all of their toys stayed behind. And it's an old house so there are lots of toys. Maho never left either. She never left her friends. Like I did when we moved out here. I told Maho my parents made me move. 'See,' she said. 'Parents don't understand about friends. About how much we love our friends, and how special secret places are to us. You can't just leave them because papas get new jobs or are sick. It's not fair. Who says things have to change and you have to go to new places when you're happy where you are?'

I didn't want to move here and I was scared of the new school. But since I made friends with Maho and the toys it isn't so bad. I like it here now and I will never go to that school. Maho knows a way around that. She'll show me soon and the toys will help.

There are so many toys. We find them everywhere: beneath the stairs and under the beds, in the bottom of trunks and behind the doors, up in the attic and looking through holes. You never know where they're going to show up. Most of the time you have to wait for them to come to you. And sometimes you can only hear them moving about. Mama thought we had mice in the house and Papa put traps down. Maho was angry when she showed me the traps in the kitchen and in the cellar. Toys don't eat coloured seeds, she said, pointing at the blue poisonous oats, but sometimes they dance too close to the snapping traps. Twice we had to rescue them before the morning. A dolly with a china face got one of her long arms stuck in a trap in the pantry. She was squealing and the thin arm covered in black hair had snapped. When we freed her, Maho picked her up and kissed her cold face. When she put the dolly down the dolly ran behind some bottles and we didn't see her again for three nights. Then the old thing with the black face and whitish beard got his pinky tail all smashed in the trap by the mop and dustpan in the cellar. When we let him loose, he showed us teeth as thin as needles and then he crawled away.

Three nights back, when Mama and Papa were supposed to be sleeping, I know Papa saw a toy. There were plenty of them out that night, skipping mostly. The first of them came out of the fireplace. 'Hello,' a little voice said to me. I was only dozing because I was too excited about the playing, so I wound Maho's silky hair off my face – it goes in my ears and up my nose too – and I sat up in bed. 'Hello,' I said to the little thing down on the rug. They don't like lights, so you only see them properly when they get real close, but even in the shadows I knew I'd seen this one before. He was the one with the top hat and little suit. His shirt is white, but his face is all red and his eyes are black and shiny like marbles. He went round and round in a circle on skipping feet and in the room I could smell sneezes and old clothes. But Maho's right: you get used to the smell of the toys.

She sat up beside me and said, 'Hello.'

The toy stopped his dancing and said, 'Hello.'

Then we heard the drum, but we couldn't see the musician. He was in the room with us. Under the bed, I think, and playing his leather drum. He shines like the brown shoes that I once saw made from alligator and he creaks like old gloves when he moves. As usual, when he played the drum, the clown in the dirty blue and white pyjamas came out to dance also. All around the bed he went with his shabby arms thrown up towards the ceiling and his head flopping back. His mouth is all stitched up and his eyes are white and bobble on his cloth face.

I leaned over the bed to get a better look.

'Best not to touch *him*,' Maho whispered into my ear and her coldish breath made me shiver inside. 'He's very old. He once belonged to a boy whom he loved very much, but he was taken away from the boy by parents. So he climbed inside the boy's mouth to fix the broken heart.'

I wanted to ask what happened to the boy, but Maho turned her head to the door so that I couldn't see her face. 'Your papa is coming.' But I couldn't hear a thing. I looked at her and frowned. 'Listen,' she said, and she took hold of my hands. Then I heard a floorboard moan. Papa was outside in the hallway, going to the toilet. Papa was not well at that time. That's why we came here, so that he could rest his head. He never slept very much at night and we had to be careful when we played with the toys. 'Some toys are out there,' Maho whispered. 'He might see them again.' She was smiling through her hair when she said this, but I didn't know why.

The man with the top hat skipped back inside the chimney. Under the bed the drumming stopped.

The next morning my family sat at the kitchen table. We never ate in the dining room because Mama couldn't get rid of the smell. She tried to find cheerful music on the radio, but it sounded all fuzzy so she turned it off. Her mouth was very tight so I knew she was angry and worried too. She gave up on the radio and pointed at my bowl. 'Eat up, Yuki,' she said, then looked at the window. Rain smacked against the glass. Watching the water run down made me feel all cold inside.

Papa said nothing. He just looked at the table next to his bowl. His eyes were red and his chin was bristly. When he kissed me that morning I shouted out for him to stop. All night I'd been wrapped in soft black hair and his chin felt like it was covered in pins. And he still wasn't looking any better, even though he didn't have to go to work any more.

'Taichi,' Mama said. She was upset with him. Slowly, Papa lifted his head and looked at her.

'Eat or it will go cold,' Mama had said. She had fried the rice with eggs the way that he liked, with salmon on top that gets warm from the steam. Papa tried to smile but he was just too tired. He looked at me instead. 'Finished?' he asked.

As my spoon clunked in the empty bowl his eyelids flickered. I nodded.

'You can go.'

I climbed down from my chair and ran into the hall.

'Sit still for a while,' Mama cried out. 'Or you'll be sick.'

I walked down the hall, then took my shoes off and sneaked back to the kitchen door that Mama closed behind me. My parents wanted to talk. First thing in the morning they would talk to each other, but they would stay in different rooms for the rest of the day. Papa would mostly sit in a chair and stare at nothing, while Mama kept busy with washing and cooking and cleaning. One day she was crying in the kitchen by the cookbooks, which made me cry too. She stopped when she saw me and said that she was 'just being silly'. But at night I often heard Mama shouting at Papa. When this happened Maho always held me tighter and put her silky hair over my ears until I fell asleep.

'What is it? Tell me, Taichi. I can't help if you don't tell me,' Mama said in the kitchen that morning, and in a voice that was quiet but also sharp enough for me to hear through the door.

'Nothing.'

'It can't be nothing. You haven't slept again.'

'It's nothing. When it stops raining I'll go out.'

A bowl hit the side of the sink. Mama then had a voice full of tears. 'I can't stand this any more. This isn't working. It's making you worse.'

'Mai, please. I can't… I can't tell you.'

'Why?'

'Because you would think I'm crazy.'

'Crazy? You're making yourself crazy. You're making me crazy. This was a mistake. I knew it.'

'Maybe. The house… I don't know.'

A chair scraped against the floor. Mama must have sat down. Her voice went soft and I guessed that she was holding his hand.

'Yuki.' It was Maho calling me. Standing at the top of the stairs, she waved at me to join her. Because I wanted to hear what Papa was saying, I smiled at her but put a finger against my lips. Maho shook her head and her hair moved across her face to cover all of the white bits. 'No. Come and play,' she said. But I turned my head back to the kitchen because Papa was talking again.

'I saw something again.'

'What, Taichi? What did you see?'

His voice was all shaky. 'I have to go to the doctor again. I'm going crazy.'

'What? What did you see?' Mama's voice was going high and I could tell that she was trying not to cry again.

'I… I went to the toilet. Last night. And it was there again.'

'What, Taichi? What?'

'Sitting on the window sill. I told myself that I was still dreaming. I stopped and I closed my eyes and made sure that I was awake. Look at the bruise on my arm where I pinched myself. Then I opened my eyes and *it* was still there. So I pretended that it wasn't. That it was just a bad dream. I ignored it. But when I came out of the bathroom, *it* was still just sitting there. Watching me.' In the kitchen they stopped talking, and all I could hear was the rain. Thousands of little drops hitting the wood and tiles and glass all around us.

'You were dreaming,' Mama said after a while. 'It's the medicine, Taichi. The side-effects.'

'No. I stopped taking the medicine.'

'What?'

'Just for a while to see if *they* would go.'

'They?'

'Yuki. Yuki. Come and play. Come,' Maho whispered from behind me. She was coming down the stairs on silent feet.

'I don't know,' My Papa said. 'A little thing… with long legs that hang over the window sill. And its face, Mai. I can't sleep after I see its face.'

'Yuki, look what I found. In a cupboard. Come and see,' Maho said from behind me and reached out to take my hand. When I turned around to tell her to be quiet, I saw that her dolly eyes were wet. So I went up the stairs with her. I can't stand to see Maho cry. 'What's wrong, Maho? Please don't be sad.'

She led me into the empty room upstairs, at the end of the hall, and we sat on the wooden floor. In there it's always cold. There is only one window. Water ran down the outside and made the trees in the garden all blurry. Maho's head was bowed. Her hair fell over her white gown all the way down to her lap. We held hands. 'Why are you crying, Maho?'

'Your papa.'

'He's sick, Maho. But he'll get better. He told me.'

She shook her head, then lifted it. Tears ran down from the one wet eye that I could see through her hair. 'Your mama and papa want to leave. And I don't want you to go. Not ever.'

'I'll never leave you, Maho.' Now she was making me sad and I could taste the sea at the back of my throat.

She sniffed inside her hair. The rain was very loud on the roof and it sounded like it was raining inside the room. 'You promise?' she said.

I nodded. 'I promise. You are my best friend, Maho.'

'Your parents don't understand the toys.'

'I know.'

'They just want to play. Your papa should sleep and let them play. If he finds out about me and the toys then he will take you away from us.'

'No. Never.' We hugged each other and Maho told me she loved me, and told me that the toys loved me. I kissed her silky hair and against my lips I felt her cold ear.

Downstairs, I heard the kitchen door open and then close. Maho took her arms away and uncurled her hair from around my neck. 'Your mama wants you.' Tears were still running down her white face.

She was right because I heard feet coming up the stairs. 'Yuki?' Mama called out. 'Yuki?'

'I have to go,' I told Maho and stood up. 'I'll come right back and we can play.'

She didn't answer me. Her head was bowed so that I couldn't see her face.

'Yuki, what would you say if I told you we might be moving? Going back to the city?' Mama looked at me, smiling. She thought this news would make me happy, but I couldn't stop my face feeling all long and heavy. Mama was sitting on the floor next to me in the cold room where she found me. Even though Maho had hidden I knew that she was still listening. 'Wouldn't you like that?' Mama asked me, 'You'll see all of your friends again. And go to the same school.' She looked surprised that I was not smiling. 'What is wrong, Yuki?'

'I don't want to.'

She frowned. 'But you were so upset when we moved here.'

'But I like it now.'

'You're all alone. You need your friends, my darling. Don't you want to play with Sachi and Hiro again?'

I shook my head. 'I can play here. I like it.'

'On your own in this big house? With all this rain? You are being silly, Yuki.'

'No, I'm not.'

'You will get tired of this. You can't even go outside and use the swing.'

'I don't want to go outside.'

She looked at the floor. Her fingers were very white and thin where they held my arms. Mama sniffed back her tears before they could come out. She put the back of one hand to her eyes and I heard her swallow. 'Come out of here. It's dirty.'

I was going to say, I like it in here, but I knew that she would get angry if I said that. So I stayed quiet and followed her to the door. In the corner, in the shadow, I saw a bit of Maho's white face as she watched us leave. And above us, in the attic, little feet suddenly went pattering. Mama looked up, then hurried me out of the room and closed the door.

That night, after Papa finished my bedtime story, he kissed my forehead. He still hadn't shaved and his lips felt spiky. He pulled the blankets up to my chin. 'Try and keep these on the bed tonight, Yuki. Every morning they are on the floor and you feel as cold as ice.'

'Yes, Papa.'

'Maybe tomorrow the rain will stop. We can go and look at the river.'

'I don't mind the rain, Papa. I like to play inside the house.'

Frowning and looking down at my blankets, Papa thought about what I had said. 'Sometimes in old houses little girls have bad dreams. Do you have bad dreams, Yuki? Is that why you kick the sheets off?'

'No.'

He smiled at me. 'That's good.'

'Do you have bad dreams, Papa?'

'No, no,' he said, but the look in his eyes said yes. 'The medicine makes it hard for me to sleep. That's all.'

'I'm not scared. The house is very friendly.'

'Why do you say that?'

'Because it is. It just wants to make friends. It's so happy we're here.'

Papa laughed. 'But the rain. And all the mice here, Yuki. It's not much of a welcome.'

I smiled. 'There are no mice here, Papa. The toys don't like mice. They ate them all up.'

Papa stopped laughing. In his throat I watched a lump move up and down.

'You don't have to worry about them, Papa. They're my friends.'

'Friends?' His voice was very quiet. 'Toys? You've seen them?' His voice was so tiny that I could hardly hear him.

I nodded, and smiled to make him stop worrying. 'When all the children left, they stayed behind.'

'Where… where do you see them?'

'Oh, everywhere. But mostly at night. That's when they come out to play. They usually come out of the fireplace.' I pointed at the dark place in the corner of my room. Papa stood up quickly and turned around to stare at the fireplace. Outside my window the rain stopped falling on the world that it had made so soft and wet.

The next morning, Papa found something inside the chimney in my room. He started the search in my bedroom with the broom handle and the torch, poking around up there and knocking all the soot down, which clouded across the floor. Mama wasn't happy, but when she saw the little parcel that dropped down from the chimney, she went quiet.

'Look,' Papa said. He held his arm out with the package

on the palm of his hand. They took it into the kitchen and I followed.

Papa blew on it and then wiped it clean of ash with the paint brush from under the kitchen sink. On the table Mama put a piece of newspaper under the parcel. I stood on a chair and we all looked at the bundle of dirty cloth. Then Papa told Mama to get her little scissors from her sewing box. When Mama came back with the scissors, Papa carefully cut into the dry wrappings. Then he peeled them away from the tiny hand inside.

Mama spread her fingers over her mouth. Papa just sat back and looked at it, like he didn't want to touch it. All around us we could hear the rain hitting the windows and rattling on the roof. It sounded louder than ever before. Then I knelt on the table and Mama scolded me for getting too close. 'It could have germs.'

I thought it was a chicken's foot, cut from a yellow leg, like the ones you see in the windows of restaurants in the city. But it had five curly fingers with long nails. Before I could touch it, Mama wrapped it up in newspaper and stuffed it deep inside the kitchen bin.

But there were others. In the empty room at the end of the hallway, Papa knocked another parcel out of the chimney and took it down to the kitchen again. At first, my Mama wouldn't even look at the tiny shoe, even before we found the bone foot inside. She stood by the window and watched the wet garden. Leafy branches moved out there in the heavy rain, like they were waving at the house.

The shoe was made of pinky silk and my Papa untied the little ribbons. It opened with a puff of dust and he emptied the teeny foot onto the table. The rattle sound made Mama look over shoulder. 'Throw it away, Taichi. I don't want it in the house,' she said.

Papa looked at me and raised his eyebrows. We went off looking for more. In the big parlour downstairs while he was poking up inside the chimney, he told me the little parcels belonged to ancestors. 'This is a very old house. And when it was built, the people put little charms in secret places. Under the floors, in the cellars and up inside the chimneys to protect the house from bad spirits.'

'But why are they so small?' I asked Papa. 'Was it a baby's foot in the shoe?'

He never answered me and just kept poking around, up inside the chimney with the broom handle. Papa was very clever, but I don't think he knew the answers to my questions. These things he was finding had something to do with the toys, I was sure, so I decided I would ask Maho when I saw her later. She disappeared while I was eating breakfast and was still hiding because Papa was going into every room and searching about.

The next parcel we found was a tiny white sack, tied up with string, with brownish stains at the bottom. But right after Papa opened it and poured the hard black lumps onto the kitchen table, he quickly wrapped them up in newspaper and put them inside the kitchen bin with the hand and the foot. 'What are they?' I asked him.

'Just some old stones,' he said.

But they didn't look like stones. They were very light and black and reminded me of dried salt fish.

Papa stopped looking after that and swept up the soot from the floorboards instead. While he did this, Mama stood on a chair in their bedroom to get the suitcases down from the wardrobe. And I couldn't find Maho anywhere. She never came out all day. I looked everywhere, in all of our secret places, but I never found her or saw any of the toys either. I whispered her name into all of the tiny holes but she never answered. But when I was checking inside the attic, I heard Mama and Papa talking underneath the loft hatch. 'A heart,' Papa whispered to Mama. 'A tiny heart' was all I heard before they moved away and went downstairs.

That night, when Maho climbed into bed with me, she held me tighter than ever before and wrapped me up in her silky hair so that I could hardly move. It was so dark inside her hair that I couldn't see anything and I told her to let me go. I couldn't breathe, but she was in a strange sulky mood and she just squeezed me with her cold hands until I felt sleepy.

Outside, the rain stopped and the house started to creak like the old ship that we went on one summer. Eventually Maho spoke. She said that she had missed me. In a yawny voice, I asked her about the shoe, the foot and the little bag with the lumps inside that Papa had found in the chimneys.

'They belong to the toys,' Maho said. 'Your papa shouldn't have taken away things that belong to the toys. It was a mistake. It was wrong.'

'But they were old and dirty and nasty,' I told her.

'No,' she said. 'They belong to the toys. They put them up there a long time ago, and they shouldn't be removed by parents. They're like happy memories to the toys. Now sleep, Yuki. Sleep.'

I couldn't understand this. While I was thinking about what Maho said, I started to fall asleep. It was so warm inside all of that hair. And she sang a little song into my ear and rubbed her cold nose against my cheek like a puppy dog.

Outside my bedroom in the hallway I heard the toys gathering. More toys than ever before had come out to play. All at the same time, and all in the same place. This had never happened before. It must have been a special occasion, like a parade. They had a parade when Maho's parents left. 'Toys. Can you hear the toys?' I whispered into the black fur around my face, and then I dropped further into the deep hole of sleepiness.

Maho didn't answer me, so I just listened to the toys moving through the dark. Little feet shuffled; pinkish tails whisked on wood; bells jingled on hats and from the curly toes of thin feet; *tap tappity tap* went the wooden sticks of the old apes; *twik twik twik* went the lady with knitting needle legs; *clackety clack* sounded the hooves of the black horsy with yellow teeth; *tisker tisker tisker* went the cymbal of the dolly with the sharp fingers; *dum dum dum* went the drum; and on and on they marched through the house. Down, down and down the hall.

Shouting woke me up. Through my sleep and all the dark softness around my body, I heard a loud voice. I thought it was Papa. But when my eyes opened the house was silent. I tried to sit up, but couldn't move my arms and my feet. Rolling from side to side, I made some space in Maho's hair. It was everywhere and all around me. 'Maho? Maho?' I said. 'Wake up, Maho.'

But she just held me tighter with her thin arms. Blowing the hair out of my mouth, I tried to move a hand so that I could take the long strands from out of my eyes. I couldn't see anything. Maho wouldn't help me either, and it took me a long time to unwind the silky ropes from around my neck and off my face, and to shake them from my arms and from between my fingers and toes where they tugged and pulled. In the end, I had to flop onto my tummy and then wriggle backwards through the funnel of her black hair. She was fast asleep and very still and wouldn't wake up when I shook her.

I could only sit up properly when I reached the bottom of the bed. All the sheets and blankets were on the floor again. I climbed off the bed and ran into the unlit hall. I couldn't see the cold floorboards and could only hear the patter of my bare feet on the wood as I moved down to Mama and Papa's room. The door to their room was open. Maybe Papa was having a bad dream and was awake, so I stood outside and looked in.

It was very dark inside their room, but something was moving. I screwed up my eyes and stared at where the thin light coming around the curtains had fallen, and then I saw that the whole bed was moving. 'Mama,' I said.

It looked like Mama and Papa were trying to sit up but couldn't. And all the sheets around them were rustling. Someone was making a moaning sound, but it didn't sound like Mama or Papa. It sounded like someone was trying to speak with their mouth full. And there was another sound coming from the bed too, and getting louder as I stood there. A wet sound. Like lots of busy people eating noodles in a Tokyo diner.

The door closed and I turned around to look behind me. I knew Maho was there before I even saw her.

Maho looked at me through her hair. 'The toys are only playing,' she said.

She took my hand and led me back to our bed. I climbed in after her and she wrapped me up in all that hair. And together we listened to the sounds of the toys putting things into the secret places, behind the walls, where they belonged.

The Age of Entitlement

At dusk, when all about us faded, we walked in silence down the deserted street called Rue du Sous-Lieutenant de Loitière that neither of us knew how to pronounce. Ahead of us, even though we could not see its surging beyond the white stone and slate-coloured buildings on Quai du Canada, we knew the sea was going black. That street was closest to the ocean and appeared more than empty. It was dead.

The streets of Arromanches were not ruined. Not so much as a window was broken. Nor were they all yet derelict; though I was never sure which were and which were still occupied. The flags had been taken down; the tanks and field artillery, preserved since the Second World War, were rusted, the cafés and museums had closed, and the veterans who once visited here were long dead. But more than the desolate and sombre inland reach of the town, huddled into itself and shuffling away from the seafront, the actual buildings facing the ocean were lifeless, spent, somehow, as if they had already been overcome.

We could sense the ocean's swallowing of the watery light, and we could hear the endless tumult of its cold choppy heaving, the great restless sighs. Insensible, timeless, the water pulled us down to the shore and into a terrifying orbit. To think I once regarded the sea with fondness, its fragrance and bird calls producing a sense of comfort. Now the mere thought of its existence as we are erased, nation by nation, made me shudder. And that morning, right after we arrived at Le Havre, while standing before the great expanse of water, my inner world was crushed to a thing insubstantial. As with my perception of the black infinite depths above the earth, the water's unbreathable immensity felt closer to the land than it had ever been before. Too near, somehow. In Arromanches this feeling was acute.

My heart beat fast. Panic swelled up my throat. I gulped at the cold air. 'The sky is closer. The sea is closer. The light is going out.' When I said this to Toby on the street called Rue du Sous-Lieutenant de Loitière, he smiled with no warmth and too many teeth. I desperately wanted reassurance, but he was delighted by my discomfort.

Our relationship had always been an unbalanced thing. I amused Toby, and took care of the practical matters that he required to make these journeys. I think they were the only reasons that he tolerated my fretting, anxious presence at his side. Like an old relative or servant, deferring to someone younger and more powerful and spoilt and knowing: that's how he made me feel. I despised him.

'It's good shit.' He was referring to the contents of the little brown glass bottle he often kept inside the breast pocket of his tatty Gore-Tex waterproof. I had barely touched the drug; earlier that day, in our room at the guest house, I had taken a mere sip of the bitter syrup before we began exploring Bayeux at noon. But Toby had filled his mouth with it, until his teeth were filmed with the old bloodstaining of neat iodine. Which is why his eyes were still glassy, and why he had lain down in the wet overgrown grass of the War Cemetery beneath the abandoned Musée Mémorial de la Bataille de Normandie and stared at the dismal grey sky, all afternoon, in silence. He was content to lie among the unkempt graves of five thousand dead soldiers whom no one has the energy to honour any more, after all that has happened so quickly in this world.

Toby has no interest in recording the *experiences* any more either; or of talking about them; or relaying them to me; or making sense of them. He was content merely to endure the episodes, in silence, over and over again. He said nothing to me besides, 'But are they willing to be forgotten? That is the question, my dear.' And he had giggled like an infant after he'd tempted the fallen, so brazenly, to appear.

That was the nature of my fear, close to the shore in Arromanches, of things being pulled in at me, on that vacant street, and all at once too. My gaze was drawn to the grey stone walls, bordering the weed-wretched gardens, at the rear of the once grand hotels on our right. Then my vision groped to the windows above, set within bricks seared by salt and lashed by wet winds for centuries. And in the second-storey window of the building that neighboured the derelict church, I saw a figure.

I stopped and inhaled so sharply that I unleashed a tiny scream that turned and fled back down my throat.

The figure's scrutiny had alerted me to its presence; it had been watching me and then suddenly turned away the very moment I had looked in that direction. Not vanishing, but merely turning its back to me, which I could still see, robed in something long and smooth and pale; the tone in keeping with the chalky light that the Impressionists once adored here, so long ago. The head of the figure was cowled. And both hands were pressed against the hooded face so that I would not see its expression.

'Jesus,' I said, and the word trembled on leaving my mouth.

'What?' Toby said, looking at me and frowning with a tired indifference.

I swallowed, unable to speak, clenched into the cold paralysis of a short and powerful shock.

Toby turned and followed my eyes. 'What?' he said again.

I pointed at the window. 'There.' He shrugged, so I stepped up beside him. 'There!' I jabbed my finger toward the window in which the figure still stood, exposing itself and yet pleading with us not to stare at it, not to see such grief. This was not mourning, this was desolation; I knew so at once.

'What am I looking… Oh, yeah. But what… ?'

'It moved. Turned away. Covered its face.'

'Let's go look,' Toby said, and he strode across the road to the garden wall.

'No. No,' I cried out, and I marvelled at his complete insensitivity. This figure at the window required a respectful distance; was to be looked at briefly and then left alone. I knew this instinctively. But Toby was so brash. With the feelings of others, if I am to be honest, he was a vandal and a trespasser. His incessant seeking of sensation, of the esoteric, of the weird, of visceral experience delivered in full glare, of risk and danger, troubled me at that moment, on that road, more than anything else that I had watched him do, in all of the twenty-three years that I had known him.

But I could not rationally account for why his leering intrusion here shocked me sick. This involved no swallowing of unidentified pills, no deliberate losing of oneself in strange places, no camping in extreme landscapes with unsuitable gear, no going in through dark windows, or provoking the unstable with alcohol and rude cleverness; his intrusion here would carry a heavier penalty. To impose and interfere would be sacrilegious. How I knew this I cannot tell you exactly. Suffice to say, this was a place in which a multitude had died so horribly in a forgotten war. And as Toby and I have seen, in those places where so many ended their days in great swathes through violence, their desire to remain can *invest* where they fell. Because they reach, I tell you; and they clutch for ever at where they sense the light once was. I have warned Toby of this realm that is only ever sensed or glimpsed in certain places at certain times. But sometimes this region, which I suggest is a kind of parallel non-existence, is thrown wide open. Like *here*, which accounted for my extraordinary nervousness since we'd alighted from the one ferry that each week still ends its line on this near-abandoned Normandy coastline.

Of course, that is precisely why Toby had wanted to come here, with me as his guide. He had heard *things* about the place. And I was a Labrador to a blind man. I took him across things. I led him around obstacles. He would have walked directly past the figure in the window had I not been at his side suffering an anxiety attack; the very peak of my seizure had resulted in the drawing out of… of *what*, I do not know.

'Statue,' he said, his voice dropping with disappointment, and contempt for me as if I had failed to entertain him enough with the sighting. Then, his tone buoyant, he added, 'But it's still pretty amazing.'

I felt some relief that it was only a statue, but not for long. This carving in stone of a woman wretched with grief, turning inwards and away from the world, covering her features and clasping her terror and despair right back upon her own face, made me wither; shrink before all that it symbolised in this dark and dying place. And I bowed my head and closed my eyes at the mere thought of who the sculptor had modelled this figure upon, or of what the weary yet tireless yearning from beneath the waves had *invested* into stone. I wanted to scream at Toby again that 1,807 bodies eviscerated within the salty shallows and between the neat hedgerows had still not been found. That we had to tread lightly and soundlessly, and keep our eyes and our voices down. What we had stirred up out of the derelict trenches at Vimy Ridge Memorial, during the previous summer, had made him vomit onto his own shoes. And I had fainted.

But Toby had no such concerns here, no such interpretation, as he stood before these cold, wet and mostly abandoned buildings of scoured stone, only yards away from the ghastly sea that slapped down upon the shingle and drowned the light.

The sea. Vast. Senseless. Monotonous. Dreadful. Nullifying, like the expanding, freezing abyss above us that was indifferent to this blue grain of life we stood upon. Specks upon a speck. The sea and the sky were almost touching here; *could he not feel it*? Here was extinction.

The sudden roaring of my imagination nearly put out its own light with a hiss. I squeezed my nails into the palms of my hands and said the words; the invocation. Said the words over and over again to evoke myself back into myself. Then I relaxed my shoulders, exhausted.

Toby remained at the wall, staring, enthralled by the distant stone figure behind glass. The room around the figure was dark. And then Toby spoke without any emotion, but his words made my bones ache with cold, and the skin around these bones prickled. 'There are others. Look.'

I joined him at the old wall. And I looked into the neighbouring house. A similar figure stood alone, cowled and robed, with the head turned away from the world, the face clutched. That one stood immobile too; a sentinel at a second-storey window. On the other side of the church, a third stone figure filled a side window in a miserable concrete building, the blue metal roof peeling. It must once have been a garage.

'Wonder why they are there?' Toby asked, his query sincere.

To me, the figures seemed to be sealing the empty buildings, or marking them as condemned, or as unstable, as *invested*. These statues signified places where the dead rose more freely, as the living made room: where the dead *invested* into things and into spaces. 'Let's get back.'

'This is so cool.'

There have been times in our companionship when I have dearly wished to destroy Toby, physically; this was another one of those times.

As soon as we were back inside our room at the guest house, Toby stretched out on his bed. Still wearing his coat and his muddy boots, he closed his eyes and was snoring within a minute. His muddy footwear soiled the bottom of the bedspread that the withered and yellowing old lady who owned the pension would have to scrub.

Hunger, sitting in the cold cemetery watching over Toby all afternoon, and the recent episode in the street, had weakened me. Quietly, I made my way over to the little table upon which we had placed the remainder of our lunch for the car journey from Le Havre. Inside the plastic box, I made the discovery that Toby had eaten, without my knowledge, the last two sandwiches, the bag of crisps and my chocolate bar. I looked at the tray that bore the kettle and hot-drink materials that came with the room. Earlier, I'd seen two packets of complimentary shortbread biscuits. These he had also eaten. The plastic wrappers were discarded beside the broken television.

When I realised that my grinding my teeth risked breaking one of them, I unclenched my jaw and rubbed it. And I looked again at him on the bed, his snoring now vibrating through the walls and filling the chilly air. His thin face was pale, his pinched mouth open. His curly white hair seemed too youthful for his face, like he was an old man in a girl's wig. I wanted to kick him off the bed and stamp and stamp and stamp on his curly-bitch head.

Instead, I looked away. Beyond the window, the sea and the sky were black, as if existence ended outside the glass. The sudden intense heat in my body abated and left my head aching. There was still some tea and coffee in sachets, but boiling the kettle might wake him.

I cursed myself for such an act of consideration; a human instinct he knew nothing of, because he had never displayed it once in our long friendship. Toby immediately placated any impulsive appetite that he experienced, with no regard for anyone else's needs. He was a snatcher, a grabber; or he expected everything he needed to be provided everywhere, all of the time. He was entitled. And his contempt for me was reaching unmanageable levels. But now I knew exactly what accounted for his contempt; now it all made sense to me. Now, *he* made sense. And what was worse than his revelation in the car about his family background was the fact that we cannot change our natures.

In the dark, I sat my drained and tired body down upon the end of my bed. It had gone eight.

I thought of what he had said to me in such an offhand manner in the car, and of how it had numbed me to the core. I had been poor company thereafter. In the passenger seat, Toby had read my shock and merely adopted a smirk that had lasted for the remainder of the day. I had been too proud to lose my temper, too upset to speak. I had been betrayed, and betrayal is a powerful emotion that shuts down most of the mind, besides its ability to sustain the misery of betrayal, at least until rage takes over. And this was no lovers' tiff, because we were not lovers. But we had shared a bond that only lovers share. Or rather I realised, with a cold trickle of terror and shame in equal amounts, that what we had shared for twenty-three years was the devotion of a dog to its master; a master who considered his own needs as superior to those of the dog, and was soon to abandon the trusting hound too.

In that dim and fusty room in a boarding house on the shore of a relentless tide, I could not bring myself to list all of the things that I had sacrificed and missed in life, due to my misguided attachment to this man, this *friend*. But the listing of my grievances would come in time. There was always time for the listing of grievances in the long dark days that filled my existence.

Toby would soon return to a comfortable world full of potential and opportunity and promise that I had known nothing of in the last two decades. A world that he had deliberately kept hidden from me, and had retreated to during his enigmatic disappearances over the years.

This was to be our last journey together too: without a trace of remorse, he had told me as much, in the car, on the French side of the channel. After the trip's conclusion in two days, I would be left with so many silent hours of contemplation on wasted time and youth. And the memory of him and his deception, which would become viler in my mind, would always be there to accompany me as I sank back into a directionless, debilitating and miserable poverty. He did not state this, but we both knew it to be true.

What did any of these uncanny experiences of ours now mean? Our explorations in the abandoned and derelict corners of Great Britain, a country that now hurtled backwards to the social inequality of Queen Victoria's reign, had come to nothing. And so quick was Britain's regression through history that everyone had been taken by surprise. It was possible that the society would go even further back to feudalism, and then reach the new Dark Ages with a population to match. The situation was even worse in France; the French were now but a fraction of the population within their own countryside, and only the dead of ages remained *en masse*.

Toby and I had thought ourselves unique and above the disintegrating world. But what music, or poetry, or writing, or films, or art, had our collaborations in the esoteric achieved? What had our explorations of psychic geography in a dying world ever produced? Those creative ventures we had planned, and incessantly talked about, through long hours in the squats and grim flats that we had shared together, smoked in together, and in which we had withdrawn from the fallen world together, had degenerated into recreational drug use and a perpetual staring into space. We had become degenerate and hopeless, like most of what remained of the world.

I thought of those inexplicable stone figures in this town with their faces turned away. Without Toby, my fate would become theirs: cold as stone, an installation planted in isolation, paralysed with despair, waiting for the darkness to finally take everything away.

But if I protested too much about his abandonment of me, Toby would only shrug and smirk and merely tell me that I was being 'dramatic'. And then he would be gone into the light of comfort, into a grazing of pale female flesh, into vast warm rooms, and into so much money that his wealth will only cause him anxiety at the prospect of it being shared. And I will be left behind, in a place like this: a dead corner. My existence beyond whatever tiny grim space I occupy will amount to nothing more than him saying, 'I knew a chap once…' That will be my epitaph, an anecdote briefly spoken and then sinking in the fragrant air of some noisy party in Paris, or South Kensington, or Edinburgh, where the privileged congratulate themselves on still being privileged despite all that has happened in the world.

Better for me, and for all those he and his kind have exploited, if I had smothered him right then in that guest house, with one of the musty pillows, as he lay snoring like some sated king upon the faded candlewick bedspread. Over his thin pointy face I should have pressed down hard until his vigour was stoppered.

Instead of murder most just, I abandoned the unlit room; leaving the curtains open to the darkness, to the immensity that made an even greater mockery of my foolish trust and pathetic hopes. I went down and through the silent house and into a cold night roaring with ocean.

I imagined that some place, somewhere inside this dim town, must still serve food. Maybe hot food would have made me feel better too. But I would bring nothing back for Toby; I would sate my own hunger. For was I just to wait for him to awaken from his drugged stupor, and then find him nourishment, as I had always done? And as he would expect me to do, and at my own expense? He was entitled to what I could do for him; that was the essence of our relationship. And what one group of people can do for another has been revealed as the foundation of civilisation, now that all illusions of fairness have been doused, and now that nearly everything is in ruins. Perhaps greed is the very root of our species.

I walked down Quai du Canada and avoided looking at the great imploring sea, so idiotic in its surging. I did not want to be pulled into those black, churning waters. To my left, the long line of empty hotels and bars had unlit windows. Many were covered from the inside, with blankets nailed to sash frames, or old newspapers taped to the glass.

Before I turned inland, I saw another stone figure at a window. That one had withdrawn itself further inside the room. But in the ambient glow of one of the last working streetlamps, the figure still showed the black ocean its stone head, covered with a cowl and clutching white fingers.

I walked along Rue du Mézeray and Route de Ryes. Here too everything was closed, shuttered, derelict. But in the weak light of the lamps, from the occasional lit window above street level, I caught glimpses of other stone statues in the distant gloom of the empty gift shops, or crouching in despair behind the dirty glass of bankrupt estate agents, clothes shops and cafés. Each of the figures made me start, and I made sure not to stare for too long, in case my appalled scrutiny would draw me inside an empty shop front, to stand in horror in the darkness, in the dust with them, amongst the litter of flyers advertising pizza restaurants long gone.

I walked along the wider thoroughfare of Rue Marie-Rose Thonnard and saw not a soul. The restaurants were shuttered against indifference, one sustained long enough to fade their hoardings and signage; the coaches had long departed and left no trace; the shuffling tourists were less than a memory of a distant era when holidays were taken by any but the few. The darkness had come in from the sea and refilled the places in which human antics had once occurred.

On both sides of the Channel, what remained of us now drew together in greying cities to clutch at the charity that was thrown from the back of lorries. Or we stood in long lines, day after day, hunched toward the distant promise of something of colour. France was also being closed down, village by town, as if the villages and towns were little lights on some great grid that winked out on the *Grande Retraite* towards Paris, and had left the rest of this land in darkness. On the grid, the coastline was almost entirely black now, as if the sea was coming over the rim; thick and salty and toxic.

But in the abandoned places, other regions were either opening or had always been open but obscured by irrelevance. Without clutter and noise and traffic and so much electricity, strange flowers were now opening to the moon, and curious doors and windows were being left carelessly agape and uncovered. There was no life to be had in such spaces now being revealed; just the silent staring of what had *invested* itself, and will continue to do so until an unrecorded end of everything living. But that had done nothing to dim Toby's fascination with such things in such places. Until now, because here he was saying goodbye to it all; bidding farewell to the places where those left alive were outnumbered by the dead.

Back to the sea. Toward the seaward side of Arromanches, I found an open restaurant. And I studied its yellowing menu intently through the brown glass while my stomach gaped and burned. The broad windows were tinted to protect diners from the heat; many years ago someone had thought it a good idea. In the 70s perhaps. This town seemed to have known nothing of the brief peaks of prosperity that had come and gone since the decline. Like every other place here, the people left when the tourists left, or when the factories closed, or if the fields became overgrown, and the jobs vanished.

I checked the prices rather than the items on the restaurant menu. Vanity induced me to casually withdraw the coins from my pocket and count them; I knew exactly how much money I was carrying. Along with the crisp brown sheet of a treasured ten-euro note that I could not bear to part with was the last of my benefits in coinage: three euros and thirty-four cents. I'd had thirty-two cents, but I had found two greening one-cent coins close to the cemetery and had polished them into a serviceable lustre while Toby stared at the sky, from amongst the weeds and tombstones. My half of the guest house bill, five euros, was buried at the bottom of my rucksack. That five was gone, dead to me, and was to become the property of the yellowy woman soon enough.

There was to be no rib-eye steak or *bourguignon* for me that night. It would have to be soup of the day and a cup of coffee. When I returned to Wolverhampton, whatever remained of my money would then have to be meted out for two weeks until my next benefit payment. The length of time was staggering, and recalling it made me lightheaded. I even leaned against the glass of the restaurant for a moment to regain my balance. Inside the restaurant, I noticed a woolly head, hunched over a table, feeding.

The restaurant was warm. The walls were brown and tatty and peeling. The furniture municipal. The carpet hard under my feet. I could see no staff behind the counter with the curved glass sneeze screens and little golden lamps shielding empty hot plates. Despite the scores of tables, there was only one diner: what appeared to be an old man in a bad wig and a maternity dress, gobbling at soup. I kept my eyes away from him. Beside his table was a wheelchair and a plastic supermarket bag full of children's books.

I walked along the broad counter, peeking over and muttering 'Hello' towards the dim suggestion of a kitchen beyond a fire door. No one came out.

I sat at a table by a window; there was nothing to be seen through it besides some smudges of building exteriors and the odd globe of a street lamp. I could still hear the sea. For all I knew it was as black as oil now, and welling up the glass outside the restaurant.

A meagre old woman with a man's haircut eventually shuffled out of the dim kitchen and approached without looking at me once. She dropped a menu encased in a heavy binding on the table before me, and then retreated back behind the counter where she busied herself with things out of my sight. I felt awkward and under-dressed. I had not washed in three, no four… no, at least five days. I was pungent and rubbery beneath my waterproof and knitwear. Stupidly, I envied the disabled man his ghastly floral maternity dress; at least he was clean. What had possessed me to think that I could come inside here and eat?

I raised the leatherette menu, which was the size of a stamp album and tasselled. I affected a poise and nonchalance that filled me with a hot self-loathing. As if I, a scruffy man with soiled canvas shoes on his feet, ate in French restaurants as a matter of course. I was ridiculous.

I added the price of soup to the price of coffee and then counted my own money again, inside my head, to make sure that I had enough.

The waitress came back; she knew I was English. Who else would visit here now that the Americans stayed within their own borders, with their own dead? She barked more than she spoke. 'No steak. No stew. Just lemon sole, potato gratin.'

'Soup?'

She nodded.

'Soup. And to drink, I'll have… a cup of coffee. White. Sugar.'

She snatched the menu off me.

'Bread with the soup?' I asked, and tried to keep the desperation out of my voice.

'Extra.'

'How much?'

'Furty cents.'

'Great. Thank you.'

She was already walking away from the table as I thanked her. I fretted that she had not taken my order for bread. I felt that I would die without bread. I had only eaten two sandwiches at eleven, and had been saving the crisps and chocolate that Toby had eaten for later.

But I think the soup was the best thing that I had ever eaten, and there was plenty of it. I soaked it into the two slices of white bread and then crammed them into my mouth. When I had finished eating, I sat back and sipped my coffee. Feeling magnanimous, expansive, a man of the world, I pondered a tip.

And left the restaurant without leaving one; the meal consumed most of my change, and I had deducted points because of the abrupt service. Thoughts of money had also spoiled the second half of the coffee, which I had swallowed without any memory of doing so. I had left my room in Wolverhampton the previous morning with forty euros to my name, but the ferry, petrol, guest house, the soup and the lunch that had I paid for, had left me with only ten euros to live on for a fortnight. A miserable prospect, but I had done so before, many times over the years, having eschewed a material lifestyle, as had Toby – 'because what is the point now?' – or so he'd always claimed.

Hunched over, I plodded back towards our lodging. I kept my head down to avoid the stone figures and my instinctive gaping at the sea; the horrified astonishment that I felt it wanted from me.

I was quickly consumed again by my petulant thoughts about paying for our lunch. It was not an unusual train of thought; spending what little I had on Toby inevitably began an interior discourse on the unfair division of our limited resources. But considering what Toby had so recently told me, about his father's directorship of a major surviving industry, and his parents' purchase of a large flat for their son in South Kensington in London, where he would now reside while working for his father's cremation empire, would it have been unreasonable for me to raise the matter of half the cost of our lunch?

This line of enquiry soon had me gasping for breath and slapping at the stone walls that I passed on my way back to the guest house. I even paused to scream, 'Jesus Christ!' at the black and utterly featureless sky. Cascading through my mind came specific memories, and phrases of his about our companionship. A terrific welling sensation of betrayal was the sole result of such musings.

Toby had always pleaded poverty for the twenty-three years that I had known him. I recalled his habitual rent-free living in my dismal flats and rooms. He'd always claimed to have no home address; to have successfully crafted a possession-free existence that involved living on the sofas and the floor-space of 'friends', and sometimes even in a tent on beaches and in verdant parks that no one used any more. And I had admired him for this; I had even recounted his exploits to anyone who would listen in the long aid queues. What had attracted me to Toby in the first place was his calm, his confidence, his refusal to worry, his aversion to any anxiety about money. And now I knew how such an attitude was sustained.

Back in the days when I could find work, how many jobs had I lost due to his insistence on my dropping everything and embarking on a new journey with him? Journeys that I had inevitably funded. And during that time when there was, at least, some work available to the educated but semi-skilled, how often had I called in sick when some new adventure was announced upon Toby's return into my life? What of his curious and inexplicable golden suntans that were not bestowed by any British sun? They were a result of what he had claimed were holidays provided by affluent friends, or merely 'friends of friends'. And he may well have been sunning himself on the decks of 'friends' yachts, while I had collected tickets at the dispensary, and handed boxes of powdered milk over the counter to single mothers who shouted, 'Dat's mine, innit,' while pointing long fingernails at the hundreds of parcels behind me, on the shelves holding the boxes that awaited collection.

Not once had Toby ever invited me to his parental home, which had sounded excessive during his confession in the car – the home in Suffolk, I am referring to, not the one in Spain. In fact, Toby had always dismissed his parents as tyrants, as bullies, and had claimed to have had no contact with them. For all of the years that I had known him, he had practically passed himself off as an orphan to engage my sympathy. And it was a lie; it was all lies. He was a lie. Utterly inauthentic while claiming that his life was a penniless search for the sudden emergence of the authentically weird. He was a Trustafarian and had been slumming at my considerable expense for twenty-three years.

Lies. Liar. Lies. Liar.

I ran down to the water and fell upon the freezing, wet sand and I clutched at it with my hands. I shuddered with a rage so powerful that I became blacker than the terrible sea.

And he was getting *married*. Married: how was that even possible? There were no women in our lives.

I walked into our room a little calmer, but still intent on confrontation. I would have something of Toby's fortune. I had decided this while sobbing into the stones on the beach; rocks reduced to dust by so many waves for tedious millennia. It would not be inappropriate for Toby to now provide for me; to return the favour, so to speak, by paying a pension. I also felt triumphant about eating while he'd slept, but Toby merely said, 'I'm not hungry' when I asked him, 'What are you going to do about food?' So my little victory was dashed.

I found him slouched upon his bed, smoking a joint that I had been able to smell from the ground floor of the guest house. He'd been inside my rucksack to find the little baggy, containing enough skunk for two joints, that was to have been a treat during our visit to Normandy. The baggy was now empty; he'd put all of the weed into one joint for himself. His eyes were red and heavily lidded.

'I want to see the gun emplacements at Longues-sur-Mer,' he said.

'What? Now?'

He nodded. 'They're the only remaining guns of the Nazis' Atlantic wall.'

I didn't want some drug-impaired activity at night to distract us from what we needed to discuss. 'But it's pitch-black out there.'

'So?' he said with such ironic force that it made me blink and swallow.

He looked at the end of the joint, reduced to a butt. 'There's a fortified observation point up there too. In blast-proof concrete. With those guns, they could hit targets twenty kilometres away.'

Why had this not been mentioned before? It was so typical of his selfishness; to have designs on visiting something that he would only share with me moments before he actually wanted to see it.

'It'll all be broken or locked up,' I said. But that was a futile thing for me to suggest, as those very facts would make Toby want to see the gun emplacement even more.

He looked at me and frowned. 'Was that not the entire point of the journey?'

My anger closed my throat down and made my blood hiss through my ears.

'And the fact that it will be pitch-black,' he said, 'makes it all the more worthwhile. And I'm really fucked now, so I want to be up there before I straighten out.' His teeth were brown and gleaming too, so he had taken yet another hit from the bottle that he kept inside his coat. So was I to experience it all *straight*? As he'd taken all of the drugs, it appeared that was to be the case.

He stood up. 'Coming?' He said this with such a weary uninterest, as if he really didn't care if I went with him.

'My, my, how things have changed.'

'What? What did you say?'

I swallowed; it was hard to keep my thoughts straight because I was so angry and upset and feeling rejected. If I spoke, my voice would be full of tears.

He shrugged and made his way to the door, stepping over my open and discarded rucksack. It was on the floor at the foot of my bed, where he'd left it after rummaging for the drugs.

We drove to the cliffs in silence. He asked me to park near the old cliff walk. He wanted to climb up to the guns from the sea, in the dark, like the American Rangers had done at Pointe du Hoc in 1944.

'No way,' I said.

But from the car I docilely followed him down a cliff path to the shore, where he then began moving around to the area below the gun emplacements. I trailed him along the crunching shingle, and up and over a stone groin, and then up the side of some wet rocks to the foot of a steep, grassy cliff-face that would have to be scaled as a scrabble, on our hands and knees, in the dark. The sign on the fence at the foot of the grassy cliff forbade access and warned of avalanches. In parts, the sea-facing side of the hill formed a sheer rock cliff-face too, dropping into the angry waves that smashed into black rocks. But I was to follow him and his feeble torchlight upwards? It was too dangerous. 'No way, Toby.'

Without a single word of advice or encouragement, he set off on his hands and knees. I dithered at the bottom, then followed his sounds ahead of me. I stopped after a few minutes and shouted at him to slow down and to direct the torchlight down to me. He turned the torch off and laughed. But I had climbed too far to go back down in the dark, and Toby knew this. He was forcing me to follow and I was already nearly in tears with fear.

I had nothing else to guide me; his red waterproof and his

pale curly head were consumed by the lightless night. I could barely see my own hands where they clawed at the slippery grass on an almost vertical hill. At one point, I made again to go back down, but so steep was the gradient that I was sure, if I slipped, I would just plummet into the darkness below. Descending by the same route was impossible. In a breathless voice, I pleaded with Toby again to stop, but he didn't reply. His sounds just accelerated ahead of me, as he went higher, alone. Swallowing a panic that wished to become hysteria, I too continued upwards, slowly.

A terrible universe of thin cold air reached out into the darkness behind my back and above my head; it seemed to suck at me. A cold breeze then slapped against me as I clung to the grassy rock-face like an insect. Below us, so far down, was the thunder of the sea, rushing in to smash itself against the land. It was as if I were climbing into the sky; as if I had gone through the very atmosphere and was entering the deep frozen gases of space. There were no lights at the top. A sliver of moon. No stars.

It took me over an hour to haul my trembling body up that incline. By the time I had reached the top, my mind was witless with vertigo and agoraphobia; fatigue had turned my muscles to warm water.

I stumbled through the shrubbery at the summit, and then climbed a wire fence to a mercifully level surface beneath long grass. In which I came across the derelict observation post. It was like a featureless mausoleum with a thin slot in the front for the dead to peer through. I called out to Toby and received no answer.

It took me another twenty minutes to find him up there in the darkness.

'Would you be fucking quiet,' he said at one point, from somewhere to my left.

Squinting into the inky absorbing nothingness of the clifftop, I followed the sound of his voice. By this time my breath was sobbing out of me, and my fear of how we would get back down was close to paralysing. And something terrible was up there with us. Not an individual or a shape this time, but something above us that had no form or end. I felt I could have just fallen upwards, into the sky, where the stars should have been. This was a night that would have once wrecked ships. There was no bottom to it, no horizon, no sides or ceiling. The night was a vast absence that did not end. It was not paranoia that had made my climb unbearable; it had been a justified caution at climbing over the edge of the world.

Where the fence was broken, Toby was standing on the cliff edge, staring up and outwards to sea. 'Can you feel it?' he said.

'Too much,' I cried out, and I fell to my face and grasped handfuls of long grass. A terrible sensation overcame me that my feet were then rising from the earth and moving upwards into the cold black infinity, and I screamed.

'What is fucking wrong with you?' he snapped at me. 'You are ruining it.'

Whatever blackness was attempting to wipe my presence, my very existence, off the face of the earth, and whatever it was that we had climbed into, withdrew momentarily from around my unravelling mind. I felt as if a tight hat had been snatched off my aching head. And within the lightless air, I became red and I burned wild and hot with fury.

I stood up. I walked right at him. 'Ruining' was all I could release from behind my clamped-together teeth. And then Toby came into focus suddenly, as he turned around on the very edge of the cliff. He was actually angry with me.

I punched both hands into his chest. Hard. My elbows locked tight.

And Toby fell backwards, and was then yanked straight up and into the air.

There was a whisk of nylon sleeves as his arms windmilled in nothingness. In his raking torchlight, his mouth opened and his eyes went wide behind his silly little spectacles, and then the details of his shock and fear were gone. His body surged even higher and further out too, like a kite caught on some sudden upward draught of fast-moving air. His coat flapped.

And then I heard him drop like a stone into the darkness.

I stood still and listened to the silence for a time that began to feel preposterous. Until, so far below the clifftop, I heard a distant explosion as his body struck the rocks and surely came apart. After that, I heard no more from him.

Silence thickened all about me on the clifftop. Far away and below my feet was the rush and hissing retreat of the ocean waves. There was no other sound.

I looked at the sky in awe. There was nothing to see besides forever. And the lightless canopy of the universe was not only closer than ever to the surface of the earth, it was touching the earth.

I dipped my head and clutched my face in my hands. And I shouted out into the lightlessness, cried out the inscription upon the memorial for the Commonwealth soldiers: 'We whom William once conquered have now set free the conqueror's native land.'

After the incident on the clifftop, I walked inland and eventually found a road that led down to the car. I drove back into the town, whose name I will never speak again, nor will I countenance its name being spoken in my presence.

Inside our room, I ransacked Toby's scruffy rucksack and found more than I had bargained for. His address book contained details of a vast life that I had no knowledge of. It was a thing filled with names and numbers and email addresses, and on every single page, and I will always treasure it. I now possessed his secret world. His mysteries were mine to explore whenever I wished to, if I wished to.

Inside his toiletry bag, I found his money and his drugs.

He had an ounce of weed in a baggy, and some pills. The little waterproof wallet bulged with over five hundred euros. Pin money for Toby, but I could live on less for years. I pocketed the money and drugs, his iPod and his smart little camera. I wondered if there were pictures of his fiancée on there; if so, I intended to masturbate over them at a later date.

The rest of his things I stuffed inside his rucksack and then jammed his effects deep inside an overflowing skip at the corner of an abandoned building site on the outskirts of the town. I left the guest house before dawn, leaving ten euros on the front desk with the room keys on top of the money. I drove out of town and headed for Dunkirk to catch a return ferry at midnight. With the wet-wipe tissues he had in his toiletry bag, I even wiped everything of his that I had touched and then abandoned.

I called Toby's parents three weeks later and inquired after him. His mother answered the phone. She was very posh. 'He's off' – which she pronounced *awf* – 'on one of his escapades. Who can I say called?'

Despite the fact that I had killed her son, I gave her my actual name. In the phone box, I nearly fainted with excitement.

She'd never heard of me.

He'd clearly never mentioned my name to his own mother in all of the twenty-three years that we had known each other. Again, Toby had managed to spoil a small moment of triumph. He was a natural.

But the strangest thing of all is that even now, when I ponder the fact that I have killed, I can feel no remorse at all. Toby's sentence, I feel, fitted his crimes; and his crimes were those that no surviving vestige of any criminal justice system would ever recognise. And yet the damage of such crimes had blighted a life: my life. His death at my hands made me feel renewed, invigorated, awoken and awake, if that makes sense. I felt that some small act of fairness had finally been *invested* into an unfair world that had left billions dead. I even felt entitled. And the craziest thing is, had he paid for our packed lunch on that final trip, he would still be breathing now.

Florrie

Frank remembered his mother once saying, 'Houses give off a feeling', and that she could 'sense things' inside them. At the time, he'd been a boy and his family had been drifting around prospective homes with an estate agent. He only remembered the occasion because his mother was distressed by a house that they had viewed and had hurried away from to get back to the car. As an adult, all he could recall of that particular property was a print of a blue-faced Christ, within a gilt frame, hanging on the wall of a scruffy living room; the only picture on any of the walls. And the beds had been unmade, which had also shocked his mother. His father had never contradicted his mother on these occasional matters of a psychic nature, though his father had never encouraged her to hold forth on them either. 'Something terrible happened there' was his mother's final remark once the car doors were shut, and the house was never mentioned again. But Frank had been perplexed by the incongruity of both the blue skin of the Christ and a house belonging to Christians that issued an unpleasant 'feeling' to his mother, when she should, surely, have detected the opposite effect.

Frank amused himself trying to second-guess what her intuition would be about the first home that he'd ever owned. He knew what his dad would say about the 120 per cent mortgage that he'd arranged to purchase the two-bedroomed terraced house. But once the house was fixed up, he'd have them down to 'his place': his own home after ten years of cohabitation and tenancy agreements.

The narrow frontage of the house's grubby bricks faced a drab street, cramped with identical houses that leaned over a road so narrow that two cars driving from opposing ends struggled to pass each other. But a final jiggle of the Yale key moved him out of the weak rainy light and into an unlit hallway where the air was thick with trapped warmth. A cloud of stale upholstery, cauliflower thoroughly boiled, and a trace of floral perfume descended about him.

He assured himself that the house would soon exude the scents of his world: the single professional who could cook a bit of Thai, liked entertaining and used Hugo Boss toiletries. Once he'd ripped out the old carpets, stripped the walls and generally 'torn the shit out of it', as his best friend Marcus had remarked with a decisive relish, the house would quickly lose the malodour of the wrong decade, age group and gender.

Enshrouded by a thin illumination that wafted through ground-floor windows begrimed with silt and the silvery nets, he quickly realised that there had been a mistake and that the place had not been cleared of the former owner's furniture. It was as if he'd mixed up the exchange dates and stepped into what remained of the vendor's home. 'Pure 70s, Nan,' Marcus had remarked, with a grin on his face, during the evening when he'd visited to assist Frank's purchasing decision between this two-up, two-down and an ex-council property in Weoley Castle that had needed an airstrike more than a first-time buyer.

Poking from a Bakelite fitting on the wall of the front room was a chunky light switch, the same colour as the skirting boards, kitchen cupboards and fittings: the plastic of artificial limbs used until the 1950s. But the switch was stiff and, when he'd forced it down, the ceiling fixture only emitted a smoky glow from inside its plastic shade, a shade patterned with all the colours of a tin of fruit cocktail.

He stared at the cluttered room and his distaste and irritation fashioned fantasies of destruction about everything inside it: the rosewood sideboard; the gas fire grille with its plastic coals and concealed light bulbs that would glow in the hearth; the ancient television in a wooden cabinet, the small screen concave like a poorly ground lens in a pair of NHS spectacles; the tufted sofa, exhausted and faded and reduced from an article once plush and dark but now sagging into the suggestion of a shabby velour glove dropped from a giant's hand. All of it was an affront to his taste. The furniture and appliances also made him morose, though glad that he'd been born in the mid-70s so that he'd not had long to wait for styles to dramatically change and appear modern over the next decade.

Beneath his feet a red carpet swirled with green fronds and made him think of chameleons' tongues licking fire. He looked down at the weave and his focus was drawn into the pattern. The carpet absorbed most of the dim electric light too, and drained the last of his optimism.

As if he'd just uttered an inappropriate remark in polite company, from the dusty gloom of the sitting room an odd chastening quality descended upon his spirits.

Frank reached out and touched a wall, without really understanding why he felt the need to. The paper was old and fuzzy against his fingertips, the vine pattern no longer lilac on cream but sepia on parchment. About him the warmth and powerful fragrance of the room intensified in tandem with his curious guilt.

Momentarily, his thoughts were weighted with remorse, as if he was being forced to observe the additional distress that his spiteful thoughts about the decor had inflicted upon someone already frightened and… *bullied*. He even felt an urge to apologise to the room out loud.

Only the sound of a delivery truck reversing and beeping outside stirred Frank from his inexplicable shame. The unpleasant feelings passed and he surveyed the room again.

Where to start? Before he could pull up a single carpet tack, the furniture would have to be removed. All of it.

He reached for his phone. This also meant that the terrible Formica dining table with extendable flaps would still be crowding the second downstairs room, along with the hideous quilted chairs. He checked and confirmed that all of the vendor's furniture remained in place. 'Fuck's sake,' he whispered, and wondered why he'd kept his voice down.

Frank jogged up the narrow stairwell to expel a sense of fatigue, presumably caused by the stifling air or the anticipation of renovating the house.

The master bedroom was still choked by the immense veneered walnut wardrobe that he'd seen during his two viewings of the property. Beside it a teak dresser stood before him in defiance. A bed that had probably survived the Luftwaffe's bombing of munitions factories on the nearby Grand Union Canal appeared implacable and vast enough to fill what remained of the floor-space.

One quick look around the door of the second bedroom revealed that it was also being used *in absentia* by the previous owner, as a depository for cardboard suitcases, dated Christmas decorations, candlewick bedspreads, candy-striped linen and knitting paraphernalia.

On the tiny landing, while standing beneath the white hardboard loft hatch, Frank wondered if the old woman had even moved out, or perhaps come back home. 'She's in a retirement home, I think. Couldn't cope. Went a bit funny. Dementia or something,' the wanker that was the estate agent, Justin, at Watkins, Perch and Manly, had said when Frank had asked about the former occupant's history. So why hadn't her relatives collected her things?

Maybe she had no one at the end.

Frank was overwhelmed by an unwelcome notion of age, its indignities, its steady erasure of who you had once been and the recycling of your tiny former position in the world. The same tragic end might befall him one day. *Right here too.*

He was disoriented by a sudden acute empathy with a loneliness that might have been absolute. It took a conscious effort for him to suppress the awful feeling. Wiping his eyes, he went back downstairs.

He listened to an answering machine at the estate agents and left a curt message for Justin. Then turned about in the living room and forced a change of tack in his thoughts. He visualised the transformation of the house that he and Marcus would effect: wooden floors, white walls, wooden blinds, minimalist light fittings, dimmers, a wall-mounted TV, black and white movie stills in steel frames on the walls, leather furniture, a stainless-steel kitchen, a paved yard for outside dining, a spare room for his gadgets and guests, fitted closet space and nothing in the master bedroom but his new bed and a standing lamp. Clean lines, simple colours. Space, light, peace, modernity, protection.

He had his work cut out.

On the Friday of Frank's first week in the house, the former resident's furniture was still in place, as it had been for long enough to leave the carpet dark beneath the sofa and the solitary armchair in the living room. This had prevented him stripping the walls. Until the furniture was hauled away, the kitchen was the only part of the house that he could dismantle, even though he had become fond of using it to make egg and chips, which he'd not eaten since he was at school. He also liked to listen to the radio in that room, and BBC Radio Two, which he couldn't recall ever hearing since childhood. As a result, he'd staved off pulling down the old wooden cabinets with their frosted-glass doors. There was also something cosy and reassuring about the cupboards and the little white stove. And anyway, as Marcus was due to arrive with his tools the following morning, Saturday, Frank was able to postpone the destruction until that time.

He needed groceries too for the weekend and hadn't organised himself sufficiently to shop at a supermarket, so he'd been dipping in and out of the local shop to feed himself. The store was called Happy Shop, and was conveniently situated at the end of the road. A strip-lit cave run by a smiling Hindu man. This would be his fourth trip to the store in a week. *Or had it been more than that?* Didn't matter and he was due a treat, which might just be the Arctic Roll that he'd been eyeing up the day before. *Or had that been Wednesday?* Nothing had seemed to define the days of his first week in the house; they had all been slow and pleasant.

Frank hadn't been out much that week either, and now found himself craving human company. Going round the local shops was the furthest he'd ventured all week, because the house was immensely warm and cosy and it had made him consider the world outside the front door as not being either of those things.

On leave for the first time in six months, he'd quickly slumped into a routine of slouching on the sofa each morning to watch the greenish TV screen. This had been his first opportunity for ages to relax, which must have accounted for his torpor. But the house untied his knots wonderfully; he'd slept as if he was in a coma for an hour after lunch too, until his shows came on. Not that he'd ever seen any of the television programmes before, due to work, but he'd quickly discovered preferences on the five terrestrial channels available to him.

In the cupboard under the stairs he'd found a tartan shopping trolley on wheels. It had been parked beside a carpet sweeper that he was sure he could flog on eBay to a retro nut. Having to fetch and carry so many tins all week from Happy Shop had made the idea of using the trolley gradually less of a joke as the week progressed. And before he left the house on Friday he even paused outside the cupboard and wondered if anyone young might laugh at him in the street if he went out with the trolley. But if they did, he wasn't sure he'd care.

Inside Happy Shop his usual tastes deserted him. The idea of sushi, or stir-fries, or anything with rice and coconut milk, or anything that had been messed about with, like the curries and chillies that he often ate, all running with sauce… turned his stomach. Revolted him, in fact. The store hoarded forgotten treasures from any 70s childhood and he'd spent his first week eating tinned pink salmon with a brand of white bread that he hadn't known was still baked. There had been lots of tinned rice pudding in his new diet too, a Victoria sponge, ice-cream packaged in cardboard, and Mr Kipling French Fancies for pudding. He had rediscovered his enjoyment of condensed milk and individual frozen chicken pies. And he'd bought, for the first time in his life, a round English lettuce.

Up in Happy Shop, within minutes, a packet of Birds Eye fish fingers and a tiny bag of minted peas rustled in his basket. There were four baskets at the front of the shop that smelled of newspaper and tobacco. A tin of mandarin segments, strawberry-flavoured Angel Delight – *they still sold it in sachets!* – a box of PG Tips and a jar of Mellow Bird's coffee went into the basket next. He avoided anything with onions as he'd recently gone off them.

To his growing haul, and because he missed its fragrance, he added some Pledge furniture polish that he remembered being stored under a sink in his family home; once he got busy with a duster and some Pledge, the veneered finish on the wardrobe would come up a treat, as would the rosewood sideboard and the teak dresser.

Frank had become fond of using the cupboard above the cooker as a space for treats, and had often found himself dipping into it before he watched telly in the afternoon. Inexplicably, the true purpose of the cupboard had suggested itself to him. So, in Happy Shop, he bought a bag of Murray Mints and a Fry's Turkish Delight.

Almost done. What else did he need? Washing up liquid. He seized one of the green and white plastic bottles of Fairy Liquid. He hadn't seen that packaging in years. When he smelled the red nozzle, the fragrance of his childhood summers made him giddy. Overexposed images turned in his memory: running in swimming trunks, grass blades floating in a paddling pool, the plastic bottom blue, the water warm, suffocating with laughter as he was chased by his brother, who squirted him with water from a Fairy Liquid bottle, trying to swim in the paddling pool – though the water was never deep enough and his knees bumped the bottom – but then lying face-down in the warm water for five seconds before springing up to see if his mum was worried that he'd drowned. And he saw deckchairs in his mind too, with his mom and nan in them, watching him and smiling. He was rewound to such an extent that he even thought he'd detected a trace of creosote on a garden fence, that tang of burned oil and timber.

Frank walked back to the house, dreamy and taking short steps with his head down, as if wary of hazards underfoot, until he snapped out of the new habit and walked normally.

When Marcus knocked at ten on Saturday morning, Frank jumped up from the kitchen stool but couldn't account for why he was so nervous. He was being silly, but opening the front door was suddenly a cause of great anxiety. So he hovered, scarcely breathing, inside the hall beside the thermostat that looked like something from an instrument panel at the dawn of space travel. When Marcus peered through the letter flap, Frank was forced to open up.

'Fuck's going on?' Marcus said, when he saw the kitchen. 'I brought the tiles and units with me. This shit should be long gone by now. Your stuff can't stay in my garage for ever, mate.'

But, despite his friend's disappointment, Frank craved a stay of execution for the kitchen, and hoped that he could somehow delay Marcus or persuade him not to engage in the splintering of wood and the crowbarring of those kitchen cabinets from the walls. They must have been up for decades and were still in good nick. Nothing wrong with them, in fact, so it seemed such a waste. And Frank also wanted them left alone for another reason and this motive had been nagging at him as Saturday had approached: gutting the kitchen just felt *wrong*. Bad, like violence. Like bullying.

Too embarrassed by his own sentimentality to defend them, and with a heavy heart, he helped Marcus break the cupboards away from the walls, and he'd felt like crying as they did their worst with the crowbars.

When they found the handwriting behind the first cabinet – *Len and Florrie, 1964* – Frank went into the bathroom with moist eyes and smothered his face inside one of the big lemon-yellow towels that he'd found in the airing cupboard.

The three wall cabinets and the row of cupboards were soon piled like earthquake wreckage in the yard. The sight of the pale, unpainted wood that had been facing the kitchen wall since 1964 hit him as hard as the sight of a dead pet had once done: a rabbit rigid with the terrible permanence and unfairness of its final sleep, when it had still been *loved*.

Indifferent to the inscriptions left by Len and Florrie – they had found four – Marcus cracked open tins of white emulsion and began painting the bare walls. As Marcus worked, Frank recognised that he despised his best friend.

They didn't have time to vandalise another room that weekend, and it was just as well, because Frank's relationship with the house changed during the night after the desecration of the little kitchen.

The following morning, while Frank sat doleful over toast and a mug of tea in the newly painted starkness of the kitchen, with his stainless-steel units piled up in the middle of the room, he mused that during the preceding night it was as if he'd entertained someone else's dreams.

All night he'd passed through a dark muddle of images that were mostly lost to him in the morning. But he did retain partial impressions of a room filled with the smoke of Silk Cut cigarettes, the clack of Scrabble tiles, and the Matt Monro song playing on a continuous loop from a black tape recorder, a device he'd seen in vivid detail with spatters of white paint upon the speakers. 'Born Free': that had been the song. He hadn't heard it in years. He'd also been a guest on *The Price Is Right*; had somehow been inside the show while also watching himself from the sofa. It had been his goal to win a small caravan. The contest had been compelling. Just before he'd woken, he'd been standing upon the yellow lino of the kitchen floor, counting pages of Green Shield stamps. Or once he'd thought he'd awoken, because there had been someone in the bedroom with him. Talking to him between sharp intakes of breath. A small indistinct figure had also been standing at the foot of the bed.

In the second, more vivid dream – because it must have been a dream – the standing figure had left the room quickly with its hands clutched over its face. The presence had then reappeared in the doorway as a hunched silhouette, lit by ambient light rising up the stairwell. The silhouette had taken to crouching as if in pain, and, when the figure had turned towards him, the face had remained in darkness. He was sure the person had been a woman, for whom he felt a rush of tenderness and affection and remorse, despite the shock that she had given him by appearing at the foot of his bed. When he encountered her in his sleep, he had been stricken with the same feeling of abandonment that he remembered on his first day at school.

The dream had continued and he had found himself standing behind the small figure in the spare room. In that part of the dream, she had been bent over and was mooching through a collection of plastic bags. 'You need to get ready. And I can't go without it,' she'd said to Frank, without once turning around to face him.

He'd woken at seven and discovered that his face was briny with dried tears. He'd gone downstairs to the smell of fried sausages that competed with the stink of new paint, though he hadn't cooked a single sausage in the house.

The dreams turned nasty on Sunday and Monday night and were caused by the kitchen cupboards being left outside in the rain. Like his mother's vibes about other people's houses, Frank instinctively knew that the kitchen wreckage was the cause of his troubled sleep.

On Sunday night, the small female figure had returned to his bedroom. But her agitation and grief had intensified and he'd woken to find her leaning over his face with her hands clasped across her mouth. He'd suspected that the glimmer of a solitary eye had been visible, but he'd seen no other features on the face of the woman of his dreams. From behind her fingers she'd muffled a horrible grunt.

Frank had sat up in bed, his heart hammering, convinced there was an actual intruder inside his room, but then watched the figure of the small woman fade into the dark centre of the wardrobe.

He'd quickly put lights on and conducted a search of the entire house, but there had been no one inside with him.

On Monday night, what might have been the figure of the elderly woman was inside his room again, but on her hands and knees. He might also have dreamed about a wounded animal, because he awoke to hear something mewling and fumbling about beneath the curtains that didn't sound like a person. Round and round the thing had gone on all fours, for a few seconds, bumping the walls in distress. He never saw anything and had just remained stiff with fright in the bed.

The intruder eventually left the bedroom and scurried across the landing; Frank only saw the last of it go and suspected it had been a dog because no human could move that fast on all fours. Terrified, but compelled to follow, Frank had peered inside the spare bedroom and seen the figure of the old woman, her small body covered in a grubby housecoat, with her back to him. She had been searching amongst boxes of photograph albums with vinyl jackets until she found what she'd been looking for. She'd held it before her lowered face and gave Frank the impression that she was either struggling to read in bad light or putting something inside her mouth. Frank didn't know, but could hear the woman's heavy breathing, betwixt a series of animal grunts.

When he spoke to her, the figure turned quickly and showed him a pair of milky eyes, like he'd once seen in the head of a dead sheep, and bared teeth that didn't belong inside a human mouth.

Frank had woken underneath the eiderdown in his room with his fingers stuffed down his own throat.

On Tuesday morning, he carried the broken kitchen furniture back inside the house and dried the wreckage with a tea towel. The very act of reclamation felt as necessary as rescuing a drowning cat from a canal.

Mail from Macmillan Nurses and a council mobility service arrived on Wednesday morning addressed to Mrs Florrie White. He put the letters in a neat stack beside the small toaster on the kitchen counter; he'd repaired that unit as much as possible, and then placed it leaning against the wall, set at a tilt, which didn't help the house much, but he couldn't bear another night of the broken wood being outside in the cold. The new steel kitchen units went outside and into the yard. Of course it would not be a permanent arrangement, but he couldn't settle his nerves until the swap had been made.

He spent Tuesday to Thursday on the sofa, listless and melancholy, drifting through afternoon television shows for the modicum of comfort that they provided. He also took long naps with the gas fire on; its glow and little clicking sounds reassured him more than anything he could remember. But he would often awake from these naps, because the little figure from his dreams would mutter to itself at the top of the stairs. When he awoke, Frank could never remember what it said, and there was no one up there when he looked.

Frank also spent a lot of his time staring at the pattern on the kitchen table and thinking of the rooms he'd occupied as a student: cohabits through his twenties with two girlfriends long gone; house-shares with strangers with whom he had no contact now. In the increasingly indistinct crowds of his memories, there had been an alcoholic who only consumed extra strong cider and Cup-a-Soup, and an obese girl who had eaten like a child at a tenth birthday party and spent hours locked in the bathroom. He could no longer remember their names, or the faces of the girlfriends. He tried for a while until he moved to the living room and fell asleep in front of *Countdown*.

On Thursday evening, he refused to take a call from Marcus. There had been four since the previous weekend too. All unanswered. For some reason Marcus and his calls were irritating Frank to such a degree that he put his iPhone in the cupboard under the stairs, deep inside a box of wooden clothes pegs. He hadn't had enough time to think through the changes that he'd once planned to make to the house, and he could not abide being rushed.

His sleep went undisturbed until the weekend and he found himself watching ITV from seven to nine before going up to bed. Happy Shop kept him fed with its inexhaustible variety of memory and flavour. And when Marcus arrived on Saturday morning, Frank never answered the door. Instead, he lay on the floor of the living room with the curtains closed.

At the end of his second week off work, he called the office from the public phone outside Happy Shop to tell them that he wasn't coming back.

On the Monday of his fourth week in the house, Frank finally went out for tools. Not to renovate the property, but to try and repair the kitchen. That task could not be put off any longer.

The act of leaving the house was excruciating.

Twice the previous week, when he'd been cooking in the wrecked kitchen, he'd looked up because he was convinced that he was being watched from the doorway, as if caught doing something wrong, or eating something he had been told not to. The imagined presence had been seething with a surly disappointment and dark with hostility. That room had become the focus of an intensification of the restlessness growing since the Saturday when he and Marcus had assaulted the cabinets. The kitchen was the heart of the house and he had broken it.

There was no one physically inside the house with him, and there could not possibly have been. But the repeated sounds of small feet padding about the lino, while he napped in the lounge during the afternoons, suggested, to a region of his imagination that he little used, that a bereft presence was repeatedly examining the kitchen. The first time he'd heard the shuffle of feet, he'd actually worried that the former owner of the house had escaped from her retirement community, or worse, and let herself back inside what she believed was still her own home.

Frank recovered quickly from the sudden frights, and within the confines of the comfortable womb of the terraced house he eventually found the supervising presence acceptable, even deserved. Nor could he think of a single reason to doubt his instincts that amends had to be made. Within the house such things were possible.

But navigating his way through the world outside the house, which no longer felt so familiar, defeated him. When he went out for tools, his attempts to move on the Pershore Road wasted him before he'd reached the bus stop in front of the bowling alley.

Unpredictable tides of energy, and the staring eyes of pedestrians and motorists, had seemed to pull his thoughts apart and then compress him into a muttering standstill. He was thinking of too many things at the same time, but then forgetting one train of thought at the same time as another began.

The pressure the city exerted upon him was tangible. Uncomfortable, like a head-slappy wind on a hilltop, or a coat pocket caught on a door handle. Unless he was inside the house, or Happy Shop, he didn't fit in anywhere and was in everyone's way. And so his recent life had been reduced to quick forays outside the house, because he was unable to cope with anything else and wasn't wanted anywhere. Never had been. The house had opened his eyes. And there was now something wrong with one of his legs; a pain that started inside a hip. So he should keep off it.

On the day he went out to buy the tools, the further he ventured from the house, the greater was his physical discomfort and his confusion. Frank lit endless cigarettes for the slight comfort they promised. Silk Cut. He'd started smoking again at the weekend after being driven by an unstoppable urge to light up during the National Lottery. At the bus stop, fat pigeons had scurried around his feet and watched him with amber eyes.

After boarding a bus, he'd made his way upstairs. With his bad hip it had been similar to standing upright in a rowing boat. Sitting by the window as the bus trundled toward Selly Oak, where he knew there was a DIY store, he'd looked down at the streets for women wearing tight skirts and leather boots; such a sight usually made him dizzy with longing. Now the women and their clothes just appeared ordinary, and he felt dead to the previously strong images. This impotence led to an incredulity that such a part of himself had ever existed.

From a seat in front of him, a mobile phone began to ring in a girl's handbag. The noise distracted Frank from what had seemed like important, meaningful thoughts that he could barely remember a few moments later. He'd groaned aloud. The girl spoke in a loud voice. 'Oh, Jesus,' he'd said, wanting to take the phone from her hand and drop it out of the window. He'd wanted to hear it smash on the asphalt below.

Muttering under his breath to prevent himself swearing aloud, he was forced to listen to the stranger's conversation. The girl's voice was controlled and sounded too much like a prepared speech to be part of a natural discourse. There were no pauses, or repetitions, or silences; just her going *blah, blah, blah,* and addressing everyone on the bus. It was not a phone that she was holding, but a microphone. Perhaps the most disappointing thing about getting older, he'd mused, was to still be confronted by childish actions and behaviour, these increments of self-importance and vanity that he now observed all about him whenever he left home.

By the time he reached the Bristol Road, Frank had felt sickened by his aversion to everything around him. A hot loathing, but a fascination too, and a pitiful desperation to be included. In one mercifully brief moment, he'd also wished to be burned to ash and to have his name erased from every record in existence. He was rubbish. No one wanted him around. He'd dabbed the corner of one eye with a tissue and had wanted to go home, back to the house.

As the bus brushed the edge of Selly Oak he'd fallen asleep. And awoken to find the vehicle had trundled and wheezed into streets he didn't recognise. He'd slept through his stop and found himself in a bleak part of Birmingham that he had never seen before. Somewhere behind Longbridge maybe? In a panic, he'd fled down the stairs, alighted and then stood beside a closed factory and a wholesaler of saris.

Everything there was inhospitable. Self-loathing had choked him. *Can I not leave the house without a map?* He'd lived in the city for ten years, but he recognised none of this. It was as if the streets and buildings had actually moved to disorient him while he'd slept on the bus.

He'd followed a main road in the opposite direction the bus had taken, but grown tired and eventually turned his face to a wooden fence surrounding a building site and there suffered a paroxysm of such contained rage that it had left him with a broken tooth and cuts on the palms of his hands. Clenching his jaws together and grinding his teeth, he'd felt the enamel snap on a tooth at the side of his mouth. His cheeks had filled with grit. But when the tooth snapped the tension had passed from his body, leaving him confused and expecting shockwaves of agony. But there was no pain and he'd decided against going to a dentist. He didn't know where the dentists were in the city. He'd then noticed the little half-moons of blood on the inside of his palms, made by his own nails. It had been so long since he'd bitten them; his nails were like unpleasant, feminine claws. How could they have grown so much and he not noticed?

Trying to retrace the bus route and find a landmark, Frank became hopelessly disoriented. He went into a tacky women's hairdressers, which was the only place that he'd been able to find that offered him any sense of familiarity, to ask for directions. Girls in heavy make-up had exchanged glances when he found himself unable to speak. He'd just stood and trembled before them. After throwing his arms into the air in silent exasperation, he'd left the shop, crimson with shame. Speech only returned to him at the kerb where he'd stood muttering. Some people had stared. A taxi had taken him home.

These things never used to happen to him, but he had a notion that the potential for such a slide had always been in place. In the back of the taxi he'd hidden his face inside the lapel of his overcoat and bitten his bottom lip until his eyes had brimmed with water.

Two days later, or it might have been three or even four, someone knocked on the front door, and for a long time too. So Frank had hidden by lying on the floor of the spare room. He'd heard voices outside, talking in the neighbour's garden, and he'd known that they were trying to look through the back windows of the house.

For the rest of that afternoon he'd chain-smoked Silk Cut cigarettes and didn't relax until it was dark outside and *Coronation Street*'s theme tune was booming through the living room. The thought of going out to buy food had made him feel nauseous, so he'd stopped tormenting himself with the idea of leaving the house.

He tried again to fix the broken cabinets to the kitchen walls, but only succeeded in making his fingers bleed. He'd gone upstairs to wash them, but when he arrived on the landing he couldn't remember why he had gone upstairs. He went and lay down on the bed instead. And around him clouded the smell of perfume, old furniture, stale carpets and chip fat. The radiators had come on with a gurgle. He'd felt safe and closed his eyes.

Sometime in the night, Florrie came into the room on all fours and climbed onto the bed. She sat on Frank's chest and pushed a thin, cold hand inside his mouth.

About These Horrors: Story Notes

'Where Angels Come In' is much like my earlier story 'Mother's Milk', in that I attempted to tell a horror story from the point of view of a child, or from a childlike state. It's the time in our lives when most of us probably suffered our most intense terrors of the imagination. And for me the first draft of a story of this nature isn't planned, but is anticipated in the form of a few images, and often adapted from a voice announcing a few lines in my imagination. I have scant idea what the story will make itself into; they're expressionistic for me too, I go deep to find something that impacts on me, no matter how strange the image, and I don't approach the stories rationally. What comes out in the first draft does need extensive rewriting, but I try to preserve the style and voice that are there from the start.

This story and 'Mother's Milk' are also a cause of regret, because I wish I had written far more stories like them at that time, when this type of voice most often tried to get onto the page. I'd like to have written a full collection's worth of stories in this style. I never did. But though this approach feels like an instinctive and natural part of my writing, it has found less of a role in my novels, and the novels have always been my priority. The process of pushing the envelope, and daring to be fresher in the use of voice and imagery, at the same time as wrestling with the more conventional, expected and more widely appreciated forms of voice and structure, is a tension that has dogged, and perhaps even assisted, my entire career as a novelist. From collisions can come sparks and maybe even new forms that combine the best of two forces.

This story has struck chimes in a few readers and editors too. Ellen Datlow and Stephen Jones both reprinted 'Where Angels Come In' in their annual best horror collections. Ellen Datlow even came back for the story for her collection *Hauntings*. *Nightmare Magazine* recently reprinted it, and the Secretari de Cultura in Mexico has translated the story into Spanish for a state-funded horror collection. The response to this story has often made me sit back and think: *what did I do right*?

It was written after my first Fantasycon, in 2004, in which the publisher/writer Gary Fry asked me to write a story in the spirit of M. R. James for the Gray Friar collection *Poe's Progeny*. Such was my enthusiasm that I wrote two stories: 'The Original Occupant' initially, and then 'Where Angels Come In'. Gary Fry used each story in a different Gray Friar collection. 'The Original Occupant' was later published in *Bernie Herrmann's Manic Sextet*.

The founding image for this story, however, came to me as I walked between two long rows of Georgian terraces in Holland Park, West London, near where I lived for seven years. I imagined glimpsing an elderly face, but one too bloodless, wasted and harrowed to be that of the living, at an upstairs window, which quickly withdrew into the darkness of the room. I held the image and, when I next arrived at the building where I was employed as a porter in Mayfair, I began writing the story. The entire first draft came out in one sitting, and I remember that writing the story slipped me into a trancelike state.

Though the story is entirely Jamesian in intent and imagery, and even features the spectres from some of his stories, it was also an anti-Jamesian story, in which I eschewed any hint of the social background and erudition of his world, the age of his narrators, and the time in which the story is set is contemporary. After all, the editor had asked for the spirit of James and not a pastiche. Since *Banquet for the Damned* this is what I have most often tried to do with the enormous influence that M. R. James has wielded upon my imagination: to try and mirror his approach to the supernormal, and some stylistic traits, while avoiding pastiche.

'The Original Occupant' was another attempt to use a particular and distinct voice, though a much older, more traditional, educated, and patrician male voice that dominated the classic era of the ghost story. I've rarely used this voice again, and wasn't sure whether to even include this story in the collection, but it has significance to me because the ideas and location in this story planted the first acorn for my later novel *The Ritual*. The mannered voice in 'The Original Occupant' too easily leans to contrivance in my ear, and when I am reading it is an idiom that can bounce me out of a story if it doesn't seem natural. It's not my voice, and I don't share its social background, and it often seems part of a consensus in English literature, embedded within the class structure. I've taken against it for long periods as a reader.

Most of my short fiction is written in the first person, though not one of my eight horror novels has been. I mention this because the short story has been a palette for experimenting with voice from the beginning of my writing. I think experimentation also accounts for why I'm often told that all of my books are different from each other; *how* something is written, both the narrative and the voice, or voices, is something I never stop mulling over, before, during and even after I've finished a story or novel. *Is this right?* is a common question that I ask myself. Another question is: *so who is actually telling the story?* I make no criticism, and have often envied their consistency, but there are writers with long careers who seem to have written every book in the same way and in the same voice. I think I'm incapable of that dedication to a single style and approach.

I also began writing *The Ritual* four years after finishing this story (though that novel is written in a very different way, and tries to break with the literary, in some ways, and to marry itself with the cinematic), and that's how long it can take for me to realise an idea fully enough to attempt it at novel length; generating ideas is never a problem, but how they should be written is a perpetual puzzle. But this story was an attempt to offset the horror; to tell stories within stories, from three characters, varying from a narrator to reported conversations to correspondence; but the primary narrator is only ever offering hearsay. This was intended to create layers of distance from the actual horror, before bringing it forth at the very end.

At this time, I was also seriously considering emigration to Sweden or Norway. I'd visited and travelled in Scandinavia many times from 2000 until 2005. My original, lunatic aim was to live in a *Fritidshus* too, for one entire year, in order to see what kind of fiction I could produce in twelve months of isolation within a wilderness. I remain relieved that I came to my senses.

'Mother's Milk' dates back to the mid-90s and is the only fiction from my earliest period that I have allowed to survive.

So critical were the comments of tutors on my creative writing master's degree in 1997 about my work submitted to workshops and tutorials that I remember suffering a sense of hopelessness and feeling genuine despair about my writing and writerly aspirations. It is the only time that I ever considered giving up (albeit briefly!). But the tutors were absolutely right about the incoherence in my writing at that stage, and never intended to inflict any real damage – in fact, they practised a very genial bedside manner – but young writers can be as fragile as old eggs.

In order to crawl before I could walk, as opposed to trying to run as a more sophisticated writer that I certainly wasn't, I decided to *infantilise* as a writer. So I stripped myself back to year zero in voice and intention and revisited an early version of this story in 1997; a story in which I had written very simple sentences in a childlike voice. I was now interested in clarity, voice and effect above all else. So, I rewrote the story until every image rang true, until I could hear, taste and see what I was describing. I'd been over-writing, over-confidently, for years until 1997, and had produced a collection of short stories and a short novel by the mid-90s; I'd even sold a popular erotic novel to a mid-size publisher. But nothing from that period I consider salvageable besides 'Mother's Milk'. The year 1997–98, in which I received formal instruction on my writing, was therefore pivotal for me.

'Mother's Milk', submitted to workshops on that creative writing course, was the first piece of my work that was widely appreciated by those who read it. In the first place, it took a friend to persuade me to even put the story into a workshop; I was embarrassed by the strange voice and the grotesque themes in the story, particularly in a place like St Andrews, but I privately acknowledged that the tale was an authentic catch from deep within my imagination. Ultimately, the way the story was received was one of the most confirming experiences I had as a fledgling writer.

The second most confirming experience at this stage was Ramsey Campbell publishing the story in *Gathering the Bones* in 2003. This was my first time in print as an author of horror and the weird. Prior to this, I'd sent 'Mother's Milk' to a well-known horror magazine to have it sent back with a comment that it was too descriptive and also badly written. Discouraged, it was only years later in 2000–1 that I'd shown the story to my editor at Virgin, the late and much missed James Marriott, who was a devotee of horror and wanted to see something I'd written in that vein. Without my knowledge, James passed the story on to John Coulthard, who passed it on to Ramsey Campbell. My first rune had truly been cast. And out of the milky blue I received an email from Ramsey in which he explained that he liked that the story contained 'the texture of a nightmare' and wanted to publish it in *Gathering the Bones.* Ramsey then helped me into print as a novelist too, by recommending that I send my first supernatural horror novel, *Banquet for the Damned*, to his UK publisher, PS Publishing (Ramsey also wrote the introduction to that first edition of the novel, published in 2004). I do sometimes wonder whether, if 'Mother's Milk' had been dismembered on that creative writing course in 1997, I would have subsequently learned to write as openly as I do in my horror fiction.

A first draft of 'Yellow Teeth' was written sometime in 2004, but was revised and extended a few years later after Tim Lebbon, James A. Moore and Christopher Golden invited me to write a story for a collection they were compiling, *British Invasion*, that Cemetery Dance were publishing. Writing this story mirrored a difficult period in my existence in London, stretching from 1999 until around 2005, in which my living arrangements, and my personal standards, were often severely compromised by having very little money and working at night. This forced me to live in some shoddy places and to cohabit with, quite frankly, people with the most appalling habits, who may even have been suffering from personality disorders. That whole period was a maelstrom of sleep deprivation, poverty, despair, conflict with others within small living spaces, and grave anxieties about my future. This story was a reflection of my being inspired while down (you always have writing to turn to). But my experiences in my first years in London really manifested in the novel *Apartment 16* (I was twice asked by mental health professionals, after they'd read *Apartment 16*, if I suffered from schizophrenia).

During these early years in London, as well as working as a porter, writing one erotica novel each year and putting the finishing touches to *Banquet for the Damned*, I also felt that most of my energy and capacity was being wasted in just coping with my existence in London. And once I'd begun this story, I was convinced that it was a novel too. Problem was, I already had two novels on the go in different fields, and so I decided to leave 'Yellow Teeth' as a long short story and to revisit the ideas and characters sometime in the future. And I did revisit them in 2015, with my novel *Under a Watchful Eye* (as it is called at the time of writing), which is scheduled for publication in early 2017.

'Pig Thing' was another early story, written at a time of personal and professional despair, and while I was living above an old pub in London in 2000. One evening, I tried to recall a time when I was happy as a child in New Zealand, and this story came out. Not so much horror from a child's point of view but a story from an omniscient narrator who interprets the experience of children in jeopardy. I think the happy memories about my enchantment in a sub-tropical environment, as a child, became mixed with the oppressive weight of the dark atmosphere that had enfolded me in London, and produced an odd story.

In the first version, the story stops as the two children climb inside the freezer to hide from the pig thing, after having lost an elder brother and both parents to it. I never submitted the story anywhere on spec, but did offer it, years later, to two small presses who asked me for a story. Each of them rejected 'Pig Thing'. It was too subtle for one, and 'went nowhere' for the other. Years later, Danel Olson invited me to write a second story for his *Exotic Gothic* series. As 'Pig Thing' was Gothic in tone and set in New Zealand (the stories in this series could not be set in Great Britain or France) I showed Danel 'Pig Thing'. He suggested that I write a second part to the story, to make it longer, and I'm glad that I did. The story was published in *Exotic Gothic 4*, in 2012, but I place it towards the beginning of this collection because the first version was actually written in 2000. It has also been subsequently reprinted by two annual best of horror and fantasy collections.

'What God Hath Wrought?' was the first of two stories

I've written for Conrad Williams, when he has edited multi-author horror collections. This story was written for *Gutshot*, an anthology with a western theme, published by PS Publishing in 2011. I read a great many westerns as a boy, and loved western films, particularly those that involved the US Army, so I jumped at the chance to be included in *Gutshot*. As an adult, I'd also become a fan of Cormac McCarthy's fiction, and had read all of his westerns. It was from the latter that I took most of my inspiration for this story's atmosphere, while the actual plot and action owed much to my former exposure to westerns. I wanted a collision of pulp fiction with something else more lyrical, to suggest that greater forces and epic histories existed behind the action of the story.

Writing this story also coincided with an enormous research project that I was undertaking for my novel *Last Days*, in which I studied cults from various eras and cultures, including the Mormon Church. This cult, or movement, has a history perfectly suited to horror, because of its blind faith in the dubiously numinous and supernormal. Its origins contain moments of such spectacular fantasy and obvious confidence trickery that I am still genuinely amazed to see the faith thriving and growing in the modern age. I suppose this story is also my sole contribution to the zombie subgenre that was all the rage in 2010 when I wrote this story.

'Doll Hands' was started after midnight as I worked as a nightwatchman in a swanky apartment building in Knightsbridge. This was in the latter half of 1999, or even in 2000. During the early hours of a shift, at this time, I also began recording a series of grotesque prose expressions of isolation and horror that would eventually become my novel *Apartment 16*.

I often wrote on a second-hand early incarnation of the laptop computer, which used floppy discs. Some of these discs, including the ones containing many of the earliest *Apartment 16* fragments, or *Down Here with the Rest of Us*, as the project was called at the time (without yet forming into a novel), were lost during one of my relocations from one wretched room in London to another wretched room in London. I still dream of a scene that involved a starving cat and a pigeon with one leg, and remember being as inspired as I'd ever been while writing that scene, but it is lost for ever… a casualty of war… and may have given me the idea for the lost paintings, more like nightmares than actual artefacts, that came to fruition in *Apartment 16*. But at night, as I'd sit for twelve hours behind a reception desk in that building, before the front entrance, my reflection would appear slightly warped in the glass of the front doors, and my bald white head would seem large and distorted, and would contain a small face above my scrawny shoulders, clad in a grey uniform. That reflection literally mirrored my morbid thoughts and low spirits, and seemed to encapsulate my existence. And the narrator for this story was born.

I finished 'Doll Hands' years later in Mayfair, during another porter's job, at a time in which I'd almost given up any hope of escaping a fate of unskilled, uniformed, low-paid work that could be terribly demoralising. At a real low point, I tried again to express my feelings and impressions within a short story that featured the actual buildings, though in the future, in which the few survivors on the earth were horribly disfigured and had become as much animal and monstrous as they were human. The end of humanity, in effect, with its final industry and purpose being cannibalism. This story also really demonstrates to me how the anthropomorphic horrors of Francis Bacon's paintings have touched my writing. As an influence, he is probably up there with M. R. James, and Bacon's effect really ran wild in *Apartment 16* too. More than any other artist, in any medium, I think Bacon best distilled the very horror of existence. So this story was one of my own 'Bacon' paintings, and another attempt at depicting the childlike voice and perception, because of the strangeness that can be added to the horror; that strangeness amplifies the feeling of horror in the reader but *not* necessarily the narrator. Is there not instant horror when presented with a recounting of vile behaviour or horrible events by a person for whom such behaviour and events are normal?

Again, it was a story that was knocked back a couple of times by editors who had asked me for a horror story, and perhaps this even disenchanted me about the mileage that this kind of style (beyond my own distorted head) had *out there.* But the story was rescued from the abyss by Johnny Mains, who was putting together a members-only collection for the British Fantasy Society, entitled *The Burning Circus.* Johnny was very enthusiastic about the story, and even reprinted it in Salt's short-lived *Best of British Horror* series. Ellen Datlow later picked the story up too, for her collection *Monstrous*, and it has been translated into Russian and German. Moral of the story: sometimes you just have to get your strangest work before the eyes of the right editors.

'To Forget and Be Forgotten' was written for Danel Olson's *Exotic Gothic 3*, with a setting in Flemish Belgium, one of my favourite places on the planet thus far visited. Antwerp may even be my favourite European city and I've visited it even more than Stockholm. But the story, setting and characters are drawn from my own deep well of portering experiences in West London, though less expressionistically in this story than in 'Doll Hands'.

The scene in which the porter is asked to watch over an elderly heiress for a few minutes, a woman who hasn't walked in twenty years, is true. It happened to me. And, in the nurse's absence, the resident did stand up out of her wheelchair and began to walk while shrieking out a woman's name repeatedly. My presence made her very agitated too, so I did hide behind a wall in the kitchen to stop her getting even more distressed. It was perhaps the longest ten minutes of my life and left me a bit shaky.

Movements inside empty apartments, and strange atmospherics in these old apartment buildings, were also commonplace (footsteps running and walking down empty staircases that you are standing on were not uncommon), as were the incredible ages of the wealthy residents. Rumours and gossip about the residents' secret histories – which defy belief because such tales never reach the tabloids – were also rife. I actually tried to compose a memoir about being a porter, and wrote an opening ten thousand words. Though all of my stories in the memoir were true, it was rejected by the six literary agencies that I approached with a proposal. Where comment was given, the proposal was rejected for being 'unrealistic'. One agent claimed it was 'too sinister and unpleasant' to publish. What did they want from me?

The final image in the story was suggested to me by Danel Olson. He felt the story needed one final detail. He's a finisher.

'The Ancestors' was written around 2005, after a request for a horror story based on a cinematic style. I chose Asian horror, as I'd seen a lot of it by then. The themed collection was delayed and delayed and then never happened, but I'd still written my story for it, and then I mothballed it for years. It was first published in what was to be a doomed venture, *The British Fantasy Society Yearbook*, though a volume did appear in 2009 for society members.

This story featured another of my attempts to evoke horror, as effortlessly and guilelessly as I could, by using a juvenile voice in the first person. It is probably the least revised piece of work that I have written, along with the transcripts of the interviews in *Last Days*. The Japanese child in my imagination just narrated the story to me and I wrote it down, as did the interviewees in *Last Days*, and I struggled to find much that I wanted to change after a first draft had bled out in one continuous stream (though that doesn't mean that these pieces are perfect). The nightmare of a toy with long legs and a horrible face that waited upon a landing for the sleepless to discover it was actually endured by a friend and his father, and in the same house, in which they both worried they were going mad and suffering from hallucinations. I couldn't forget their story.

'The Age of Entitlement' is unusual in this collection, because it doesn't feature an obvious monster. I wrote this story for Ian Whates's *Dark Currents* collection (Newcon Press), published in 2011, and I made sure that my story was more speculative in tone – something that I had rarely tried in this way before.

The location comes from a battlefields tour that I took with my brother in 2010, which we began in Normandy. But the sudden appearance at the window of a building of a stone statue of a woman with her hands over her face relates to an experience I had, with my heavily pregnant wife, in Aberystwyth. The sight of the woman stopped us in our tracks. For several airless seconds, in which I became rigid with fear, I was convinced that I was looking at a ghost. But someone had, for some inexplicable reason, placed a memorial statue in an upstairs window of their home. The world around us suddenly became very Robert Aickman.

Evidence of the colossal but incomprehensible loss of life in the Great War – my brother and I visited dozens of cemeteries in France and Belgium – had a strong effect on me. And a sense of such loss came together with that image of a grieving stone woman that I'd seen at a window in Wales, in the same time frame. Complementing this was a not uncommon experience for me in London, in which I became acquainted with people who were, for their own reasons, concealing the fact that they were very wealthy and had very wealthy parents. One friend even managed to fool me for years. But they were always people whose seemingly carefree approach to life, and confidence, and inability to suffer regret, made me feel neurotic in comparison. So I imagined a Patricia Highsmith Tom Ripley situation, in which a wealthy man had fooled his companion in this way for decades, without realising that his friend was an evolving psychopath. Admiration, I suspect, can easily turn to resentment in the right circumstances, and even violent murder in some cases.

'The Age of Entitlement' is a class rage, quiet apocalypse, psychopath story. I've always liked it and was grateful that a publisher whom I'd never considered writing for encouraged me to be more speculative with a short horror story.

'Florrie' is the second of three stories that I have written over the years for Jon Oliver's horror and weird fiction collections, published by Solaris. It's also my favourite of the three. It's a rumination about age, about becoming sensitive both to age in other people and to the evidence of the past within the buildings that you occupy. As a man who has lived in many old buildings and rooms, poorly or improperly decorated, that are like archaeological digs to a lay social historian, I've been peculiarly sensitive to suggestions of who has filled these spaces before me. In my room above the pub in London, a resident (or was that an inmate?) who had lived in a single room within the building for 25 years casually mentioned to me that a sex offender had been arrested in my room (and caught red-handed), and that the room had also been the scene of a long period of explosive domestic violence (I was never able to scrub the dried black blood off the radiator – it had adhered to the metal and hardened like resin). Each of those true horrors made it into my novel *Apartment 16*.

A touching tale from my own family also made it into this story. The kitchen in my grandparents' house was being renovated by my sister and brother-in-law, and once the cabinets were removed it was discovered that my grandparents had written their names on the wall, alongside a date, in pencil, to commemorate the time when the cabinets were first fixed there. It was a simple elegy to their beginnings in that home, and it was a detail that I wanted to include within this story, as well as other details that I have observed in the old houses I have lived in or just passed through. I often imagine that the past still exists in a close and not always completely intangible form, though as a mostly unseen presence and more strongly in certain places. Perhaps it's not only my imagination.

Publication History

'Where Angels Come In' originally appeared in *Poe's Progeny*, edited by Gary Fry (Gray Friar, 2005).

'The Original Occupant' originally appeared in *Bernie Herrmann's Manic Sextet* (Gray Friar, 2005).

'Mother's Milk' originally appeared in *Gathering the Bones*, edited by Jack Dann, Ramsey Campbell and Dennis Etchison (Voyager, Harper Collins, 2003).

'Yellow Teeth' originally appeared in *British Invasion*, edited by Christopher Golden, Tim Lebbon and James A. Moore (Cemetery Dance, 2008).

'Pig Thing' originally appeared in *Exotic Gothic 4*, edited by Danel Olson (PS Publishing, 2012).

'What God Hath Wrought?' originally appeared in *Gutshot*, edited by Conrad Williams (PS Publishing, 2011).

'Doll Hands' originally appeared in *The Burning Circus*, edited by Johnny Mains (British Fantasy Society, 2013).

'To Forget and Be Forgotten' originally appeared in *Exotic Gothic 3*, edited by Danel Olson (Ash Tree Press, 2009).

'The Ancestors' originally appeared in *The British Fantasy Society Yearbook 2009* (British Fantasy Society, 2009).

'The Age of Entitlement' originally appeared in *Dark Currents*, edited by Ian Whates (NewCon Press 2012).

'Florrie' originally appeared in *House of Fear*, edited by Jonathan Oliver (Solaris, 2011).

Acknowledgements

A very special acknowledgement goes out to the late James Marriott, to John Coulthard and Ramsey Campbell, who got the ball rolling for my short fiction many years ago. My gratitude extends to all of the other editors who often prised these stories out of me, and had the faith in the first place to want a story from me for their collections: Gary Fry, Christopher Golden, Tim Lebbon, James A. Moore, Danel Olson, Conrad Williams, Johnny Mains, Guy Adams (who requested a story for the BFS 2009 Yearbook, though no editor's name appears on the publication), Ian Whates, Jonathan Oliver, Stephen Jones, Ellen Datlow, Steve Haynes, Victor Blázquez, Dan Coxon, John Joseph Adams, Adriana Diaz-Enciso. I must also acknowledge the persuasive powers of Jen Kitses, who talked me into workshopping 'Mother's Milk' in a creative writing class in 1997. Thanks also to my father, Clive Nevill, who first read ghost stories to me and opened that door.

In order to better publicly appreciate the many people who created the hardback, I want to warmly acknowledge the patience, expertise and wisdom of Brian J. Showers of Swan River Press, Dublin, who has mentored me on producing the hardback edition and pretty much shone a light onto every aspect of independent publishing, from the printers to postage concerns and every detail in between. Couldn't have done it without him and his considerable experience in producing collectable books. And thank you to Andy Howarth and Mark Radley of CPI for helping me turn these horrors into a printed book that isn't horrible to hold, look at or read. The work of my old friend and colleague Toby Clarke is also much appreciated in designing the jacket, as were the text design skills of Peter Marsh. I'm also heavily indebted to the artist, Mister Trece, who gave me permission to use three of his paintings for the jacket and endpapers; they seem to expose the roots of nightmares. Something I also try and uncover, like deeply buried nerves, when I write.

Many thanks to the managing editorial team of Tony Russell, Paul King and Robin Seavill, whom I have relied upon in my professional life for many years.

A very special mention must go to my clever wife, Anne, who has assisted me with developing Ritual Limited into more than just a name on the files at my accountants. Could not have done this without her.

Finally, let me thank every reader who has decided to own and to read this collection of selected horrors that have roared, or even just dripped, out of me over the last twenty years.

Lightning Source UK Ltd.
Milton Keynes UK
UKHW011510110520
363092UK00008B/1017

9 780995 463035